DIGGING UP BONES

By

Augustus G Van Slyke

Books by Author:

Book I – DIGGING UP BONES

Book II – FINDING MAGGIE'S BLISS

ANGELS NEVER LIE – Memoir

Disclaimer:
The book is based on actual police reports, victim accounts, and confessions by perpetrators. This story is pure fiction. Resemblance of characters and places in this book is coincidental, thereby protecting the guilty, unfortunately.

ISBN 13: 9780978568924
ISBN: 0978568923
Library of Congress Control Number: 2013920309
CreateSpace Independent Publishing Platform
North Charleston, South Carolina

For the boy who was tied to the side of a barn in Wisconsin and killed at the hands of his adopted father and who's last words were-
"I'm cold, pa."

Edited by
Pamela A Van Slyke
and
Valerie Valentine

Preface

William M. Messenger
December, 1949, age: fourteen years and six months

"My name is William M. Messenger. The 'M' is for Miles, William Miles Messenger.

"I got scars on my back, legs and arms. I smoke a pipe and an occasional cigarette.

"First of all, this isn't my story. Secondly, I've got secrets. I can tell a few, though you can't go telling on me on account of the ongoing investigation.

"About me: I'm five feet, eleven inches and growing. My hair is brown and, when combed, I comb it straight back, then pull a little of it forward, down by my eyebrows.

"The Messengers adopted me. Pa needed help on the farm because Ma couldn't have kids.

"I can swear a blue streak, too, but I mostly quit that by the age of nine. That's when I was introduced to my angel. I can fly. It's true—Ralphy taught me. I can do it most of the time, when I'm in the right mood.

"I told Pastor Swain about seeing angels. He got mad and kicked me! He said I had no right to see one. So I said my angel didn't like the way he lured good folks inside his church building and how he makes them ashamed enough to *pay* to hear him talk of the Good Book. That's when the old boy came unglued.

"There's more I want to tell you, but you gotta promise to keep all this a secret. I don't wanna get the Sheriff or me in Dutch.

"Ma and me don't think much of Pa, either.

"Ma said to me once, 'Boy, I don't think Pa ever had a mother. I think a bird shit on the fence post, and the sun hatched 'im!'

Intro

Kathryn sat in the front row, last seat on the left of the small stage. Gordon looked her way and winked his patented wink. She smiled and nodded.

"My wife is sitting in the front row, ladies and gentlemen, as she always does. She's here for me, for encouragement and comfort. I kid her now and again. I say that she accompanies me to these speaking engagements in case I have a girlfriend." There were a few snickers rumbling through the audience of nearly two hundred who had come to hear his story. It always seemed to break the ice. By the grace of God, Gordon had reached his seventies, pushing toward eighty.

"Miracle stories tend to be gushy and predictable. This is not. It's the story of truth. I leave no details out, the gore and bloody details; it's all here, warts and all.

"As I often say, what you are about to hear is two connecting stories. *If* you find that it's William's story more than mine, you'd be right. He'd be happy about that, you see; he likes to get into my head.

"William's story is what brought me here with you. It is about life and its connection to others. You never know how a stranger's life will alter the course in yours, even if you but glance at an unknown person. It can and will affect some part of your existence. William's plight changed my life and that, too, is the truth.

"It was he who helped me dig up the bones I buried long ago. I didn't ask for help, nor did I want to revisit the past. But I had to, you see. To help him, I had to confront my past. William wasn't much different than any other fourteen, fifteen-year-old. It's the circumstances, not age, that make a difference in one's life, that's all.

"I was still pretty much a low-level Sheriff in a small town in Middle America. My life was a train wreck from hell heading toward oblivion. Little did I know that what transpired in the final days of December back in nineteen forty-nine would lead me on a journey to defend the helpless. The innocent.

"Today they're called 'throw-aways.' That's the term given to children who are deemed to have been so severely tortured physically, mentally, and spiritually that they could never be healed enough to live a normal life in our society. And why *is it* that society has to put labels on kids and toss them aside? They say animals are dumb.

"William was one of those kids. I tried to save him. Ironically, he saved me. Such is the heart of children, pure and innocent, like the face of God, some say.

"Will talks of angels. My story does not. He says he showed me his angel. Was it an angel? He says it was. Maybe. Maybe it was the DTs. My story says nothing about a God, at least not on purpose, I don't think.

"I have many stories to tell, and Kathryn insisted that I write them down. This is the first one, the story that started all the rest. Hadn't even one gray hair on my Irish red head. "It all started with a letter. My deputy found many letters that Will had written. They were meant for me to read as evidence in case something happened to him. Something did, and it was horrible.

"Oh, perhaps this will sound . . . eerie. I'm going to tell you folks something *more* than what I know. You're the first to hear of this. Take it to heart.

"I'll begin the story at the time I was in the hospital, back in the first half of the last century, December, 1949."

CHAPTER ONE

"Bastard. That ugly bastard!" Nurse Anne bellowed. "We'd better get back to our stations before someone starts looking for us. Dry your eyes, honey. I'll cover for you until you pull yourself together. And thanks for sharing, Pam," she said as she gave her a final hug and a light kiss on her neck just below her ear. Pam hugged her back and kissed her on the lips.

Anne's head was spinning with the new revelations and no one to talk to, no one to tell them to. Still trying to clear her head of all the pieces of a puzzle yet to be completed, she also remembered there was a new patient in room 101, the one with a broken nose and shattered jaw. She desperately wanted to see him, but first things first: she needed a rest and a cigarette to clear her head.

The rain had quit, and the sound of distant thunder had quieted down. Will was outside of his body again. Raphael stood with him in his room as they gazed out the window. Lecturing him on his new surroundings and those around him, he continued, "Remember, William, you're here for special reasons, and we'll discuss all that in detail when the time is right. For now, Sheriff Maxwell, Nurse Anne, and Pam Darling will need to sort out their lives. You must let them be. Your role is to be their friend, that's all. As hard as it will be, and it will be, you'll have to allow the universe to work on their behalf. Their voices need to be heard. Let God do the rest. *You* are the connecting tissue that has been missing in their lives."

William stood silent for a moment before saying, "Like listening to pretty Miss Darling's thoughts and words?"

"And listening to the words of Nurse Anne as she reads to you. Absorb the words, thoughts, and loving care that each one brings to you."

"Ralphy, I got enough trouble just sloppin' the hogs."

***

Anne was daydreaming in the nurse's lounge next to the cafeteria in the basement. Her Italian lover had her in his arms at on the bottom of the gondola, both humping away as it floated unmanned along the canal in Venice. Then Pam stepped in.

"Excuse me, Anne, but the Sheriff, Gordon Maxwell, wants to see you when you're available." Still in a dream state, Anne nodded and Pam disappeared, closing the door.

Rose petals were floating down from the heavens onto the two naked lovers, spent, their bodies glistening, he on top of her as she gazed skyward. Then, from out the billowy clouds came a beautiful, white, shimmering feather descended, gliding to and fro, finally coming to rest in her lover's butt-crack. Quill down, feather straight up.

"Goddamn it! Why do all my dreams have to end like that? It was such a beautiful, sensual, lusty dream, then it ends so, so . . . fucking *stupid!*"

Shaking it off and running her hands through her hair, she crushed the cigarette in the ashtray. Anne hoisted herself out of the overstuffed brown leather chair, and ambled out of the lounge and back to her routine.

I can tell him, what? She had doubts. How *could* she tell him about something called the LOC, Will, with the cuts, the bruises, and incisions, all healed in less than a week? *Yeah, Right! I don't think so.* She blocked it for the time being as she entered the patient's room. How would she tell him about the photos of children Dr. Bullock has? *It isn't a crime to have pictures, is it?* Her mind was racing, waiting for the right moment to present itself.

"Good afternoon, Sheriff Maxwell. How is the old Sheriff doing today?" Gordon could only look up at the nurse and smile. His mouth was swollen, aching from the surgery, wires, and stitches. She could smell his stale breath. *Yuck,* she thought, *a boozer.* She checked his pulse.

He appreciated a woman's touch, a warmth he hadn't been accustomed to since his wife left him years ago. He tried speaking, but it hurt like hell. His eyes were swollen, almost shut, and his upper and lower teeth never separated.

"You're mumbling, Sheriff. If you want more sedatives, please nod." He did.

"Oh, by the way," Anne continued. She lifted his head and dropped two codeine-coated tablets in his mouth through a gap where a tooth used to be. "You know, young William is just down the hall and coming out of his coma. He's been calling your name in his restless sleep. Apparently, you two know each other. Would you like to see him? I think it would do him some good if you'd go down there. I mean, I'll wheel you down or I could accompany you as we walk down there. What'll it be, Mr. Sheriff?"

Gordon swallowed the pills by drinking the glass of water through a straw that she held for him, and nodded in agreement. He tried to speak, but the words dribbled out like droplets of unwanted saliva.

"You're mumbling again," she teased. "I'll be back after I see the rest of my patients. By that time the medication will have had time to work. We've got to talk. I'm serious. Something—*strange* is going on around here."

Again he nodded, not knowing what the hell she was talking about. He laid his head back on the pillow, thinking of that crazy dream of Will in his bedroom. He just could *not* get it out of his mind. He wanted a brandy, too.

CHAPTER TWO

An hour had passed before Anne could return to check on Gordon. The codeine was working, and he decided he would try walking to Will's room.

As he shuffled along the corridor with her toward Will's room, he caught a whiff of her perfume. It was so pleasing to his senses, like something his wife may have worn, or even his mother; rest her soul. Anne was strong and self-assured: something he wasn't.

Gordon grimaced as a sharp pain in his mouth brought him back to a horrific memory that had been blocked for years. His father, a staunch third-degree Catholic Knight and a strict high school principal, backhanded him for telling him about an incident at the seminary.

He was troubled and wanted to tell his father about something that had happened, so he started in. "Allen and Kip are fourteen-year-old freshmen like me, Dad. They're twins and ultra polite. They're a little shorter than me, have light brown hair, and real skinny. They wouldn't hurt a flea, but Dad, we ah, I mean the other students and I, are quite sure those two priests who came to the seminary just this year did something bad to those boys.

"Gordon," Clifford Maxwell asked, "is this going to be one of your long *fantasy* stories, again? If it is, you're going to get a beating, so help me . . ."

"Dad! Listen! Just once, hear me out. The incident occurred when the two priests took Allen and Kip with them to the Church-owned cabin on Lake Winnebago, north of Capital City." He was trying to tell his overbearing father the story exactly the way it was told to him.

"They're young priests. Maybe still in their twenties. They know all the latest songs, and movies and such, and are fun to be around, but they make me feel uneasy, like a little *too* friendly, sometimes. Anyway, what happened was, they performed *un*-natural acts on the twins."

All he could remember was seeing the back of his father's thick hand as it smashed into his face and split open his upper lip.

"I won't hear of it! Now say no more on that subject," his father roared. They were sitting across from each other at the breakfast table in the too-small, crowded kitchen of their home, a brown-bricked bungalow.

"But, Dad, you always told me to tell the truth, and that's what I'm telling you." He raised his heavy cold hand again, then . . . hesitated. This time Gordon looked away from his angry father and brought his head down as he brushed the back of his hand across the warm, oozing blood coming from his ear. A ringing developed that wouldn't quit. He wanted to tell him what they told him in his room late that Sunday night when they returned from the weekend with the priests.

"Alright then. Tell me what he told you. I'll be the judge of what's fantasy and what isn't. Go on with your sinful friend's accusations."

"This is how Kip, the skinniest one, told me."

"On our way to the cabin, Father Long was driving, and my brother Allen was in the front seat. I was in the back, sitting with Father Smiley. Father Smiley put his hand on my leg just above my knee, squeezed and said, 'I'm your friend.'

"I didn't know what to say. I didn't know what he was up to. Then he did it again—moving his hand higher up on my thigh.

"'Want to be special friends?' he asked."

"Stunned, I just sat still, and said nothing, as he continued on and rubbed my crotch. He unzipped my pants. He rubbed and pulled my penis up and down. I had a hard-on. This was no game. I was embarrassed. I was numb."

Gordon watched his father close. Rarely did his father let him talk this long. Clifford Maxwell's eyes were closed tight. His lips moved in prayer, timed with each movement of a thumb to a new bead, as he clutched tight to the black jagged rosary beads. His face was flushed as droplets of sweat formed on his forehead. Gordon took a long breath and continued with Kip's story.

"He said, 'It's just between us, *special* friends.' Then he took my hand, put it inside *his* pants and made me do the same to him. His penis was already thick and hard. He put his arm around my shoulder and said, 'This will be our little secret,' and then Father Smiley tongued my ear.

"When we reached the cabin, another priest and a boy greeted us. The boy was introduced to us as Alfred Unser. "Alfie is my prized student in catechism," the short, slim Father Kempler exclaimed. Father Kempler had his arm around the slight-built fair-haired boy as he spoke, then kissed him on the cheek and mussed his hair. Alfie just stood there half smiling, red-faced, looking us over.

"Later that night the three priests were drinking brandy in the kitchen and they gave us rum and Cokes. We all drank several glasses and smoked cigarettes, too. We thought we were big shots sitting around in just our swim trunks, drinking and smoking with the priests, even peeing outside in the moonlight, the six of us. They taught us dirty Irish folksongs the first night and we went skinny-dipping.

"While we were in the water, Father Long suggested that we play underwater tag. A priest always touched my genitals. Grabbed and massaged them, too, as we stood around talking about dating girls with the water up near our shoulders. I could tell it was happening to Allen and Alfie, too. All of us, including the priests, were getting hand jobs. Allen, Alfie, and I never made eye contact while we stood with the priests in the water. The fun ended. We felt ashamed. We had sinned.

"The second day started out kinda normal. We knelt in the main room and prayed the rosary in the morning, then went swimming. In the afternoon we went hiking, paired up, priest and student. I was forced to jack-off Father Long, again, on our afternoon hike. I almost got sick.

"The second night started out the same as the first night. All of us were sitting on the two couches in the main room. There was a twist. We were paired off, each one of us with a priest. We had nothing on but our trunks, like the first night. We were smoking and drinking Cokes and rum.

"Father Kempler had a Bell and Howell movie camera. He brought it out and put reels of film on it as we drank, and giggled at dirty jokes that father Smiley told. Father Long got a white bed sheet and hung it on the wall in the main room. The reels were all pornography.

"We watched three different movies. We were also introduced to blowjobs that night, and were forced to trade partners. Allen and I had to take turns with Alfie as Father Kempler took pictures with his Kodak. Paired off again with different priests, we went into separate rooms. It went on for hours.

Kip said to me, "I'd never done anything like that before. I didn't want to do it. Father Smiley threatened to tell my folks that I was a queer if I didn't give him a blowjob. What could I do? Afterwards, I threw up. I still feel sick inside, Gordy," he said to me.

He looked his father square in his eyes as Gordon said to his father, "I know how you feel about priests and Catholicism, Dad, but that ain't right, no matter how you look at it."

Clifford sat erect and silent, thumbing the piercing jagged black beads faster and faster. Blood dripped onto the tablecloth just below the tightly gripped rosary. Clifford's face contorted strangely as he silently prayed faster and faster as he jerked the beads through one hand, then the other, harder, faster.

"He told me, Dad. He didn't know how to tell his folks about what happened. Kip said to me in a matter of fact way that night, that all of it was new to him. He always expected that he would have a girlfriend—someone his own age. *They* would experiment with sex, *not* a priest. We are supposed to look up to priests, Dad. He's not a queer. They were, scared; yes, but, the priests were going to tell their parents."

"Enough!" Clifford Maxwell slammed the bloody rosary to the floor and stood. He was wringing his blood-wet hands as he began pacing the kitchen floor.

Gordon continued the story to the day Kip and Allen were sent home.

"The day they were to go home, Dad, they came up missing. Allen and Kip's parents came to pick them up. They parked near the front of the seminary like everyone else.

"They were expecting to see their two sons standing on the steps with suitcases in hand. But they weren't there.

"Kip and Allen were never seen again. There were rumors. Father Cheney said that it happens now and then. 'It's rare,' he said, 'Sometimes Satan gets ahold of sinful children and they just up and disappear.'"

Gordon's raging father said, "If that's what Father Cheney said, then, by God and his avenging angels, that's what happened. Case closed!"

His eyes were red and glaring as he stepped around the small kitchen table, grabbed Gordon by his shirt, and pulled him up and out of his chair. With a sweaty, stone-cold face, nose-to-nose with his, he spoke, "You will speak *no more* of such nonsense. If you do, I'll chop you up and throw you out like *garbage.* Hear me, son?"

Gordon loathed Father Cheney. Now, he felt the same toward his own father.

He knew he couldn't tell his mother *or* father about being forced to dig a grave, either. Not now, anyway. That would have driven the old man over the edge.

Father Cheney said it was the final resting place for priests. There were small graves behind the red brick house that served as a convent. White wooden crosses. Three rows deep. No names. Sometimes, he dreamt of bony skeletal arms, reaching up from the graves. It almost seemed as if they were pleading for something. He'd wake in a cold sweat. Confused. Frightened.

The perfume and gentle hands of Nurse Anne holding his arm and hand brought him back to the present. "When I get out of here, I've got work to do."

"Sorry, Mumbles," Anne said in a monotone voice, "I can't understand what you're saying." She did, though. She was thinking about the work he had to do.

She tapped on the door.

"Hey, wake up, Junior, you have a visitor!" Anne exclaimed, pushing the door wide open. "Look who's here to see you."

Will rolled toward the door and opened his eyes slowly. Squinting from the glare of the hall light at the two figures, Will hoarsely whispered, "Well, I'll be, go to Helen's hat shop, if it ain't that old dog, Sheriff Maxwell."

Taken aback by Maxwell's face, Will continued, "By God, Sheriff, you look like you kissed a brick wall at fifty miles an hour."

Anne all but jumped out of her skin as she heard Will speak for the first time since he was hospitalized. She was amazed at his quick recovery. After a few minutes of verbal bantering from Will and muffled attempts at speaking by the Sheriff, Anne broke in, "I have to make my rounds. Will, welcome back."

How could anyone come to so fast from a six-day coma? And what about the stitches? Anyway, she was delighted to see Will out of the coma and speaking freely. She felt good about that.

The Sheriff? She thought. *There's got to be a way.*

The dreamer took a deep breath, exhaling as she stepped out into the hallway, her thoughts betraying her. Instantly, a movie played in her head. A dozen Italian men danced naked, each extending a red rose to her as she stood among them, fully dressed. Contented, she smiled with thoughts from Thoreau:

There's nothing in the world I know-That can escape from love—For every depth it goes below—And every height above.

CHAPTER THREE

Gordon sat silent, looking at William as he lay back down on the bed. "I'm tired, Sheriff," he said, "You talk. I'll listen." Will closed his eyes and went into a dream state, half awake, and half of him went to another plane.

Gordon nodded as tears began to well up. Wracked with the pain of guilt, he rested his second chin on his chest and let the tears flow. How could he have allowed this to happen to his young buddy? Why couldn't he, the Sheriff of Pine Nut, stop the child beatings sooner? What could he have done to prevent it? These questions and more came crashing down on him. They would not cease. Tormented by guilt, he felt impotent, useless, and undeserving to wear a badge, a badge of courage, honor, and trust.

"Yeah, right, courage. Give me the evidence, God, and I can stop harm to all children in my charge here! You know that, God!" he screamed, grinding his teeth. "If you are a God, help me. Give me a chance to make things right." He pleaded.

While Gordon poured his heart out to the Universe, high above the clouds far beyond our planet, peering at the distant shimmering orbs, Will was in conference with archangel Raphael.

"Whadya, er, excuse me. *What* do you think, Ralphy? Do we let the ole boy in on our little secret?"

"William, you're a child of God, as is the Sheriff and all people of this planet, yet only a tiny fraction of beings here has been able to pierce the veil to go to the other side like you have."

"I do what I can to get myself out of the way of spirit, you know that."

"Yes, Will, I know and you know, but this is not for just any mortal. Everyone has a path to follow. They'll get to where you are and farther, someday. I'm afraid for now it will be too much for Mr. Maxwell to comprehend. You saw what happened to him when he saw you in his room."

Will pondered the angel's statement. "What if I tell him what happened, would that be too much for him?"

"You can tell him," Raphael said. "It won't help him."

"What if I tell him about you and flyin'?" Will asked.

Raphael shook his head and began fading out as they made their descent back to Earth. The archangel leaned and whispered, "That's fly*ing!*"

Back in the room and under the covers, William looked over at Sheriff Maxwell's battered face and felt sorry for him. *Geez,* he thought, *I scared the shit right out of him.*

"Hey, Mumbles," Will said with half a grin, "I have something to tell you, but you have to keep it a secret."

CHAPTER FOUR

Raphael re-examined Gordon's dreams and thoughts of the early morning hours, on the day he entered the Pine Nut hospital.

The morning snow was blowing in through the bedroom window. Gordon had passed out hours ago. His cheeks and nose were rosy colored. It matched his red hair. He lay crosswise on the bed, face up, head near the half-open window with his plaid shirt partially unbuttoned and his boxer shorts on backwards and torn open. The wind blew the snowflakes in, landing in his hair and face as he snored and coughed his way to semi-consciousness.

In the dimly lit, tiny cluttered kitchen, his empty brandy bottle sat on the counter. Open and empty green cans of Del Monte corn, beans, and peas stood among the cans of fruit slices on the counter by the sink that overflowed with unwashed pots and pans, dirty dishes, empty glasses, and silverware.

His aching, throbbing head began to move left, then right as he moaned. *No, no, why? I should have known . . . I killed the kid, my little buddy.* He was having a nightmare, as sleep was interfering with his drunkenness, or was it the other way around? In either case, it was about Will and his inability to keep him safe before the big roundup the two of them were working on.

He was ashamed of himself. The few times he went out in the country to Will's house, Gordon wanted to snatch him up and take the poor, battered, lovable dark-skinned boy home with him. He always wanted children, and often dreamed of having them fill his house with love and happiness; something he rarely felt in his own youth as an only child in his strict religious parents' house.

The sting he felt from his first visit haunted him and stayed in his guts forever. It happened when he put Will's Pa in jail for being drunk and kicking and punching a bony, broken-down old plow horse tied to the side of the feed mill just off Main Street.

Upon his arrival at the farmhouse, he saw both Will and his mother, she at the screen door in a tattered and torn plain buttoned dress, nondescript apron, and fat bloody lip with swollen cheeks around her eye sockets. Her shoulder-length brown hair was tangled and bloody; William, resting on one knee, in his bib-overalls, bloodied and sweaty, hunched over the post he was tied to outside near the shed and barn. Will was just a little brown-eyed nine-year-old lad at the time.

Gordon's thoughts bolted to a country setting of the all-boys junior seminary he attended. He saw himself as a young freshman sitting naked on a solid oak chair facing the rector, a bishop, and a few of the priests who taught at the seminary along with Opus Dei priests, and other *special* visitors. The scene took place in a secret room, which the student body was aware of, but unsure of its whereabouts. A chosen few were led there blindfolded with hands in cuffs behind their back as a form of punishment and, of course, humiliation.

Until the new bishop arrived from Iowa, no one student had ever known of the eerie dark room. They didn't need to. The use of the room wasn't intended for the seminary students until *he* arrived. Its purpose was for the occasion of dark, unnatural, *unsacred* ceremonies.

Inside the twenty by thirty-foot enclosure were tables, chairs, and a makeshift stage. It consisted of two old banquet tables pushed together with a dark green rug used for flooring. There was also a makeshift, wooden, three-step portable stairway at one end of the long table.

Directly in front of the stage were three plush armchairs with folding chairs on either side. Several rows of chairs were placed behind the first row.

The cold, sterile atmosphere had a hint of ammonia emitting from the freshly scrubbed oak flooring and was dimly lit with a small, lone lightbulb dangling from the high dark ceiling immediately above the solitary wooden chair. Aside from the entrance door, there was only one other door, which looked more like a broom closet door. It was in the back of the room, behind the stage.

Gordon's mind played like a movie as he watched himself sitting there with arms tied behind him, unable to cover his manhood. He began to stare at the moving mouths of the shadowy men in black sitting in the folding chairs. They chanted in Latin, *"Mea culpa, mea culpa, mea maxima culpa."* Then, they chanted something gothic and unrecognizable to Gordon while one clergy member at the end of the table waved a large canister of incense attached to a small chain held high, and rocked it to and fro. The solemn-faced men were also tapping their feet on the bare floor in unison and did so for what seemed an eternity. Young Gordon would jerk his body and turn his head, as the sudden burst of a bright light would attack him from a single flash camera.

As silence overcame the dark, dank room, the one who sat in the middle of the three chairs in front stood and proclaimed in a loud thunderous voice, "I offer you up to the cause. You *are the chosen one!"*

***

William was standing in front of the dresser mirror in the bedroom, using God-Thought, something that Raphael had taught him, and to his amazement and amusement, became visible as Sheriff Maxwell tossed and turned in his bed with drool coming out of the corners of his open mouth. Fading out and fading in, Will was fascinated and continued practicing his disappearing act in front of the mirror.

Maxwell laid flat on his back with mouth open, stopped breathing for a few long seconds, then let out a snort and a cough as he rolled over onto his stomach toward the little pine nightstand that held a cracked glass-framed picture of his ex-wife. The sudden cough produced a small chunk of phlegm. It flew out, hitting the picture in the upper right corner and rocked it enough to make it fall forward off the table, smashing to bits on the pine wood floor. The crash woke the Sheriff. He rolled onto his back and opened his blurry, stinging, bloodshot eyes.

As he fought to focus, he saw something odd. He rubbed his eyes with the palms of his hands and refocused his sight only to see Will in front of his mirror, appearing, disappearing, and then reappearing. He closed his eyes, thinking he was still dreaming and mumbled, "He's alive, the kid's alive."

Will, watching him through the mirror, turned to Sheriff Gordon Maxwell, took a breath, and in the deepest and loudest voice he could muster, commanded, *"Hey,* you old sidewinder, there's work to be done. It's time to rise and shine, boy!"

Maxwell's jaw dropped to his chest. His eyes grew to the size of cup saucers. He bolted upright and lunged to the opposite side of the bed, away from Will, and slammed full-bodied against the light blue-painted solid brick wall, then slid to the hardwood, with his chin bouncing off every single brick on his downward slide to the floor already littered with frame, picture, and broken glass.

William faded from the mirror.

CHAPTER FIVE

I f the Sheriff's jaw hadn't been wired shut, it would have dropped to the floor.

He listened intently to William's story. Gordon sat staring at the green-colored corner, next to Will's bed.

Shaking his head as if it would take him back to the reality he knew before, and through his wired shut jaw, he proclaimed, "Oh *horse* shavings! How in God's good Earth is anybody going to believe all that nonsense about flying, angels, and junk like that? I mean you've got to be *real* sick to even *think* that kinda stuff. Do you know what they call that? *Bla*sphemy, that's what is. It's blasphemy!"

Of course no one could understand him, even if someone were there to hear it, which they weren't, but Will knew what he said, even if he couldn't understand all the words.

"You're mumbling again," Will whispered.

Gordon Maxwell was getting pissed off about his new nickname. His face turned red with anger, but because of his current condition, he couldn't do a whole hell of a lot about it. Still processing all the information just received, he looked to Will and asked, "So, if you got an angel, does that mean everybody's got an angel?"

"Yupper. I have two. That's what I've been told by the one I've seen anyway."

"I suppose their names are Amos n' Andy," Gordon mumbled. "When you fly, do you fly alone or are you in a flock?"

"Actually, Sir Mumbles, they're important angels and, no, that's not their names. I've heard Amos n' Andy on the radio. Laughter keeps people from goin' goofy. Anyway, let me know when you want to see one, and I'll make special 'rangements for a private viewing just for you. How'd you like that, Mr. Black and Blue and red all over?"

Coyotes were howling, and they could be heard from the cold frosted window. Gordon flashed back once again.

He sat in his chair in Will's room as his memory became a time capsule. Once again, he was taken back to his high school seminarian days. He could still see himself just turning fourteen years old, standing naked in front of all those men dressed in black. It was his first trip to the secret sacrificial room. The thought of it made him shudder.

One priest, the one who cuffed his wrists behind his back, was now pointing at his penis and laughing as he commissioned the others to listen. "Now, doesn't his penis look to be the same size in the paintings by Michelangelo?" The entire room erupted in an echoing laughter. For the first time in his life, Gordon Maxwell felt ashamed of himself. It wouldn't be the last time by any stretch of the imagination. There was more to remember about that day, but he refused to acknowledge anymore. Not now, anyway.

He drifted away in thought about the last couple of days and imagined all the hurt his young buddy had been going through. He was amazed that Will had pulled through that God-awful beating by his father. Now he, too, was in pain, stitches and all, feeling frustrated at not being able to speak and be understood.

He sat looking across the room at Will, who was telling him of angels, spirit guides, and flying, wondering if his buddy had become a little daft after his beating. *Really*, he thought, *who talks about angels except the people in church, and even then, only while they are in church. Ain't nobody I know talks about them in public, anyway.*

Will closed his eyes and drifted back to sleep as the door opened next to the Sheriffs' chair.

"Psst. Come, Gordon," Anne whispered. "I've got to get you back to your room, stat! Dr. Bullock just arrived, and he looks like he just had lunch with a pack of werewolves."

The effects of the medication were intoxicating for the Sheriff as he sat in his chair next to his hospital bed, fast asleep. He stayed that way all day.

When the night shift came in to do their nocturnal rounds, Nurse Anne was right there for all of her patients. "Next stop, the Sheriff," she said out loud while scanning through her patients' charts. Looking down at the clipboard, she raised her right hand and tapped on the door before opening.

"Oh, Gordon, are you awake? It's time to check your vitals." Gordon was still in his chair and listening to a radio program. It was Bob Hope on the NBC radio channel. It was his 1949 inaugural Christmas special for the troops in Okinawa. Gordon was laughing so hard, he had tears rolling from his eyes. Anne turned the radio down and sat on the Sheriff's bed facing him.

"May I call you Gordon?" she asked.

He turned from the radio, a little dejected, as he was enjoying the one-liners from Hope and listening to the laughter of the troops, but he half-smiled at her.

"Gordon or Gordy is okay with me. I've been called worse by worse people," he said with a sly grin. "I feel a little better, so when can I get the wire off?" he mumbled.

"It usually takes a few weeks for your jawbone to heal enough before we do that. You're becoming quite colorful around your big beautiful eyes. Gordon, that nose of yours, I'm afraid, it may have a new look to it." She took his vitals and checked the bandages. No doubt that he was on the fast track for recovery.

"Gordon," she began and reached over and took his hand in hers. She stopped mid-sentence and looked at their intertwined hands.

"I've got to get out of here," he mumbled. "You have to help me, Anne. I have important work to do that involves William."

Anne was startled by his quick comments, but joined in. "More than William, I'm afraid. There are other children in harm's way, and important people are involved in these things, whatever it is."

"I know," he said. "It involves people from here to Capital City and beyond. I need to get out of here so I can get my work done. I need to badger Will's old man. He knows more than he's willing to say, but I'm going to get that son of a bitch to give me names, so help me Hannah!"

"I need you to rest and heal, Gordon. That's all you have to do, but I'll tell you something. Please, don't tell anyone about this, but Ms. Darling and I have seen pictures of half-naked children among Dr. Bullock's belongings in his little black bag."

"Well, that son of a bitch!" Gordon said, "I had a hunch about him, but I couldn't prove it. I know about the pictures. William snuck me a couple of them just days ago. We have more info, too. I was getting ready to get things done statewide. I ran into roadblocks on this thing, though. By the way, nurse, do you know about Pastor Swain?"

"Yes, Pam told me," she said with irritation in her voice. "I know the sniveling little bastard. He's the father of Pam Darling's child, and he dresses in women's clothing."

Gordon listened but turned his head toward the mirror on the wall behind the radio and let out a startled laugh as he pictured the pastor in a pink chiffon dress. When he did, the saliva shot through his teeth, wire, and lips, spraying everything within range, including his own face. Swallowing hard any remaining fluids in his mouth, he said, "Let me out of here, nurse!"

"I can't. Not yet anyway. You need medication. You need rest. You need shots. Sheriff, *look* at you. You're a goddamn mess!"

He squeezed her hand. "Please."

"I know, and I'm going to help you. Pam and I will help you. We want to get Dr. Bullock, but no one is to know, do you understand?"

He nodded as he wiped the mess off his face with a sleeve.

"We need each other's help, but you have to stay and heal. I'll do what I can and report back to you," she said, talking fast. "I have my rounds, hopefully a nap, then I'll be back.

"By the way, your deputy, Mickey Zaugbaum, called to check on you. He had no message. The gals at the front desk told him you couldn't speak, however, he said he'd be around tomorrow."

"Sleep sound when you get the chance, Nurse Anne. Will's father is in jail. Will and I were working on a ring of people that involved his old man, church officials, scout leaders, a couple of state legislators, and other hotshots and now that includes Doc Trent Bullock and God knows who else, and He isn't tellin'. Now let's cut to the chase. We've got to get information on a few key people. Do you think you can help me?"

"Oh *hell* yes, whatever needs to be done, we'll make it happen, I know . . ."

"Do you have time to pull the wire out of my face now?" Gordon interrupted. "Time is running out, I'm afraid."

"We'll get it done," she said, and pressed his hand on her right breast, then back to his lap. She let go of the now mutual grip. She leaned over and kissed him on the cheek, and when she did, the light flickered and one of the radio tubes blew, leaving a little puff of blue smoke coming up from behind it.

Gordon frowned. "Thanks for the memories, Bob."

"Damn it! You'll have to find a new room. They don't have many with a radio. Will's room has one. You don't mind sharing with Will? Bullock will just have to allow two to a room. He hates that. It's one of his rules. One patient. One room."

Without waiting for an answer, she called an orderly to send him back down the hall to Will's room.

There they were, near each other in separate hospital beds with the big shining iron railings, Will chatting up a storm like usual, and Gordon lying there with his mouth wired shut, a broken nose, and two black eyes. He was in a world of hurt, yet anxious to get on with the business of protecting and serving the people of Pine Nut and its surroundings, especially the children.

"You sure are a sight for sore eyes," Will said. Feeling drained, Gordon said nothing.

"Well, *ain't* you a sight for sore eyes?"

For a moment he lay silent, then raised an arm off his chest, gave him the finger, and rolled over.

Will knew how much his friend liked to listen to the radio and began to tease him. "You just never know about electricity, huh, Sheriff? 'Course it's only a theory. What if there really is no electricity, it's just a part of the mind, then what? Besides, old Bob Hope is probably back stage right now playin' with Marilyn Monroe's boobies."

Gordon gave him the one-finger salute again.

"You know, I think you'll heal a lot faster in this room, Sheriff. I got a lot to talk to you about."

Gordon interrupted and said, "How the hell am I going to heal in here with you yappin' all the time?"

He thought, too, about what Will said about Bob Hope and wondered *how* he knew he was listening to his show down the hall in the other room.

"Sheriff, you know, you did see me in your bedroom at your house."

"Oh *ba*-loney! You were just a bad glass of brandy or rotten meat I had the night before. I remember it, but I don't want to remember it, if you know what I mean. You weren't really there . . . were you?" He raised his head off the pillow looking toward Will for an answer.

"I can do it for you now, if you wish." Without waiting for an answer, Will removed the sheets, floated from the bed, and hovered a few feet off the floor at the foot of the Sheriff's bed.

Gordon's eyes rolled as his body went limp.

Old Ralphy was right.

A green orb appeared at the foot of his bed just then and a voice was heard. "Like Pam Darling, you'll let Gordon sort and talk things out for himself. He's not a believer. Just know that your voice is being heard in more ways than you'll ever know."

Gordon drifted off to sleep as a quiet peace overtook restlessness and throbbing pain from his injuries, for a while, anyway. He woke up an hour later.

Guilt returned. He felt helpless as he thought about his young roommate being damn-near beaten to death.

I should have prevented it, he kept thinking.

Will had a feeling. It felt good, as if healing was taking place and it was happening to his buddy, Sheriff Gordon Maxwell. Will just cast his loving eyes on his buddy lying there with more bandages between the two of them than the drugstore in Pine Nut had on its shelves.

"Sheriff Maxwell? Are you there, Sheriff? Come in, Sheriff Maxwell, wherever you are."

Gordon rolled toward the boy in the bed next to his.

Will spoke again, "Would you like to be pain-free for a while, you old coot?"

Gordon nodded.

"Then it's done," Will said in whispers.

A strange sensation came over Gordon. It felt as if hot needles were striking at his jaw deep from the inside and also within his broken nose. He felt a queer dizziness yet in a good way, a way that he couldn't explain. He could hear snaps, cracks, and pops within his jaw and nose.

"Those pills Nurse Anne gave me are starting to kick in, I think. Aside from some kind of weird tingling sensation happening inside my head, I don't feel sore at all." Gordon got off the bed and stood in front of the mirror rubbing his face. *I gotta get me some of them pills to take home*, he thought.

"You don't have to take anything home, Sheriff," Will said, watching him examine his face in the mirror.

"Why's that, little buddy? Do you think one of your angels can help me?"

Will responded. "You could use one. Just ask one for help."

"I'll do that," Gordon said, thinking he was goofy.

"Anyway, Sheriff," Will said, "you don't have pain anymore. And another thing, Nurse Anne and Pam Darling have found something for us. Dr. Bullock is in on the bad stuff. They found pictures of children in his doctor bag."

"I know about the nurses knowing. There's a lot of loose ends to be tied up now, so I have to get out of here and get to work. I need to know *who else* around here is in on it. I'm feeling totally overwhelmed. I'll need more help."

"You'll get it," Will said. "I don't hurt, and I'm going to fly out of here tonight and help you get your work done."

"Oh, right. You're just going to fly out the window like Superman and round up the bad guys. Is that it? Like they do on the radio? It only takes Superman a half hour, and that includes a commercial," Gordon said in jest.

"Something like that. You think I'm full of horse shit, don't you?" Will asked.

"Well," he said, trying to get comfortable as he sat on the side of his bed. "I wouldn't use those words." He thought a little more, then said, "Maybe you are a little daffy, but not full of horse shit, *exactly*." Gordon pondered a few things before continuing, "Your language has gotten a lot better since you've been here, I can tell you."

There was a long silence between the two as the corner next to Will's bed turned green. Gordon saw it, but didn't acknowledge it. He didn't have to. Will knew, of course, but he had to test the poor guy just a little.

"Sheriff," Will said, "if you touch your nose and tug on that wire just below your ear, I bet you won't feel any pain."

"I'm not touchin' nothin'! Leave me alone."

"If you touch your nose and feel no pain, you owe me five bucks," Will challenged.

"You're on." The Sheriff brought up his right hand, and, as he did so, stood and took a step to the mirror so he could watch this event himself. Gingerly he put a finger on his jaw just below one ear. With care, he pushed the finger on the skin, pressing to the bone. "I don't feel it. I mean, there's no pain. By God, Will. I can move my jaw."

"Now, look at the corner over here by my bed. What color is it?"

"It's that shade of green I see once in awhile."

Will said to himself, *Hey, Ralphy, you do good work!*

"It's gone! Now, it's here again. Wait. Now it's green! What the . . .?"

"I know, Sheriff, I know."

Gordon interrupted, "But something ain't right. I can't explain it, but I got a feeling inside my guts like something is wrong."

Gordon couldn't sleep. Thoughts were spinning out of control. He paced the floor for hours.

The next morning, Ms. Darling popped her head in the door and said, "Sheriff Maxwell, there's a message for you. Your deputy is in the lobby and wants to see you. I told him to meet you in your room. I'll take you down there and walk you back, and . . . *what* are you doing out of bed?"

Gordon grabbed his open gown from behind to cover his bare butt as he turned away from the mirror to face the voluptuous platinum blonde, Ms. Darling, who had a body of every truck driver's dreams.

Gordon said nary a word about his recovery.

"I'd love to go for a walk with a beautiful nurse," Maxwell said, trying to smile.

"You're mumbling, Sheriff," she said with a twinkle in her eye. "Can't understand a word you say," and she put her arm around his waist and led him out of the room.

As they were leaving they both looked back; not at Will, but at the color green. Gordon had as big a smile as he could with the wire and bandages, but a smile nevertheless. As he felt knots of fear growing stronger in his stomach, his smile left and a feeling of helplessness returned all but paralyzed his being.

CHAPTER SIX

As Pam and Gordon entered his old room, the lights flickered and the electricity went on, then off again. Pam stepped past Mickey Zaugbaum to the window, pulled open the curtain, and raised the blinds for light. Their eyes followed her to and fro, and back to the doorway. It was as if they were seeing a centerfold come to life in a nurse's uniform. She winked and said smiling, "I'll see you later, Sheriff."

Blushing, he turned to Deputy Zaugbaum and nodded.

Mickey was a thin wiry guy with small round eyes. He talked fast, couldn't control his dark brown hair, yet had a neat moustache to the corners of his mouth, and wore pants about two sizes too big for him. The belt that held his shirt and pants together flopped over in front, and his shirt came out of his pants in the back. Half the time his butt cheeks were cracking a smile. He had a heart of gold. He always said, "For a dollar, I'll give you the shirt off my back."

Folks liked him, but they didn't like that he was a Yankees fan. People would get on him once in a while about it. After all, he was born and raised for half his childhood in the Bronx. Though he didn't miss the Irish neighborhood, he clung to many of the old habits, and his favorite baseball team associated with those "Big Apple" days of his youth. He could be sly when he had to. And dumb, dumb like a fox when it was necessary. His wife loved him. So did his kids.

"Sorry I didn't introduce you to my good-looking nurse, Mickey, but she's mine, all mine," Gordon teased through his wired jaw.

"Lucky you. How good is she, anyway?" Mickey questioned, but then turned his thoughts to the reason he was there.

"Listen, Gordy, I've got to tell you what's going on in town and the news out at the farm where Will lives. First, no one thought William would be alive from what his pa did to him. I got a full confession, then some from his old man, and that ain't all. There's a hell of a lot more. Pa Priestly called me in to his cell and, when I got there, he wanted to confess. So, I got a chair, sat down, and got ready to hear all the particulars. Did you know his last name?"

"No," Maxwell said as he shrugged. "Nobody did."

"Oh, also, I got that new wire recorder, the magnetaphone you bought a few weeks back, and I brought *it* in, too, and plugged it in."

"Good job." Not only was Gordon proud of Mickey for thinking fast, he was also relieved.

"Sorry, you're mumbling." Mickey continued without skipping a beat, "And he spilled the beans on how long he'd been beating and whipping Will and his wife. He did it for years, Gordy, fucking years! It's a funny thing, though, he was telling it to me in such a calm, matter-of-fact way. It was goddamned eerie!

"We'd be able to send him away for the rest of his life on that alone, except for one thing."

"What's that?"

"He asked for a notepad and pencil last night around ten p.m. I didn't see any harm in it so I gave it to him. I checked on him later, about eleven thirty p.m., and he was lying on the cot, writing stuff down. This morning I came in with food from the café, and the goddamned dirtbag was hanging from the bars of the door. Yup, he used the straps of his bibs, wrapped them around the top bars, and he was just up there hanging in his shorts, stiffer 'n a board! Scared the bejeezus out of me!

"I dropped the food and called the doctor's office here at the hospital. Bullock wasn't around, but I got hold of Doc. Jenn, and she came from across the river to help out and pronounce him dead and all."

Gordon was busy taking notes and snarled at his deputy.

"Couple of questions. One, did you get everything on the wire that pertains?"

"Yes, all of it."

"Two, did he mention any names?"

"Yeah, I figured out how to rewind the damned thing and play it back. He mentioned several. One or two keep daily diaries."

"And three, do you know what they were doing?"

"I got an idea. It ain't good, I'll tell you. This is big stuff. If what old man Priestly said is true, like what the LOC does and how it brainwashes kids *and* adults, we got a big job on our hands, and it's just the beginning! It could mess up the whole county something furious. I found the notes and pictures that William had hid around the farm. This is big time, Gordon. We got some ass kickin' to do.

"There's something else, and I don't know what to do about it, so that's another reason why I have to talk to you. I think we should get help from the governor on this, Gordon; at least the attorney general's office."

Gordon shook his head. "No, no, no. We're going to take this on ourselves." Gordon backed himself to the chair and sat down, still clutching his notepad in his left hand and pencil in his right. He paused as his mind moved onto snippets from the past. "I'm going to get this caper under control, Mickey. I've got to do this myself. I mean, me and you." *If the attorney general were to be involved, he'd be the one to make all the calls.*

His face reddened from the anger. The anger that he thought he had under control was beginning to slip up on him again. Memories from his hidden past were coming back in flashes between thoughts. At times he had trouble knowing what was real and what was fantasy. This much he knew: these were no fantasies. He was watching them again in full color.

He thought he'd erased those days and nights of his time at the junior seminary forever; at least the priests hoped so.

"It's my duty to do it, and I feel I'm up for it, for the good people around here." Gordon felt light-headed and held tight to the chair's arms.

He had another flashback. Again, he was fifteen, naked, tied to the chair feeling helpless, afraid, angry, humiliated, and ashamed. Just thinking about it after all these years brought the feeling of hate back to him. He hated himself. He visualized slashing his wrists, hanging himself, anything to get away from it as he felt those same feelings that he'd had so long ago.

There he was on the little makeshift stage tied, naked, and helpless as seven priests stood in a small circle around him, chanting. Sometimes they would shout a phrase from the Bible, but never in unison. Each recited scripture from time to time, then teased him for not obeying, for questioning, for not feeling remorse, or not being more Christ-like. The words "Shame on you!" came back to Gordon Maxwell like a cold hard slap in the face.

"*Shame* on you, you perverted *twit*," Gordon remembered one of the priests saying. Then, they walked circles around him as he sat trying to hide his privates, his young manhood. They chanted and called out to him, "You are the devil's child! You can never be in God's Graces. God *hates* you. He doesn't like your mother *or* your father! You are a child from the City of the Damned and to *hell* you will go!"

It went on and on until they reached a point where they just stood in place. By that point, the men in black had broken the teenager. The fifteen-year-old Gordon Maxwell was sobbing and shouting. "Stop it! You bastards, STOP IT!" he shouted through his tears.

They laughed. At that point the short, balding priest, Paul Cheney, made him repeat, "I'm not worthy of God's love." He then touched Gordon's nipples with his index and middle fingers and rubbed them until they became hard. The priest then massaged his stout bare chest and firm nipples as he'd done many times in the hallway, while testing him on his knowledge of prayers. He'd rub them, twisted them, and pull them until they were purple. Father Cheney would pinch them harder and harder, twisting them until Gordon backed away. He would chuckle and say, "I'll see you during confession time. I'll be your confessor."

Gordon repeated, "I'm not worthy of God's love," both whispering and at the top of his lungs.

"Say, 'I'm a bad boy,'" the short balding priest demanded.

He felt ashamed, as he did with the incidents in the hallway, yet followed that order and half a dozen other orders after that. Tears streamed down his cheeks until there were no more tears to shed, and that's when it happened.

The men in black took a few steps closer to him, dropped their pants and had a circle jerk. Some of the men got immediate erections, held onto and massaged the penis of the priest next to them until they all were hard.

Paul Cheney was the lone exception. He didn't get an erection. Instead, he stepped away from the others, stood in front of the helpless teen, and peed on him. He arched the stream of urine so that it splashed Gordon in the face for several seconds. Gordon closed his eyes tight, holding his breath for as long as he could. He opened his eyes. When he did, he got splattered again, and it entered his mouth. He tried spitting it out, yet he swallowed. It was just a reaction, but he hated himself for having it happen. He had to breathe and, when he did, it went up his nose to the back of his throat. He swallowed again as he turned his face one way, then the other.

It was no use. The priest just followed him with his stream of urine. He sat there, tied to the chair, soaking wet with the urine dripping from his head, face, and the rest of his naked body as the group of men in black mocked him.

There was no more room for shame. He wanted to die. When Father Cheney finished and zipped up, he bent over Gordon and said with a grimace, "Shame on you! Shame on you, Gordon Maxwell. God hates you. I might tell your parents. Or better yet, bury you alive, with the others."

Gordon Maxwell was in disbelief. He thought he'd forever erased that episode from his memory back then, yet, here it was, just as if it happened last night.

"Gordon! Look at me, Gordon. Mickey urged. "I know you want to handle this yourself, but frankly I don't see how. You're all broke up. First of all, nobody can understand what the hell you're saying, and

31

just look at your face. You look, well, I don't wanna say useless, but maybe helpless would be a better word."

Gordon was about to blow his stack. His face turned as red as could be, and his jugular vein on the side of his neck stuck out and was pounding hard. He slammed his fist against the wall behind him and cracked the plaster around it.

"One more thing," Mickey said as he tiptoed away from the half-crazed Sheriff, heading for the door. "We have a couple of children missing. The Hornsby's kids.

"Mrs. Knee, the teacher at the old one-room schoolhouse a couple miles from Pa's farm, you know where it is, she stays there during the week at the Hornsby's farm just north of Pa's place.

"Anyway, Mrs. Knee was telling me she was out back getting wood for the fireplace when a long, shiny black car stopped in front of the house. A man got out, and she could see him. He was dressed in black, a long black coat, black fedora, and rubbery boots. He headed for the front door.

"She started for the house, slipped on a patch of ice near the old water pump by the garden, twisted her ankle, and hit her head on the frozen ground. By the time she got up and hobbled around to the front of the house, the man was pulling back onto the road and was gone. 'It was a Buick,' she said, 'a newer, black Buick.' That she was sure of."

"And?" Maxwell blurted out, losing his patience. "And?"

"Well, she got up to the front steps onto the porch and yelled for Timmy and Margaret. She felt sick inside because she didn't see or hear the kids. She looked everywhere and called their names, but they were gone. Their coats and mittens were still in the closet. It looks like we have a kidnapping on our hands to boot."

The pills and acids in Sheriff Maxwell's stomach were having a negative reaction, and it reached a volcanic-like eruption as the teetering Sheriff hoisted himself from the chair and made quick, uneasy steps to the room's sink, leaned over as the wretched tasting yellow bile spewed through his wired jaw and splattered into the sink, oozing down the drain. He washed his hands and rinsed out his mouth.

CHAPTER SEVEN

The days were turning into nights and night into day for Nurse Anne. She was poring over the latest revelations concerning Ms. Darling and Dr. Bullock, as well as Sheriff Maxwell's dilemma and Will's amazing recovery. She needed rest, but rest would not come, not yet. It was the end of her night shift, and she stayed to talk with Pam. She felt they had to talk and plot out the next step, whatever that may be.

She had learned that the local Lutheran minister, Florien Swain, had forced sex with Pam as a fifteen-year-old minor and got her pregnant some sixteen years ago. She was put on a train and sent out west to live with total strangers until she had her baby. Then and only then could she go back home.

Also there was the ugly matter of Doctor Trent Bullock and the way he treated Pam. On top of that, the sick bastard has pictures of children, some in sexual poses, in distress, wearing little or no clothes. *That son of a bitch needs to be castrated!*

Raphael and Will were hovering near the ceiling in the nurse's lounge above Nurse Anne. Will blurted out, "Castration?"

Raphael stood with his hands in the pockets of his denim trousers. "I just want you to know what's going on."

Will didn't say a word. He just hovered next to his angel with a shit-eating grin.

Pam stepped into the cafeteria, donned in her white nurses' dress and shoes. The top two buttons of her blouse were left unbuttoned. They couldn't be buttoned. Her more than ample breasts wouldn't allow it. The nurse's cap was pinned atop her sexy shoulder-length platinum blond hair.

She was such a good-looking, well-stacked, voluptuous temptress that the male patients got a hard-on when she walked into their room. If they couldn't raise one, they should've been pronounced dead at the scene.

She walked with sheer grace to the counter, past a table where two interns and a male nurse sat conversing and scanning the morning paper's sport section. The chatter stopped as they followed her swaying hips to the counter. She picked out a sticky bun. She never knew the correct name of the sinful pastry, so she called them sticky buns. What she did know about them was the thick caramel and crushed pecans always stuck to the sides of her teeth in and around her gums toward the back corners of her mouth, back where her wisdom teeth used to be. They must have a thousand calories. They tasted so damned good, though.

At the end of the counter, and after she paid the cashier, she reached for a thick white ceramic cup and set it on the counter. She poured herself a hot cup of black coffee. Pam liked it straight up. No sugar. No cream.

Walking carefully, she balanced her coffee and sticky bun to a table near the back wall where she caught a glimpse of another white uniform. "Hey, Anne, what are you doing here? You should be in bed and curled up around a young hot stud in a fit of unabashed sexual passion."

Anne smiled as Pam placed her coffee carefully on the table and sat down.

"With who? Is there an Italian or any man in this podunk town under the age of forty?" Anne crushed out her Pall Mall in the ashtray on the nearby table.

"A few," Pam replied. "Those who couldn't pass the test to be drafted, a few who live out on the farms, and ah, I get your point," she said as she took a bite out of one corner of the gooey bun.

Exhausted, Anne leaned in and rested her head on her crossed arms on the table as Pam gnawed and chewed on her breakfast roll. "Got any ideas of what we should do?"

Pam put a finger in her mouth, and with her fingernail, got a piece of lodged caramel off one of her molars, swallowed it, took another bite, chewed and chewed until it was swallowed, and chased it with a slurp of hot coffee.

"Gawd, you make a lot of noise with that stuff," Anne mumbled.

Wiping the corner of her mouth with a napkin, she said, "Mmm, more fun that way. I feel I get my money's worth. What do you call these things anyway?" Pam didn't wait for an answer.

"Caramel pecan breakfast thingy?" Pam crinkled her nose, "Naw, that ain't it. I'll just call 'em sticky buns."

Anne lifted her head, straightened herself, and said, "We have some serious business to talk over."

"To be sure," Pam said as she wiped the corners of her mouth, still digging into the far recesses for the last sticky pieces of pecan and caramel, tipping the cup to wash it down. "A lot of serious business, and I'm afraid it concerns me, at least two people I know and what all else I haven't figured out yet."

"Why you?" Anne asked.

"Unfortunately, I'm closest to at least two of the assholes in this mess. I get the feeling that Dr. Bullock knows Will's father better than he lets on and, what's more, I know from Pastor Swain a long time ago that he and Will's Pa would meet late in the evenings sometimes and talk with a third shady character. Now I know it was Dr. Bullock, but there was another guy; I can't think of his name, maybe I never knew it, he was a short balding puke of a man when I last caught a glimpse of him. Plus, there were one or two others they talk of but never mentioned around me until just the other day."

Anne was stunned. "You just now figured out that the guy you've been banging, Doctor Bullock, is a pervert and fools around with children?"

"Jesus *Christ,* Anne, I only discovered those pictures a few days ago myself! Maybe I've been in denial! I've been *fucked up,* used, abused; you name it. I had no one to confide in, until you came along. From now on, Anne, I'm on the offense. I'm going after them. I need help. Can I bum a cigarette?"

Anne passed a Pall Mall her way, flipped open her Zippo, and lit it for her.

"Sorry, Pam. I apologize. I'm tired and not thinking straight, I guess."

"I've been a little ditsy, too. I *got screwed!* I need help now, and that's where you come in. Somebody has got to help me. I don't want to get hurt, you know?"

"I know, I fucking know," Anne said.

Anne lit a cigarette for herself, took a long drag on it, and blew out a couple of smoke rings. She thought for a few seconds and sighed. "It's too bad our Sheriff isn't in the best of shape to help us."

"Ah, who needs men anyway? That reminds me," Pam said, "Dr. Bullock wants to come up to my apartment tonight for, ah, for . . ."

"I'm not surprised." Anne pushed forward in her chair. "Hey, why not make up an excuse to go to *his* house, not yours, and maybe you could do a little snooping. Perhaps you could find something there that you can tell our wounded Sheriff about. See if you could come up with more of those pictures and, God knows, another name or two, anything tangible that the Sheriff could use and arrest the slimy bastards." She slumped back in her chair. "I'm not sure how, though."

"I thought about that this morning while I was taking a shower," Pam said. "Perhaps a cocktail, a special cocktail."

"What do you mean?" Anne asked as her eyes widened.

"The kind one makes for the bad guys, like in the movies, let's say," Pam said with a quick blink and malicious smile, "and then they just sort of fall asleep for about seven to nine hours."

"I know that kind of cocktail you're talking about, and where to find it. We need the key to the pharmacy," Anne said.

Pam shrugged. "And that's the one key I don't have."

Anne took a fast and final pull on the Pall Mall and crushed it out in the brown plastic ashtray on the next table. As she exhaled the smoke out of her nose, she nodded. "All right, time to go to work." With a coy smile, she put her hand in a front pocket. "I forgot to hand this in after signing out for it last night." She handed Pam a long bronze key.

Raphael and Will faded out, and Will slipped back into his body on his hospital bed, still grinning that grin.

They stepped away from their table and hugged. Anne whispered, "You be careful, girl. Any trouble, just call and I'll come a runnin'."

Pam had her arms locked around Anne and squeezed a little tighter before letting go. "Wish me luck." The men in white sitting at the table watched.

As the nurses walked by, Anne looked their way, saying, "We're lezbos." Pam laughed out loud.

Anne drove her new, shiny gray nineteen forty-nine two-door Chevy coupe with a three-speed transmission on the column home to catch up on some much needed sleep, while Pam Darling prepared to make her rounds with Doctor Bullock.

She received extra pay for being the doctor's assistant, and cash "under the table" for being his secret mistress. She liked the money and had a tidy sum building up in her savings account. She didn't mind that part at all. Pam had earned every penny of it and then some. Since it came from what she termed "combat pay," she felt that she was more than entitled to it. Bullock's money was for services rendered.

No one knew about the cash that she'd collected from Pastor Florien Swain over the years, either. As far as she was concerned, he could never *pay enough* for her ride on the Illinois Central. Her west-bound train was in Kansas City. It was there she made the connection on the Southern Pacific Railway. It took to the iron and she rode those rails to Phoenix, Arizona.

Pam stayed with a Mormon family in Gilbert Arizona, not far from Phoenix. They cared for her during her stay. She had never met them until she arrived at their front door. Nice people. They put her baby in a good home with loving parents.

She sometimes fantasized about what she would say if someone confronted her about taking the pastor's money. Pamela would turn on her charm. Some people may well call it extortion. Pastor Swain agreed, however, with Pam to the terms of fifty dollars a month until their baby boy was twenty-one years old. He couldn't bear the repercussions if the word were to get out that he had fathered a baby by a fifteen-year-old girl. His reputation would be ruined around Pine Nut and, worse, he would certainly be drummed out of the Lutheran church when the elders found out about the baby and the money leaving the weekly coffers. On the first of the month, Pam got a fifty-dollar bill and still did.

She saw herself in those daydreams, turning a coquettish smile toward the inquirer with her pouting ruby red lips, big, dark, doe eyes surrounded by milky white skin, saying, "A girl like me needs a little milk money to get by on, honey." That's all it would take, and they would turn on their heels and walk away. That's how she saw it, end of questions, end of story.

Other women may have demanded the money, and lots more of it. On the other hand, the judges in nineteen thirty-five may have decided in the man's favor. After all, the judges were male, and the female was usually the seductress, regardless of age, especially Pam Darling. She just used the term "milk money," and the two men forked over the cash. She never had a reason to feel guilty about taking it, either, not until a day ago in Will's room, when she had her epiphany. Pam had other ideas, bigger dreams, and they were beginning to look good to her. Maybe her past could be rectified, the wrong righted. Pam wouldn't have to put up with the nonsense much longer. She knew, now, what she had to with them, one at a time. It would be just a matter of believability. With Trent, a guy couldn't just pull the wool over his eyes. He was a sharp man: mean, sly, revengeful, yes; gullible, no. She also knew his drinking habits. He enjoyed wine. Hard stuff was his weakness. A couple of house whiskeys and poor Trent became a messy babbler. She would buy a bottle and bring it to his house.

Pam, on the other had, could drink a sailor under the table without batting an eye.

She made her way to the front desk situated just a few steps across the hall near the front doors of the brownstone and brick hospital, up five steps to two thick Victorian doors with heavy lead-etched glass windows. The front desk was where one could find the answers: room numbers, cafeteria, bathroom, and more.

Ms. Darling was standing next to the receptionist going over the charts for Will and Sheriff Maxwell. As she was reading them, she turned to go to the Sheriff's room when she felt a hand touch her left arm just above the elbow.

"Good morning, Ms. Darling. Anything there I should know about?" he asked in a monotone voice.

Startled, yet keeping her composure, she didn't look up from the charts. "Not really, Dr. B. Everything seems to be falling into place today." Flipping the pages, she continued, "No concerns, no problems, no emergencies," she ended, still looking down at the notes on the clipboard.

"Perfect!" he said, raising his voice a little. "I feel great today. I have a few phone calls to make and a meeting to attend, so I won't be making my normal rounds."

"Something wrong?" she asked.

"Nothing to worry about. You're a good girl, Ms. Darling, a *very* good, little girl," he said as he ogled her inviting behind. He reached down and patted it hard, then pinched it.

Pam didn't move. She let him have his fun and didn't mind that the receptionist saw it all.

It wasn't that she didn't care. She did. It's just that she had other ideas, like letting others see what was going on, so that when the shit hits the fan, and she felt it was just a matter of time, it would come back to the pompous ass a thousand fold, just as the prophecies Pastor Swain lectured about on Sunday mornings. For some, they would be roaring into view, like a snowball from hell.

Trent walked Pam down the hall and around the corner, out of sight from everyone in the building. "Say, Ms. Darling, you have such a beautiful and firm behind. I'd like to see more of it. It just so happens that I'm free this evening, all evening. I'll be at your apartment tonight, say around seven? How's that?" he said with a devilish grin, his eyebrows jumping up and down like Groucho Marx.

Here it comes, she thought.

"Listen, Trent, you tiger you, I have a cousin from Chicago who's staying with me for the next few days. She's old enough to be my mother and a bit prudish. Elaine came here last night on the Greyhound bus all the way from a little town with a funny name in Arizona. But, I tell you what, dear heart. I'd love to be with you tonight just to get away from the religious old bag, even if it's just for a few precious hours with you."

"What's so funny about the name of the town?" he asked.

"Well, it's called Gilbert. Ever hear of a town called Gilbert?"

He smirked and said nothing. Pam caressed his arms and shoulders as they embraced. She had no visitor at her house, and she didn't even know anyone named Elaine. But Gilbert *is* where she had her baby.

Trent turned and walked back toward the front desk, and as he rounded the corner he slipped on something on the floor and fell on the hard marble floor. Pam rushed to help him up. "I'm okay, Ms. Darling," he said as he reached and picked up a long white feather with a green quill. Sitting on the floor with the feather in his hand, he questioned, "Now, where do you suppose this damn thing came from?"

Gordon was washing his hands at the sink next to Will talking to him about the recent events and telling him about his pa.

". . . and that's how Mickey found him, Will. I'm sorry I couldn't be there. Maybe I could have prevented it from happening," he bemoaned as he wiped his hands dry.

"What could you have done? Besides, he can't hurt anybody anymore." Will looked up at his buddy and, after a few thoughtful moments, said, "Why was he so mean and ornery?"

"I don't know, son. I don't know. He wrote a suicide note, too, which I'll let you read as soon as I can. By the way, I didn't even know his last name until Mickey told me. Never knew his first name, come to think of it. Do you?"

"Priestly. He wouldn't tell anyone though, and I don't know why. I don't know his first name. Maybe he never had one. You know Pa; he wouldn't say shit if he had a mouthful."

Gordon continued. "Folks in town knew him as Pa. Everyone called him that, and that's what he responded to. Pa Priestly. I have to tell you something else that neither the doctors nor the nurses know. I don't feel any pain, like you said, 'I won't feel any pain.' I don't know how, pills or what, but I feel great! Last night I pulled the wires out of my mouth. It didn't hurt, and there was no bleeding. I still wear the bandages so they won't notice, but I made a decision to get the hell out of here today, to start gathering the information needed to get to the bottom of things because, as they say on the radio, 'the plot is thickening.' Will, there's one other matter to contend with. Timmy Lee and Margaret Lynn, your neighbors, are missing as of yesterday."

Startled, Will said, "*What happened?* How come they're missing?" He knew about his pa because Ralphy had told him last night. He told Will many things about Dr. 'B,' Pastor Swain, a man he'd yet to meet, the Catholic priest, but no mention about Timmy and Margaret.

With a pained expression, Gordon responded, "Late yesterday afternoon, Mrs. Knee was watching the Hornsby kids, as she always does, when a big, black Buick rolled up in front of the house. She was in the backyard, saw it, and began heading toward the house, when the man in the black Buick drove off. She had a real sick feeling and ran to the house, calling the kids by name. She couldn't find them anywhere. Their coats and mittens were still in the house."

"You go, Sheriff! You go, now! They're my best buddies. They helped me and took the notes I wrote to give to you a few nights ago. So you find them. I'll get out of here, too, but in the meantime, you ask for help from your angels!"

"I think maybe your pa knocked the stuffing out of you. I don't know if I believe in angels," he said, shaking his head.

As Gordon got up to leave, the emerald green color in the corner of the room next to Will's bed deepened, then pulsated. Sheriff Maxwell's eyes widened as he watched in amazement.

"Don't piss off the angels!" Will shot back. "Don't fight it. They're as real as your feelings for the nurses, Sheriff."

"Oh, they're cute and cuddly, but I don't have special feelings toward them."

"Sheriff? With all due respect, I have to say, *bullshit!*"

Gordon rolled his eyes, knowing full well he'd been caught in a lie. He walked out the door, down the hall, and out to the street to wait for his deputy to pull up. He was thinking of the bottle of Five Star brandy in the bottom drawer of his desk and how good it would taste. *His desk, his bottle, his office.* He also thought about what Will had said about angels, and *how did* Will float or know about his feelings toward the nurses? Pills, it had to be the pills.

Will was right about the pain thing, he thought. *I don't know how it happened, but I'm glad it happened. If I have to call upon an angel to ease the pain, I'll do it.*

"Angels, if there really are angels among us, can you get my sidekick, the skinny little Zaugbaum, here now so I don't have to freeze to death waiting without any coat?"

There was a puddle of water at the curb, so he stepped back and took a few steps up to the big wide oak tree and leaned against it. As he did so, he saw Dr. Bullock drive his big tan Oldsmobile out onto the street from the back parking lot with Pastor Swain in the passenger seat and a shorter man in black in back, leaning forward, resting his arms on the back of the front seat. The Sheriff stood to the opposite side of the tree, away from the driveway, as they went by. He was close enough to be able to look inside the auto as it passed. They were looking at black and white photographs, the one in the back flashing them to the doctor and pastor in the front seat, as they made their way down the street and out of sight.

He turned his attention to the oncoming car from the opposite direction up the street. It was his squad car with Deputy Mickey

Zaugbaum at the wheel, driving like there was no tomorrow. He stepped to the curb as Mickey pulled up next to him, splashing the Sheriff's pant legs and shiny black Wellington boots with freezing muddy water as the front tires sloshed through the puddle. "Nice shot, Zaugbaum!" He climbed into the passenger seat and slammed the door shut and looked up to the ceiling, saying, "Coincidence."

"What? Oh, sorry, Sheriff. I didn't see the mud puddle 'til it was too late."

"Mickey. I wonder if you could do something for me."

"Anything, boss."

"Listen. You go to Pastor Swain's services, don't you?"

"Every Sunday, Gordon. I even pass the basket and usher. I'm a damn good Lutheran, don't you think?"

"Count the money, too?" he asked, wiping mud off his Wellingtons.

Mickey nodded. "Oh yeah. I'm the treasurer of the men's club. I do a few things besides chauffeuring you around the countryside, you know." Mickey muttered under his breath what he'd like to say out loud. *If you only knew how I cover for you on the days when you're drunk on your ass.*

Mickey could cover for anybody. He was good at it, and he knew it. He could work under cover for the government if he ever got the chance.

"Good. I want you to go over the Pastor's records and see what he receives from the basket and what he records and if it matches up."

"That'll be easy, Sheriff. I know to the penny what's taken in on a given Sunday. I write it down and enter it in a ledger that's kept in the back of the church. He looks at my ledger and copies it onto his. He has other monies coming in from the elders upstate, too, you know."

"Two sets of books? If there's any discrepancies, notify me ASAP," Gordon said.

"You got it. As luck would have it, tonight's the night I do the bookwork."

Gordon leaned toward Mickey, looked him in the eye, and said, "Can you deviate a little from your routine and do the books this morning?"

"I was hoping you'd say that. The office is ice cold this morning. No heat."

Gordon looked at him sideways, "No heat? How come there's no heat?"

"I forgot to order more fuel oil. You always did it. I just forgot," Mickey said sheepishly.

"One other thing. If Doc Bullock or anyone else is with him, I want to know what's said between them. Got it?"

"I didn't fall off the turnip truck yesterday."

Snow was beginning to fall. There was no wind to speak of as white satiny sparkles graced the leafless limbs of the bare trees and blanketed the brown ground. The tender aroma from the wood-burning stoves was in the air as the smoke rose from the surrounding homes of Pine Nut.

Will stood near the window ledge and watched as a cardinal pecked through the snow at bits of breadcrumbs he left on the outer portion of the window's brick ledge. He was thumbing through Thoreau as he heard footsteps in the hall. They had a familiar sound. He set the book down on the window's edge and slid between the covers as the door opened.

"Nurse Anne," he said, faking a startled tone. "What brings you in during the day?"

"I couldn't sleep. I just came by to grab the book on the spiritualist Madam Blavatsky. I'll be trying to get some rest on the couch in the nurse's lounge. Will?" she continued. "There's something I have to tell you, and I don't think anyone has had the nerve to tell you, but your mother is here, too, up on the psych ward."

"I know," Will said. "Don't ask me how I know. It's okay, Nurse Anne. I'm okay with it."

"She'll be with us for awhile. She's, well, she's out of it. Your mother has had several grand mals to boot. She out of it for twenty minutes at a time during seizures like that."

Will interrupted, "Could you check on her medication for me? You see, sometimes the pharmacy gets the epilepsy prescription wrong or fills it with the wrong dosage. Either Doctor Bullock originally wrote it wrong, or the pharmacist gets it wrong. Please, the problem is getting the right dosage, and she needs to be re-examined by a doctor *not* from this area. I believe with my whole heart and soul after that's done, she'll be fine as long as she gets the right kind of medication."

"I'll be sure it's done as you say," Anne confided with a surprised look. "You must have learned a little while I read to you or something. Your vocabulary has changed, and you seem much more mature for a fella your age. You're not the backwoods country boy who was brought in here last week, that's for sure. What else can you tell me, young man?" she asked.

"Lots! I have to keep the vocabulary as it was before I got here. I screw up once in awhile, but play along with me and I'll tell you all about it."

"I'm all ears."

"Grab yourself a chair and sit down, 'cause what I'm about to tell you, you just ain't gonna believe, sister. It's alright," he said as he got up and out of bed, walked to the window's edge again, and sat down.

Anne became rattled, and her hands went to her white uniform pockets searching for the matches and Pall Malls.

"I'll tell you what I know, all of it, but dammer, you've got to keep it a secret. You can't go round tellin' every Tom, Dick, and Harry, 'cause it's just too important not to. Do you understand?" Even his usage of language couldn't get her to laugh this time.

"I'll tell you, but you have to promise on your hypocritical nurse's oath you ain't tellin'."

"I won't breathe it to a soul, son," she said, trying to still her shaking hands to light her cigarette.

"Okay, here it goes, but one other thing. You're making me nervous watching you be nervous. Light one for me. I ain't had one since I've been here."

He told his story from the beginning, including his pal, Ralphy, flying, and the inside scoop on Dr. B and Pastor Swain, with their involvement in the secret society. Everything he could remember and then some came flying out of his mouth fast and furious. Awhile later he finished his story and several Pall Malls.

"And that's the way it is, Nurse Anne. I appreciate all you've done for me, especially reading to me at night. I learned a lot with your help. I'll revert to my abnormal use of words when I get excited or angry. You know what I mean? I tried telling old Ralphy about that, but he's rather stern about those things."

Nurse Anne sat cross-legged for a moment. She didn't let on about her doubts. "So you might swear a blue streak when you get pissed off, is that it?"

"Damn straight!"

CHAPTER EIGHT

Clutching the brown paper bag in her left hand, she steadied her right hand and pressed the doorbell to Dr. Trent Bullock's beige brick, two-story Victorian house. There was a full moon, and a cold wind blew.

He came down the steps from his upstairs bedroom to the foyer. She could feel his presence before the porch light came on over the doorway. Her hair stood on end. In a flash, his face appeared in the ornate window on the thick wooden door as he peered out at her. At first glance, he looked like Bela Lugosi as a vampire. The light went out. All of a sudden, he was gone. He reappeared as the door swung open. He grabbed her arm, looked about, then pulled her in and locked the door behind them.

"Thank you for making me feel welcome," she said facetiously. "Couldn't Igor let me in, or did you give him the night off?"

"I'm just checking, that's all," he said, shrugging off her curt remarks. "Let me take your coat and hat. What's in the bag? Good wine, I hope."

Trent helped her with her coat and placed it on the oak coat tree in the foyer next to his.

"Getting a bit nippy, isn't it?" he said, trying to make small talk.

"Yeah, nippy," she echoed. "Sorry, I didn't bring wine tonight, but I did bring whiskey; bourbon, actually. I wanted to find just the right bottle of wine for us, but Vinney's selection was less than desirable, unless you wanted Ripple or Dark Port. Keith Whitherspoon, the town drunk, pleaded for a dance with me. I obliged and grabbed this and got out of there." She took it out of the bag and handed it to him.

With a sneer, he took the bottle from her and scanned the label. "I'll have a taste of Mr. Jack Daniels here first; then step down to the wine cellar and see if I can dig up something more worthy for tonight."

They sat together on the brown crushed velvet loveseat in the dimly lit living room, talking about the patients at the hospital, though neither had any interest. Trent set his empty glass down on the coffee table in front of the couch. The bourbon was taking effect. He was at ease in his house with Pam Darling. It was a rare occasion. For him, women were for sexual gratification when necessary and little else.

There was a thorn in his side. A prick he couldn't get out. "Country boy. Amazing, he's still alive. I can't get over it. How old *is* the god-damn zebra, Ms. Darling?"

"The records say he was born in thirty-five." She said.

"Ah, good year," he said. "Adolph Hitler was in power almost two years by then and putting those of the Purple Triangle, gypsies, homo-sexuals, and crazy loons in concentration camps. Smart man, a great leader for the world, yet people try to make him out to be a damned fool and a mad man!" Bullock was on a roll. "He wasn't, you know. Adolph was a shrewd and calculating man of vision. He could have ruled the world. With a little more time, mankind would have been better off today," he ranted.

"You know, Ms. Darling, I have a solid source who told me that he cut a deal with the head of the Catholic Church, the grandest church in all the world."

"Why would he do that?" she asked, not really giving a damn.

"And why not? From nineteen seventeen to nineteen twenty-nine, Pope Pius the twelfth had served as the *nuncio* (papal legate) to Bavaria while living in Germany. He had the pope eating right out of his hand. He instructed his bishops to ensure the parish priests in Germany and even in New York City would speak highly of the Führer during all Sunday masses. He had them pray for a successful outcome of the war for the mother country, Germany."

"No!" she stated, trying to sound interested.

"It's true. The Pope turned on the Führer only when it was clear the war was going to be won by the Allied Forces.

Pam, bored with his rants, tried unsuccessfully to get his attention by hiking her skirt. He glanced at her white silky thighs, but kept on.

"Ah, it was in the mid-thirties that Hitler had the camps built and the gas chambers installed. The Pope knew about them. He got letters with sketches from those International Bible Students, as the Jehovah Witness called themselves back then, but burned the letters. Never said a word about the systematic torture and killing of the insane, gypsies, homosexuals, least of all the goddamn Jews; in fact, I think he took a certain amount of revengeful joy in it for the killing of Jesus two thousand years ago! I bet you didn't know that, Ms. Darling. Few people know that even now. It's a damned shame how the war turned out, *but* there is a glimmer of hope."

Ms. Darling tried hard not to get up and leave. She shook back her silver-blond hair and said, "Why don't you fix me another drink, Dr. B, while I freshen up a little." She removed her pumps from her cold aching feet and opened her blouse by unfastening the third button to help calm him down. This time it worked. He watched with delight as she undid the button. His eyes were fixed on her sumptuous, braless, lily-whites.

"Why, yes. Yes, of course, Pam, darling. The bathroom is down the hall to the right, just before you get to the kitchen. Why don't you make yourself another drink while I go down into the cellar and round up a good bottle of tasty wine for the evening."

Pam smiled and nodded. She made her way along the hall to the bathroom as he stepped toward the kitchen. To the left of the back door was the doorway to the cellar. The old wooden steps creaked as he descended to the dark, cold, musty cellar.

CHAPTER NINE

Will and Ralphy were making the rounds that night. The first stop was to the fourth floor of the hospital. Will floated in to sit with his mother. He found her asleep on a small bed in a dimly lit room that overlooked the parking lot and cornfield in the distance. The walls were lined with pads and the windows had metal bars across the thick panes of glass. At least it was warm there, and she got plenty of food to eat and no dishes to wash.

The staff was treating her well. Will checked on her daily, either physically or via God-Thought. From there, Ralphy and Will drifted across town to the Sheriff's office to drop in and see what was going on. Deputy Zaugbaum was laying out the ledger and other papers from Pastor Swain's church office on the Sheriff's desk.

"You got that furnace up pretty high tonight, Zaugs," Gordon said as he sat in his chair behind his desk.

Mickey turned from his paperwork and said, "I didn't want you to freeze tonight. I felt guilty about not ordering more fuel oil the other day."

Gordon grinned. "You *should* feel guilty." He then pushed himself away, stood, and took a step to the front door. "You get everything in order. I'm stepping out front for some fresh air." He stood on the front step and breathed in the cool night's air while stretching his arms up over his head, clasping his hands together.

Back inside, the deputy pranced around the desk, placing the items in chronological order with times and dates, making it easier for Gordon to read and comprehend.

"Ralphy, I'm going in to take a closer look at what he has there on the table."

"That's fine. Breathe now and go within."

Will took a deep breath, held it, let it out, then sailed down toward the side of the solid brick building next to the alley way. He was getting closer and noticed a window. He hesitated, *the window or the wall?* Will prepared to enter.

At the same time, Mickey was leaning over the desk, making sure he had things in order. Just as he began straightening one last paper, Will slammed into the wall.

The sudden burst of noise caught Mickey by surprise. He found himself spread-eagle across the desk with papers flying about the room.

Will managed to get himself stuck half in and half out of the office wall. His head was through, including his arms and shoulders, but that's all. The rest of his torso, butt, and legs were left dangling on the building in the alleyway.

Mickey spun in the direction of the commotion. All he could see was a bright yellow light. He stood motionless. Not breathing nor moving a muscle, his eyes were transfixed on the yellow orb on the wall by the window.

Mickey, while staring at it, inched his way off the table, eyes glued to the strange, intrusive glow.

Will had to figure something out and fast. He did the only thing he could think of. As Mickey began tiptoeing toward him, William cocked his head, looking right at Mickey with his eyes bulging wide from the sockets, and said, "Boo!"

Mickey scrambled around the desk, his legs pistoling wildly, as he raced out through the front door, smacking into Gordon. They tumbled to the sidewalk, with Zaugbaum clinging tight.

Gordon pushed him away in disgust, got up, dusted off the snow, and tried to remove the clumps of the cold white stuff that had piled up in the back of his neck and down the inside of his shirt. He peered at Mickey. "What the *hell's* the matter with you, for chrissakes? You act like you've seen a ghost!"

"Practice. You need more practice, Will."

"Damn. I thought I had it right this time. I scared the poop out of him *and* me. The deputy kept staring at me."

"Saying 'boo' works just fine. No one is going to believe him, anyway. Gordon may question a few things. That too, shall pass. Come. We got places to go."

The place was a mess. Papers scattered from desk to floor, to the sides, and all the way to the far wall. "I swear on a stack of Bibles, two prostitutes, a grandmother, and a newborn babe, that's what happened. That's what I saw!"

Gordon shook his head, emptied the pot of coffee, and made fresh. "Tell me, deputy, did that ghost say anything to you?" Gordon asked as he thought about Will's gibberish about angels at the hospital.

"Yes, he did, as a matter of fact."

"And what was that?" the Sheriff asked as he spooned at the coffee.

"Well-ah-he said, he said, '*BOO!*'" Gordon tried hard not to laugh. He couldn't. He laughed. And laughed hard.

CHAPTER TEN

Again, Will and Ralphy were above Bullock's house. Blushing, Will was enjoying the show that Pam Darling staged for the groggy and intoxicated doctor. Archangel Raphael spoke to young William: "This is not for you."

"Crap."

Raphael wore a white, collarless shirt and green corduroy pants that evening. His hands, as always, were halfway in his front pockets as he spoke. "You know, William, until you entered the hospital, her life had been pure hell."

Will's cheeks flushed as he watched the shenanigans and the sensual Pam Darling below. He didn't hear a word.

Raphael interrupted Will's train of thought. "You have to help your friend, Sheriff Maxwell. He wants to find Timmy and Margaret. He'll need your help."

Raphael placed a hand on Will's elbow, saying, "A special place awaits us, Will. It's a place of knowledge and learning. Some call it the Hall of Records."

"Timmy and Margaret are my friends," Will said. "I really don't want to hear that something bad is happening to them. I won't like it, Ralphy. I'll get angry. I'd rather be with them."

Raphael stepped back, cocked his head, and said, "A: you don't know where they are, and B: you're with me. You cannot be in two places at one time. Either you come with me to a place of learning and knowledge, or stay here alone."

William had encountered a major dilemma. Would he choose to try and find his friends or go with his angel? If he went with his friend, he knew he'd be engulfed in the loving arms of God's unconditional love. He would see and feel majestic panoramic views, and once again the feeling of absolute bliss.

"Oh Ralphy. Can't you make it possible for me to be in two places at the same time?"

Archangel Raphael began to lose his physical appearance, and a bright green bubble took his place as he spoke. "William, if you choose not to go with me now, you won't be able to help your friends. You've been given a gift. Your decision is requested. Do you choose to leave this world now and enter the place you call heaven, or do you want to stay for the sake of the children?"

William, flushed with anger, became frustrated. He let out with all his might a series of profanity-laden angry statements directed at no one in particular.

"Anger will get you nowhere. In time, your questions will be answered. Events happen for reasons not yet known to mortals." Raphael was sincere and firm. "Just remember, *love will find a way*. Love will also help you find a way to move from point A to point B. Remove the anger in your heart. Once that's done, you'll be better able to penetrate any wall between you and those you love, even brick walls. Until that time, you will not be able to do so.

Remember, fill your heart with love, remove anger, and you'll be able to move as angels move via thoughts of pure intention. *That's* called God-Thought."

Raphael returned to his physical appearance as he and Will lifted up and away from Pine Nut and the rest of the world. It felt as if they were away for months, even years. It was so peaceful for the young teenager, even as he was being pulled away from the learning center, back to Earth.

They floated down once again above the scene they had left. Time had stood still.

"It is time for you to renew your thirst for the rights of the little ones. You haven't lost a second. Do good work."

William nodded and took a deep breath as he once again peered through the doctor's roof.

Will tried to digest the information he received from the learning center and to focus on Pam Darling's plot.

She had removed her clothing and stepped out of the bathroom wearing Dr. B's bathrobe. In her hand was a packet of strong sedatives to mix with his drink.

He was rummaging down in the cellar. She looked around the kitchen for his glass of bourbon and found it on the counter next to the icebox. She opened the packet and shook the white sleepy substance into the glass, where it rested on top of the half-melted ice cubes.

As she opened the icebox for more cubes, she could hear him climb the creaking stairway to the door. Pam shut the icebox door, grabbed the bottle of bourbon, and poured it into the glass. Making her way to the sink, she topped it off with water and stirred with her finger. She was licking her middle finger and holding the whiskey glass in her other hand as Trent stepped back into the kitchen and set his lusting eyes on her.

"I see you got yourself a little more comfortable, Ms. Darling. My bathrobe fits you nicely," he said, staring.

She removed her finger from her mouth and gave him such a seductive grin that it would melt the polar ice cap. Stepping toward the doctor, she planted the most erotic kiss on his lips that he'd never felt before. Pam sucked so hard on his tongue he thought for an instant he might lose it altogether. He melted and became aroused.

"Here you go, Doctor." She handed him the glass of bourbon and took the wine bottle from him. "You take this with you upstairs and get out of those frumpy clothes you're wearing, and I'll be in the living room waiting for your touch. The lights will be off and candles burning, Doctor. Now, hurry."

Instead of hurrying, he took a long pull from the glass. Becoming anxious, she raised her hand and ran it through his combed-back, greasy, thinning, and graying hair. She leaned in like she was going to hug him. Instead, she placed her teeth on his earlobe, bit down hard, splitting the skin, whispering, "Go now. I'll be on the couch . . . waiting. Hurry back."

He turned and proceeded to the stairs with the glass of bourbon in one hand and rubbing his throbbing, bloody earlobe with the other.

Minutes later, Pamela was sitting on the doctor's lap and their wineglasses were empty. "I'll pour us another glass doctor, sit tight." She reached for the wine bottle. Her breasts, now exposed, brushed across his chest. He closed his eyes, smiling.

"Did I ever tell you about the new Catholic priest who resides in Richland Park on the other side of the river? He says mass at St. Lawrence there on Saturday nights."

Pam filled the glasses thinking *here we go again.*

Miffed, she said, "No, tell me about him," pulling the robe tight around her.

"He's a Norwegian. A Norwegian, who wiped out his mother's savings account, hopped a freighter to Denmark, lied through his teeth and bribed his way into obtaining a German passport under an assumed name. He took on the name of Stöver, Charles Stöver, and joined the Nazi Party, enlisting in the German army."

Pam tried to look interested. It wasn't easy.

"The poor man was just devastated at the outcome of the war. He reclaimed his original name, bought another fake passport, and with a good amount of money that he stole from several church lootings, he now has a certificate and whatever other credentials needed to be known as a Catholic priest, arriving in America four years ago, in the late fall of 1945."

"He must have known a great deal about that religion," she said, yawning.

"It's funny how life works. He never attended a Catholic service until he arrived here. He was a goddamn Lutheran. His name is Svendly Pervasions. How's that for a name?"

"You're so wise. You know so much about people and foreign languages," Pam whispered as she tickled his chin, then bit the tip of his nose and licked deep inside his right ear.

"College, my dear," he said, grinning at her playfulness, "And the study of higher learning.

"There was a close-knit society that I belonged to at Boston University that had ties to a Catholic outfit in St. Louis, Missouri. It still exists. On occasion we would get together and discuss our views on the war and the so-called Jewish question and things like that.

"Then, of course, there is your *special* friend, Pastor Swain. Well, he likes to play dress up. He was there, too."

It was old news to her, yet she smiled, as he continued.

"Recently he's been slipping over to Reverend Pervasion's house out on the edge of the prairie to discuss the exploits they've had with kids. Now, that's between you and me and the man in the moon, right, Ms. Darling?"

Pam hated him. She hated Florien Swain. However, she loved the money she received the first Tuesday of the month. From that she could smile all the way to the bank.

"I already forgot what you said, Doctor," Pam said as she began to remove the belt from his pants and unzip his fly. Reaching in, she grabbed a handful of his manhood. *Just as I suspected, limp like a cold dead fish. He couldn't get an erection if Mae West knelt before him with her mouth wide open, saying, "Aah."*

He moved and slipped her off his lap. He stood up fast. He felt dizzy and plopped down with his arms at his side. "Something's wrong." He put a hand to his forehead. His face contorted into a confused look as he said, "Perhaps it was that damned bourbon. I may have had too much to drink, Pam," he said, slurring his words.

"Let's go," she said as she helped him up again. "We'll have a special little party upstairs. Just the two of us, Trent, you devil you," she said with a sly grin. "We're going to party hardy. I'll be so good *and* so bad, you'll sleep like a baby all night long, you big hunk of a wild man, you!"

He teetered with a drug-induced, warped grin. The special cocktail was working according to plan.

"Tomorrow morning, I'll be gone, and no one will be none the wiser," she said as she put an arm around him and helped him up the stairs to his room. She sat him down on the bed.

She didn't know how to say it or what his reaction might be, but ask she must. "Speaking of boys, where are those pictures? I'd like to look at them, too."

"Oh," he said as he lay down across the bed on his back, he pointed downstairs, whispering, "In the cellar under the staircase." His eyes rolled, and the lids came down, resting at half-mast.

"Out cold," she whispered to herself and took off his shoes, removed his boxer shorts, but left his undershirt and socks on, then started for the door. She glanced at the neat stack of keys, coins, and papers on top of his dresser. She noticed a small leather notebook. "Aha." Wasting no time, she slipped it into a pocket of the robe.

She bounded down the stairs and glided through the living room into the kitchen, and opened the cellar door, pausing. All was quiet. She took a breath, saying, "Lord protect me. Help me find what I'm looking for."

She proceeded to touch each plank of the cold wooden step with her bare feet while holding tight to the belt of the oversized bathrobe with one hand and grasping the rough wooden rail with the other. She searched for a light switch but couldn't find one. As she took another step, something brushed the side of her cheek. Startled, she almost let out a scream. It was a string hanging down from the lone lightbulb dangling above the staircase. She pulled once, and the light flickered but stayed on.

CHAPTER ELEVEN

Tiptoeing the rest of the way down, she rounded the stairs and crouched under the staircase, peering at the far end of it, looking for a door.

After a few seconds, her eyes adjusted. She could see the outline of a small undersized door. She looked toward the cellar doorway just in case, then took another deep breath as her heart pounded fast against her chest. She kept low, stepping to the old wooden door; she put her hand on the cold doorknob. Pausing for any noise from above, her hands shaking. She'd done nothing like this before worrying that the crazy lout would somehow wake up.

Hearing only silence and the cold winter wind whistling through the trees outside, she applied pressure on the doorknob, turned it counterclockwise, and pulled. It didn't budge. She tried harder with both hands; still it didn't open. She stopped. *You can do this, Pamela.* Taking another breath, she turned the cold brass knob clockwise and gave it a quick tug.

It opened a tad and, as it did, it made a low creaking noise. Sensing success, she pulled again with both hands. This time it flew open so fast she was startled and thrown off balance. She let go of the door and found herself falling, banging her head on the back of the steps and landing on her butt, bracing herself with her hands at her side.

Rats scurried out of the short doorway and ran across her bare feet. She started to let out a scream, but muffled it with her hands. She got up and reached in on the sides of the door, hoping she would find a light switch, to no avail.

"Damn." She turned and ran up the steps. Padding to the living room, she grabbed one of the candles still burning on the coffee table. She glanced up the staircase, stopped to listen for a few seconds. Hearing nothing, Pam stepped to the front window, peered out, and saw light snow flurries and clouds passing the full moon while the sounds of swirling winds were blowing through the doorjamb.

Her mind went back to the task at hand, and she looked again up the staircase to Trent's bedroom. *All is quiet*, she thought, *the old boy's going to be out for many, many hours.*

Back in the cellar, she entered the small damp room under the stairway. More rats scurried from the light and scooted under the wine rack on the far side of the cellar. The dark walls emitted a strong musty odor.

On the dirt floor were two wooden military footlockers and an old faded traveler's chest. Hanging on a long rack were overcoats and black shirts with a ring of stiff white collars that hung at the far end of the pole. She moved one of the footlockers close to the traveler's chest, sat on it, and opened the faded green footlocker.

Inside on top, there was a tray with pockets and bins. "Photos?" she whispered. She moved the candle closer. They were pictures, all right; old metal rectangular four by six pictures taken around the turn of the century. As she leaned in, she saw an image of a boy with his mother. It was Trent. His mother wore a puffy shouldered, long pleated dress that stopped just above her high-top laced shoes. Her hair was piled high under a feathered hat tilted to one side. She had a tight grip on him as she held his hand in hers. He was wearing a suit coat, white shirt, matching knickers, argyle socks, and shiny shoes. He didn't look happy, and neither did she.

Casting the light about, she could see a stack of photos in each of the pockets and bins in the tray, lots of them. Family photos, nothing of use. She sifted through other bins and pockets in the tray and found some coins. She picked one up and saw it was a twenty-dollar gold piece. Suddenly, she found her hand in hundreds of gold pieces. It was then that she noticed leather grips on both sides of the tray.

She tilted the candle to spill melted wax droplets on the dirt floor, then set the candle on the hot wax to stay upright and steady. Grabbing the grips, she tugged, then lifted the tray up and out of the chest and set it down next to the candle. Underneath the tray was an olive drab army coat and cap.

She pulled out the doctor's old World War I army uniform. Pam remembered him telling her he was a medic during the Great War, the war to end all wars. Between the coat and pants was a framed picture of him in uniform and on the back was written, "Age 18, nineteen-seventeen." *That makes him fifty years old,* she thought to herself. The bastard lied about his age.

She closed the lid, sat on it, and opened the traveler chest she had sat on earlier. She hastily rifled through it. Nothing of interest, she thought, just old pictures of him in medical school, an old stethoscope, newspaper articles of his graduation from college, letters sent to him by his mother, old clay marbles, and a rusted tin soldier; nothing of what she hoped to find. She pulled the second and last footlocker to her and opened it.

On the top tray laid a black leather-bound booklet. She picked it up and turned over the cover flap to the first page. The inscription said, "Welcome to the *Legionnaires of the Christo,*" signed S. Pervasions. It went on, "I will introduce you to another fine doctor one day when we get to Brazil. Some call him the Angel of Death, but you know him as the great pioneer of the medical world, Doctor Josef Mengele."

She dropped it back in the tray and brought the candle up to look at pictures under the booklet. She saw one with a young Pastor Swain and another high-church official. It was a picture taken prior to World War II and, as she brought it closer to her, she could see in the background that it was taken in Rome. Another picture, almost the same but with a different official, *a cardinal?* She wondered. Swain stood with two others; one was a priest, she knew for sure. This time she recognized the third person.

She had seen pictures of him in the newspaper and at St. Lawrence Catholic Church in Richland Park. It was taken at the Vatican and she could now make out the other man, too. The three men she was now staring at were Svendly Pervasion, Florien Swain, and Pope Pius XII! "Oh, Mother Mary," she whispered in astonishment.

Underneath that photo were letters. She opened an envelope and saw that they were written in Italian and German, all addressed to Dr. Bullock. She pulled the tray out and set it aside to see what was underneath. She brought the candle closer. There, in front of her, were black velvet bags closed at the top with a narrow silk ribbon.

Opening the first one, she reached in and pulled out the contents. It was a fistful of paper currency, hundreds of twenty-dollar bills. *Why does he hide it?*

Pam reached in and pulled out several moneybags. Under the moneybags were several envelopes, each filled with photos. She laid the moneybags aside and put the envelopes in one of the pockets in her robe.

Again, she reached down toward the bottom of the wooden footlocker, and this time pulled up several manila folders. She set them on the chest next to her and opened the first one. "*Ha!*" Pictures of children. Dozens of pictures. Some were pictures of adult caucasian males with children sitting on bamboo-framed beds. The children were Asians.

Turning several of the pictures over, she saw place names stamped on the backs of the pictures Indochina, Siam, Burma. She opened another envelope. This time there were pictures of Caucasian children in familiar Western settings. They, too, were with male adults sitting or standing, facing the camera in only their underwear.

Some children were naked, lying spread-eagle on beds with hands and legs tied to the bedposts. She picked out one picture and started to tear up. There she saw a boy about nine years old standing naked and holding the erection of a man with one hand.

The face of the man wasn't visible. All she could see was the full body and sullen face of the boy and the lower half of the man. He had a large mole on his side. It looked somehow familiar. Electric pulses bolted through her. But where did I see it? Pam couldn't remember, not now, anyway.

"Oh my God." She couldn't look at any more photos; they made her sick to her stomach. She put it all back in place, minus a few pictures, a bag of money, and a handful of gold coins, which she put in the front two pockets of the bathrobe. She grabbed the candle and stooped going through the little doorway of the cubbyhole, closed the door, and started toward the stairs but stopped.

The floor creaked from above. Again and again.

"Oh shit!"

CHAPTER TWELVE

"All right, Will," he said to himself, "set your intentions in a loving manner and place yourself deep into God-Thought and try it again. 'Now, before you go in,' Ralphy would say, 'you might want to see what the inhabitants are doing.'"

He set his eyes and his intentions on the inside of the house. The walls began to open up. He felt himself being light and focused. In an instant he could view the living room. He saw the lone candle in the front room. Then he saw movement halfway down the upstairs staircase. It was the doctor in his stocking feet with this undershirt half on, and nothing else. He teetered, holding himself upright by grasping the thick oak stair railing with both hands, touching each plank, one step at a time.

I don't see Ms. Darling. He scanned the rooms.

"Keep looking," he said to himself in his own conversation, trying to stay calm. "In your mind's eye, look softly, you'll find her."

He rubbed his eyes, took long breaths, let the air out of his lungs and looked again. This time he saw her at the bottom of the cellar steps with one hand on the rail and the other with the candle standing still, listening for sounds.

Dr. Bullock's eyes were red and wild. He had made it down the steps to the foyer and reached into a long round bin where he placed his fancy canes and walking sticks. He fumbled through it, pulled out a large, thick, ornate oak walking stick, and staggered toward the kitchen.

Pam stepped up and onto the first plank, then the second and another until she was near the top step. She blew out the candle, set it next to her on the top step, put one hand on the doorknob and stood silent to listen for any noise. There wasn't a sound but she stayed frozen for what seemed an eternity. Her neck pounded as the jugular vein slammed against her skin with each beat. Bullock reached out and put one hand on the doorknob of the same cellar door. His bloodshot eyes were fixed on it as he stood there holding his breath, looking ready to kill.

Will closed his eyes as he floated forward and, to his surprise, he found himself standing in the kitchen not five feet from the doctor's side.

Hot dog. He could see through the door, and Ms. Darling was leaning on it, the same as Bullock on the other side. He closed his eyes again and found himself standing on the step just below Pam Darling. She reached and pulled the light string; it flickered and went out. It was pitch black except for tiny streams of light shining through the slits and cracks around the doorframe above and below the door. She applied pressure on the knob and stepped to one side.

Will stepped to the center. The longer Pam waited to open the door, the brighter he got.

Pam's heart was racing, and her palms were sweaty. She wiped them both on the front of the robe and, as she did, the cotton belt came undone, and the robe opened up.

At that moment the door swung open, and there stood a naked Trent Bullock with cold, murderous thoughts, his feet apart and his bloodshot eyes wide open. He hoisted the heavy stick high above his head with both hands, staring at Ms. Darling in her open robe. She froze, waiting to be slammed over the head. As he clutched the long, thick stick, his eyes rolled as the medication kicked in and his body tilted backwards farther and farther until over he went, hitting the floor like a stiff board. The stick banged against the cupboard and came slamming down on top of his head. He never moved.

Pam slipped up and onto the kitchen floor, sidestepping the doctor as he lay passed out cold. Will's eyes followed her every move. As she disrobed and ducked into the bathroom, his blood pressure rose twenty points.

CHAPTER THIRTEEN

Deputy Zaugbaum was taking pictures of the paperwork spread out on the Sheriff's desk again. Gordon was sipping hot coffee as he leaned in, examining the items *borrowed* from Pastor Swain.

"Question, Mickey. What would make a man of the cloth want to lead a double life and at the same time swindle good, God-fearing folks out of fifty bucks a month?"

"He's got no soul," an angry Mickey replied. "No soul, no heart. He's FUBAR! Fucked up beyond all repair, as far as I can tell; dressing up like a woman, fucking with the kids. All that.

"I saw some of his notes on the back of the pictures in the same drawer as the books just last week. He must have a love-hate relationship with children, too. Then there's that goddamned secret society thing with his warped, crazy cultish, Catholic fuck–ups."

Gordon's eyes shot toward Mickey, but said nothing.

"Speaking of kids, do you think Will can be at his pa's services at the hospital chapel tomorrow? Don't know about his ma, though. Nurse Anne says she's still long-gone mentally. It could be a small crowd.

"It figures," Gordon said as he set the coffee cup down to concentrate on the pictures. "People don't take kindly to suicides and women- and child-beaters. And as an FYI for you, I was baptized and raised a Catholic, too. We ain't *all* crazy."

As Mickey wrapped things up, he put the camera down and turned to Gordon. "Well, that's everything. I got to get all this shit back without Flo, ah, Florien knowing about it. I'd like to arrest him. Now?"

Sheriff Maxwell said, "To get Swain, we'd need a subpoena to search his place and get what you got, ah, what you borrowed. One way or another, we'll get *him*, along with a host of other shitheads."

Mickey said, "I'm with you, but how?"

Gordon picked up the phone to call the District Attorney's office in Capital City to ask just that kind of question.

Mickey was picking up the papers, then turned and stared at the wall where he'd seen the large yellow orb the night before.

Gordon couldn't resist. With the phone set in one hand and the receiver in the other, he raised his voice. *"Boo!"*

Mickey jumped and spun on his heels, flipping the bird at the Sheriff as he left the office to return the contraband to Pastor Swain's Lutheran church.

"No, no, darlin'," he said to the operator. "Yes, I know Halloween has long since passed. Give me the Capital City's DA's office, please. Yes, ma'am, Merry Christmas to you, too. Thank you, darlin'."

CHAPTER FOURTEEN

Anne and Pam were seated at a far corner of the cafeteria, Anne with her shoes off, both feet on the front edge of her chair, with her arms resting along the top of her knees. Anne leaned over the table, saying, "Tell me more."

"I thought he was going to kill me! He looked right through me with his wild, crazy eyes, and that's when the bare-assed shithead just fell over backwards, like he'd seen a ghost or something!"

Anne was taking a sip of coffee and half laughed. As she did, a dribble of coffee went up her nose and she started to cough. In an instant, they were both reeling back and forth with laughter so hard the tears were streaming down their cheeks while trying to muffle the laughter from the rest of those in the cafeteria.

"Oh, Jesus, I wish I could have been a little mouse in the corner and watched the whole damn thing."

Pam cleared her throat and said, "I've got the stuff from that cubby-hole in my car. It's in the brown bag on the floor, behind the front seat. When you leave, take it to Gordon."

"I'm on it, Pam. My paperwork has been turned in for the night and, just to let you know, Will slept like a baby last night. The tubes, of course, are out, so we can start him on Jell-O and broth today."

"That's Dr. Bullock's decision to make," exclaimed Ms. Darling in her most dutiful tone. They started the laughing jag all over again.

Sheriff Maxwell was on the phone with the DA. He sent Zaugs to the café for a late breakfast to bring back. As Mickey opened the door to step out, Nurse Anne was coming up the steps. "It's always a pleasure to open the door to a fine-looking woman."

"Hi, I'm Anne."

"I'm Mickey, Deputy Mickey Zaugbaum. You can call me Mickey." He nodded and puffed out his chest.

"I'll call you fired if you don't hurry up. I'm starving!" shouted the Sheriff as he stepped behind his desk with the phone in hand.

"What a pleasant surprise," he said, smiling. "What brings you here?"

She placed the brown paper bag on his desk and pulled all the items out one at a time: the velvet bag stuffed with twenty-dollar bills, faded yellow envelopes, a manila folder with dozens of photos, and twenty-dollar gold pieces. As she laid them out on the table, Gordon's smile went away. His mouth fell open, staring in disbelief at the mounting incriminating evidence amassing before him. He hung up the phone slowly, looked down at it all, and back up to Nurse Anne.

"What I want you to do now is call the hospital, ask for Ms. Darling, and tell her the brown bag is on your desk. While you're waiting for her to come to the phone, tell me where you keep the coffee. I'll make a fresh pot—for the three of us?"

"Yeah. Mickey can join us in progress."

One hour later all the paraphernalia on the desk had been looked over, the food that Mickey brought from the café had been consumed, the coffee pot was empty, and the chatter was on high speed. At moments, all three were talking at the same time and coming to the same conclusions.

"Now, let me get this straight," Mickey questioned. "Anne, you say that Pam just happened on this stuff here on the desk? Where did she happen upon it?"

Anne stood, crushed out her Pall Mall, and said, "You'll have to ask her, but really, Sheriff, think about it. Like I said, according to Pam, this is just the tip of the iceberg. There's more, much more in that cubbyhole."

"Whose cubbyhole?" Mickey looked at Anne.

"That's right, Mick. I agree with her," Gordon said. "One way or another, there's more fishies than we thought. We'll need a blanket search warrant for all of them. Whatever it takes, we need just one who'll rat on the others. By God, one way or another, we're going to get it!"

Mickey nodded and asked again, "Whose cubbyhole?"

"Nonya," Gordon said.

"Nonya?"

"Nonya damn business," Gordon said as he got up and washed his hands at the sink.

"Ha-ha. Very funny," Mickey said.

"I knew Pa was up to something beyond his temper tantrums. Will told me as much before he came to the hospital. I had hunches on a couple of guys, and I was getting closer to that fact, but I felt like someone was stonewalling me."

"Who? Mickey asked. "Any idea?"

"No. Not . . . yet. But it has to be someone in our profession, Mickey. When I tried to dig deeper into the investigation, I always felt like somebody wasn't playing it straight. I can't prove that just yet. It seemed that I was just a step or two away from breaking the whole thing wide open, but for the lack of cooperation, bodies, and funds. It's the main reason I hired you, Mickey.

"Will was slipping me notes on scraps of paper whenever I saw him. His father never let him out of his sight, so it was difficult. Pa knew he was up to something.

"I couldn't comprehend anything bigger than a local situation. How would I know it was a worldwide epidemic? All of that sick shit is beyond our jurisdiction, anyway.

"Now it's a different ballgame altogether. At last I can work on tying these people together. Something big is in the wind. I have the doctor's diary. Ever hear of something called 'Odessa'?"

Anne stood by the front window. A car pulled up. A man in black stepped out and started for Gordon's office. "Someone's coming this way," she said.

There was a lot of commotion. Everything on the desk was pulled off and stuffed hastily into desk drawers.

Mickey panicked. "Oh God!"

"It's a priest," she continued.

Gordon covered his new recording machine and set the heavy item on the floor next to his chair.

"Good morning, boys," the priest said, seeing Nurse Anne but not acknowledging her. "It's getting chilly out. Won't be long before we're singing Christmas carols, yah?"

They stood to greet the priest.

"Oh, yah, I don't know dat we met formally. I'm Father Pervasions, Svendly Pervasions. I replaced old Father Richard Nachio a few months ago over in da next county at St. Lawrence Catholic Church by Richland Park. You remember him?"

"I remember," Gordon, said, "The little questions about the altar boys. That right?"

"He's no longer in da priesthood," Father Pervasions said. "Last I heard, Richard Nachio was selling life insurance in south-central Pennsylvania. Sad case, it 'twas. Well, boys will be boys, hey lads?" he said, letting out a big laugh. No one joined in nor did they crack a smile.

"Well, okay, I'll get to da main point here. There's going to be a service for Pa Messenger tomorrow morning at da hospital. I don't know what church he was affiliated with, do any of you?"

They all talked at once. "Methodist, or Baptist," Mickey said. "No, wait, he's Pennsylvania Dutch."

Sven had a confused look.

"I heard he was a Baptist," Nurse Anne said.

"Naw," Sheriff Maxwell said. "Will told me his parents were Methodist, and his mom was raised as a Catholic. Pa read from the Good Book during the week and went to Pastor Swain's service on Sundays. Just for the record, Reverend, Priestly. His last name is Priestly."

"Ah, of course," Father Pervasions said, "Yah, I got it now. Did he by chance leave a suicide note?"

The room was silent. "No, no, I'm afraid not. I was in the hospital at the time, but my deputy was here."

Mickey cleared his throat and said, "Father Pervasions, we have to take any sharp instrument away from anyone we lock up here. It's a rule of policy. He had no pen or pencil while he was here. Also, we found nothing at his house, either."

"Well, dar you have it den," Pervasions said, "I'll stop by Pastor Swain's residence and have a little chat wit him. Top of the morning to you, men." He waved his black fedora and waltzed out to his car.

They watched through the window. Maxwell turned to his deputy and said, "Good job. That was done with a degree of smoothness. Pennsylvania *Dutch?*"

Mickey shrugged. "I felt I had to say something, and that's what popped out."

Turning from the window, they sat back down around the desk. Gordon looked up to Zaugs. "Did you tell anyone about Pa committing suicide?"

"Only you, boss," Mickey said with a knowing grin.

"Just for the hell of it, drive by Swain's place."

"Sure thing," he said. "You think he'll dress up for old Sven?"

"Don't know, but you can find out why the priest is concerning himself with a suicide note. Anyway, take the new camera with you just in case."

"Ralphy, do you remember when I asked if I could be around when Pa was at the pearly gates, catching holy hell? You said I could have a front-row seat and watch Pa's life review with all of the popcorn I could eat."

Raphael made an extra large bag of hot buttered popcorn appear and handed it to William, saying, "Let's go."

William stuck his nose in the invigorating aroma of freshly popped corn topped with warm melted butter. His saliva ran wild.

They darted past universe after universe.

"How's the popcorn?"

"Out of this world."

"I had a conversation with my boss," Raphael said. "You're not 'out of the woods,' as you would say. There's a matter of organ damage and possible failure. It'll be up to you to decide which way home."

"Do you mean what I think you mean?" Will asked.

"You'll soon have your choice to stay or leave."

"Your body is in bad shape. It can heal, however, there is a chance it won't."

They slowed, and Raphael took Will's arm as they touched down at the edge of a city. They stood outside, gazing at the glistening, spectacular crystal city. To Will, the star-studded buildings stood apart from everything else in the sky, as if he were looking at a large sparkling mural.

"This is it, Will. In there, you'll be able to see your pa's life review and more."

"Why didn't I see this before?"

"You weren't ready."

The space was literally filled with a multitude of people. The sound of people talking at once was deafening. Will held his hands over his ears as he looked at Raphael. With quiet reserve, he spoke without moving his lips.

"Use your gift of God-Thought now, and the noise will subside." Will quieted himself, and the noise did indeed soften. After one more deep breath, the resounding noise was gone.

"Now use it again to remove the people."

He did and found himself alone with Ralphy.

"This has to be the place that Nurse Anne was reading about." Will gazed around, up and down and all around, at rows and rows of tall crystal shelves filled with thick black and brown leather-bound books.

"One and the same," said Raphael. "Some call it The Akashic Hall of Records. I took you here earlier. You were too, shall I say, wild?"

"It's all true then?"

Raphael continued. "Everything you ever wanted to know is here; information about anyone and anything. Each thought, action, reaction, deed, everything said, done, unsaid, now or in the future is here. All the outcomes of our words, actions, and thoughts are kept here.

"Nothing escapes, nothing erased. The all of all is intact. All memory cells remain forever."

"You mean the life review question?"

"I mean all thoughts, words, ideas, actions, or inactions by anyone or anything, is recorded here; things good, bad, ugly, and beautiful. The loving thoughts, the nasty thoughts, terrible deeds, good deeds, the laughing, crying, the hurt, pain, and exquisite bliss is all here. It's all been recorded."

"Then there *is* a book for each and everyone?" asked Will.

"Yes," said Raphael. "There's one on you here, too."

"But I'm not dead yet."

"It matters not. Your book had to be written."

CHAPTER FIFTEEN

At the front of the chapel was a portrait of Jesus, the standard picture seen in most funeral parlors. Jesus is kneeling on a wooden step, resting his arms on the rail. He appears to be praying and looking up to the partly cloudy sky from which rays of light was shining down upon him.

The open casket was placed to the right side of the chapel, in front of the pews. To the left was the small, carpeted stage with a dark oak podium on which laid an open Bible.

Seated in a wheelchair next to the front row in the aisle and in front of the podium was Will, wearing an old off-white hospital gown. To his left was his mother. Nurse Anne had purchased a decent dress for her to wear for the services.

Ma sat there with her fingers locked, hands folded in her lap, rocking to and fro, staring straight ahead.

Will knew most of the people in attendance. He turned to see Mrs. Kathryn Knee, his schoolteacher, sitting with the teary–eyed Mr. and Mrs. Hornsby. He could see Lloyd, the barber, sitting by himself.

He glanced the other way, seeing Sheriff Gordon Maxwell with his black and blue eyes and puffy cheeks, along with Deputy Mickey Zaugbaum a couple of rows back. Just in front of them sat Anne and Pam, not recognizing the others from the hospital staff.

The Catholic priest, Svendly Pervasions, was sitting with the Lutheran Pastor, Florien Swain, across the aisle in the front row. He stood, stepped to the podium, and turned to the page of the Bible where a red ribbon divided the pages.

He cleared his throat and began to speak. He quoted Psalm twenty-three and walked everybody through the valley of death fearing no evil, along with two other psalms about fear and guilt and who are we to judge, trusting that Jesus is the Supreme Healer sitting at the right hand of God the Father.

After a few minutes of that, he closed the Bible and wiped his glasses with a white kerchief from his front suit pocket, looking toward the casket with Pa's remains. As Pastor Swain peered at Will with contempt, he began a sneezing jag that lasted for quite awhile. He sneezed, according to Zaugbaum who kept count, twenty-three consecutive times.

He continued, "All Pa Priestly ever wanted in life was a good wife and many children. He received Ma and adopted the boy child, William. He worked hard all his life and was religious.

"He told me he prayed from the Good Book, sometimes several times a day. He wore out three Bibles in his lifetime."

William thoughts were of disgust and anger. *He didn't wear them out. He cut out chunks of pages to hide pictures of frightened children and placed the words of chants and relevant information from the secret society folded inside the hollowed-out books.*

He continued, "Pa was a simple man and at the same time a complex man. He was a farmer, who was outstanding in his field."

Will thought he could hear a snicker in the crowd. It was Deputy Zaugbaum. Maxwell poked him in the ribs. He tried unsuccessfully to contain himself though, as tears were streaming from the corners of Mickey's eyes.

"Pa could drive a team of horses, repair a tractor, harvest crops, and keep his family well fed. Somewhere along the line . . ." With a scowl on his face, Pastor Swain looked directly at Will and continued, "The devil got into Pa. Why was he in jail? Did he lay a hand on the boy?" He turned now toward Gordon Maxwell as he continued. "There have been rumors as to why and how it was that the folks at the jail found Pa already dead by hanging." A few gasps were heard from the pews.

Pastor Swain looked out at the people. "We hope and pray the Lord took hold of Pa and removed the devil's grip. We pray the devious Satan stood empty-handed as God carried him in his loving arms toward those glorious pastures in heaven and set him down on fresh fields of alfalfa to live forever with God by his side. Amen and amen."

He stepped away from the pulpit and missed the single step down to the floor. He stumbled and caught himself at the first pew in front of Ma. Startled by a drug-induced reflex, she reached out, slapping his face hard. Twice. Will wrapped both arms around her to comfort and keep her calm.

Father Svendly Pervasions strode up the aisle for his turn at the pulpit. He brushed by Swain with a slight grin and whispered, "Gentle woman, isn't she?"

He opened the Bible to the pages marked by a blue ribbon, looked up and with a smile began his eulogy.

"Let us stand together and recite da Lord's Prayer."

While praying, Father Pervasions glanced at the body in the casket, as if he was thinking of the teachings of the church that taking ones own life was considered a mortal sin and, therefore, access to heaven was forbidden. *To hell he would go.* Then he chuckled at the absurdity.

Making the sign of the cross with his right hand he tapped his forehead, left and right shoulder, pressing his hands together before him near his chest, saying, "In da name of da Father, Son, and Holy Ghost. Amen. You may be seated. May God have mercy on his soul."

There was a pregnant pause before he started with a grin, opened his arms toward the heavens, lowered them, and proclaimed, "Following graveside services, da Ladies Auxiliary of da Lutheran Church will be serving coffee and homemade cinnamon rolls, cookies, and pumpkin pie. You all are invited to stop by." He snorted to himself as he thought of something clever and continued, "Have someting *sinfully* tasty and visit in da spirit of Christmas for a while."

That was all he had to say. Enough said for those in attendance, anyway, even if they *were* a bit confused by Father Pervasion's non-eulogy eulogy.

Nobody went. No one cared to go to the church basement to see people that day for coffee, pie, or anything else. Except deputy Zaugbaum: he scarfed up all the rolls, cookies, and pies he could carry and took them home.

CHAPTER SIXTEEN

Mrs. Kathryn Knee, the teacher who was rooming with Ed and Helen Hornsby, called out to Sheriff Maxwell. Clutching her handkerchief, Helen pleaded, "Please, Sheriff, what do you have for us this morning? Our hearts are breaking," she said as tears streamed down her cheeks nodding toward her husband. "We want our children back, please help us!"

"I've got the Highway Patrol and the State police working on it, doing their best to help locate and bring your children home. The good news is that there's no bad news to tell you." Gordon shrugged and continued. "And that's a good thing in a case such as this.

"We feel the children are here within a sixty-mile radius or less, and we are confident they'll be found soon. I'm sorry I don't have better news for you, but rest assured, as soon as I know something, I'll pass it on to you. We're getting new clues almost hourly. The Highway Patrol took snowprints from the Buick when it was at your farmhouse, and they are analyzing it as we speak. Hang in there, folks. We are working our butts off to return those children to you as fast and safe as we can."

She thanked him. Ed Hornsby shook his hand and asked if anyone else saw the man, the car, and the children together. Again, Gordon told him he had some good leads that he is currently checking on. He had a gut feeling, but couldn't explain it. Not to them. Not now.

Kathryn Knee went to the first pew to offer her sympathies to Ma Priestly and Will. She shook Will's hand and noticed an immediate difference in him. He didn't appear to be the same uneducated, naïve boy who visited her classroom on rare occasions. His demeanor was much more mature.

After saying hello to Ma Priestly, she turned to Will and said, "I miss having you in school, and the children hope to see you soon."

William rose from his wheelchair, stood and faced her. "It would be an honor to be in the presence of a magnificent teacher with your exemplary professionalism, Mrs. Knee. I would inhale all aspects, the very fiber of *all* education you have to offer, and use it for the utmost good within the community here, where I live," he said.

Kathryn stood speechless.

Regaining her composure, she said, "I so look forward to your return to our happy little schoolhouse." Perplexed, she nodded and stepped toward the nurses.

Two male orderlies stood next to Ma, indicating it was time to take her back to her room. Will gave her a long bear-like hug and whispered, "I love you," in her ear. Tears trickled from her eyes, but she remained silent as the two in white coats hoisted her from the pew and walked her out and down the hallway toward the elevator.

Will turned and, as he did so, he noticed Sheriff Maxwell, who was standing nearby. He made a motioned with his hand.

"Listen, Sheriff. You have to get that new recording machine you have at your office and set it up in Lloyd's back room. Don't waste time. Do it now before it's too late," Will whispered.

As he spoke, the Sheriff looked shocked. William couldn't have known he just purchased it last week. No one except his deputy knew of it. "How did . . ."

"Not now. Just do it, 'cause Dr. Bullock and the two pastors are going there now for a little meeting in the back. Let's say I've got my sources. Hurry! There's no time to lose."

"What sources?" Gordon asked.

"I *told* you about angels; pretty soon you'll have to bel*ieve*, Sheriff. And another thing, Lloyd knows—he's cutting the Bishop's hair today. The appointment was made while you were in the hospital. It'll be explained later.

He's on the same page and knows how to run the recorder. You know Lloyd; he won't say a damn thing unless it has to do with baseball. Hurry! They'll be there any minute."

The services started at ten a.m. and were completed in less than a half hour that morning. Gordon eased his way out of the chapel to spirit the recorder from his office and make the delivery.

William wheeled his chair over to the open casket, rested his hands on its front side, and stood. Pa looked younger than his age. William had never seen him look so peaceful. He'd seen his pa dressed up on Sundays to go to church, but never saw him in a suit and at peace like he was there, lying in the simple knotty pine coffin. He was well groomed. Pa's hands were folded, one atop the other. William just looked at him as his mind searched for the bright spots in his life with his pa.

There weren't many. The few good times were clouded by all the ugly times. He stood shifting the weight from one foot to the other for a long moment as he rested his hands on the coffin, touching the satin lining. He recited the Lord's Prayer. With his left hand, he reached into the coffin and touched his pa's hair.

He then bent over the cold, wooden coffin. After a few seconds he said, "I saw your life, Pa. You didn't have it so good. However, The demons you had did not give you a *get out of jail free card* to beat upon Ma and me. The way I see it, you were nothing more than a pig-fucking freak. I ain't ever going to forgive you." He eased himself back down into the wheelchair, pulled on the back of the wheels and shuffled himself toward the aisle. *You had a choice, Mister Priestly, you had a choice.*

CHAPTER SEVENTEEN

At eleven a.m. he was back in his room waiting for a decent meal, something he hadn't been privy to since he'd been hospitalized. He could smell the aroma of the food trays out in the hallway as patients were being served. He was starved. His saliva was thick, and he had to keep swallowing in anticipation. The door opened a crack, before opening all the way. Will looked up and was disappointed.

"I don't like the color of his skin." Bullock handed the chart and notes to Ms. Darling as he pulled his stethoscope out and put it to his ears.

"Sit up straight," he ordered. "Take a deep breath." He placed the stethoscope on Will's bandaged back in three different places, then on his chest. "Exhale. Another. Again. Again!" He pulled out a tiny flashlight and peered into Will's eyes and far back in his mouth. Completing his examination, he turned to Pam and put the stethoscope back in the front pocket of his white coat.

"I don't know why he didn't die. I want to have a urine specimen run on him and have it analyzed. There is organ damage from dehydration. His liver and kidneys aren't working properly. How are the wounds healing?" he asked while rifling through the small leather bag.

Her eyes darted from the doctor to the patient and back. She said, "The bandages were changed just before he went to the services for his pa. He's doing okay, Dr. B."

"Fine," he said, not paying any attention to her. "I have a seminar to attend, and I'm leaving now to go home and pack. You'll be a good girl, for me, won't you?"

"Oh yes, Doctor. I'll be good." Her eyes rolled as her glance met William's. He was holding back a laugh.

They stood outside of Will's closed door as their conversation continued. "Ms. Darling," he said, "I want to offer an apology for the other night. For the life of me, I can't remember what happened that evening."

"Really?" she said, "We mixed drinks, you know."

"But, still," he continued.

"Well, Doctor, you had three glasses of bourbon before I opened a bottle of wine from 1935, if you'll remember."

"Maybe. Suppose that's why my head hurt so bad."

"And, just for the record, Doctor," she said in a sultry voice, "you were a wild man. You almost wore me out!"

He grinned. "Pam Darling, you bring out the beast in me. We'll have to get together for a little, ah, a little Christmas party."

"Let's do that!" She gritted her teeth as her guts rolled, "As soon as my aunt leaves town."

"Oh, is she still around? I haven't seen her."

"Well, she's shy and hardly ever leaves my apartment."

"Just as well; that seminar will keep me away for a couple of days. I put an intern in charge to act on my behalf, just to let you know."

"Okay," she said, noticing a lump near his left temple.

"What happened here?" she asked, almost touching it.

Turning his head away from her hand, he said, rubbing it, "I don't know how that happened, either. I woke up in the kitchen, I think."

With a playful pout, she said, "Oh my dear Trent, you should be more careful."

Kathryn Knee was in the hospital cafeteria, and Anne was talking with her. "I haven't been sleeping well as of late," Anne confessed. "Please forgive me if I look a bit disheveled. I sleep a few hours in the morning, and again an hour or two in the afternoon before my night shift."

"There's been a dramatic change in Will that shocks me," Kathryn said, "I don't understand it. The few times I had him in class, why, it was like the first time he was around other people, as if he had lived his entire life in isolation. He was so excited and happy to be at school, but he just had no literary skills, nor did he know how to interact with others. His speech sounded as if it were self-taught, without any rules of the English language, and this morning when I saw him, he spoke like an ambassador to England!"

"Umm," Nurse Anne said with a little smile. "Well, I've been reading to him during my shift and also during the day when I can't sleep. I mean, I read books, Kathryn. I love to read books. I just read them out loud when I'm in his room."

"Whatever you're doing, Nurse Anne, it's the most remarkable job. However, reading alone in such a short time wouldn't make such a difference, in my opinion."

"You're right, Kathryn."

"Call me Kat."

CHAPTER EIGHTEEN

The two nodded to one another before they spoke to Lloyd. "What should we tell him, Florien? If I were to say dat my car is at your house and we walked here, would he believe it?"

Florien, a tad irked, had another suggestion. "Let's tell him that Deputy Zaugbaum was kind enough to give us a ride here to the services and then made a mad dash for the door when he heard about pies? And since the barber is here and we need a haircut, we thought we'd ask him for a lift? After all, the truth is easier to remember. Here he comes, now."

"Ya. By golly, dat's what I'll tell 'im." Sven said.

"Lloyd, it was good to see you here at da service." Sven said, bowing slightly.

Lloyd turned to the priest he'd never met. He'd heard about him but had never seen him until today. "I was a bit curious, as are others. You must be the new pastor at St. Lawrence. Too bad about that child found face-down in the river before the other priest left town, huh? Of course, everyone has their opinion, but I think it's too damned bad the local police at Richland Park couldn't find a connection between the child's death and Father Richard Nachio. Damn shame about that. After all, he was the last one to see the boy alive. Uh, by the way, you men heard anything about the Hornsby kids?"

Swain and Pervasions glanced at each other before answering Lloyd's question. Svendly shuffled his feet and was looking down at them as he stammered and said, "Ya, dat was a messy situation over dar at Richland Park. No. Nobody's told me anything new about da children."

Florien turned and shrugged.

"Well, say, not to change da subject, but Florien and I find dat we are in need of a haircut. We came here wit Deputy Zaugbaum. He was kind enough to give Pastor Swain here a lift, and I was at his house so we rode together. But I think he left and, er, forgot about us. Could you give us a lift to your barbershop? Of course, if you don't want to, we heard dat you're kind of a loner and . . ."

"I can be neighborly, too," Lloyd said. He was slim, stood six feet tall, thick and wild eyebrows, dark brown, thinning hair on top, and salt and peppery on the sides. His lean face and thin Victorian nose gave him a look of nobility.

"I have feelings like everyone else, you know." Lloyd was a bit disturbed by the questions of the two men of the cloth, but said nothing. He led them out to the parking lot to his car, opened the back door for them, and then slammed it shut. He got himself into the front seat and cranked the engine. *Seems like everyone needs a haircut this morning,* he thought. Before leaving the parking lot, Lloyd adjusted and then re-adjusted the side mirror and the rearview mirror.

There was a long silence before Svendly was at it again. "It's kind of chilly in da back here. Mind throwing a little heat our way? Say, by da way, I didn't mean anything by what I said earlier. I just say dat because I never see you at church services, and Pastor Swain says he's seen you in church on Christmas but *not* during Easter. Do you have a religious affiliation?"

"My mother and father used to play the accordion and sing at the Methodist church services. I mean, my mother played the accordion, my father sang wherever they were invited and would play the harmonica at times, and my brothers and I would sing along."

"Invited?" questioned the priest.

"Yes, invited," Lloyd continued. "I've got three brothers, and we could harmonize like nobody's business. In fact, as we got older, my brothers and I would sing at various denominations as well as at taverns and supper clubs. And just to let you know how good we were, when we sang in taverns and clubs, we never had to pay for food *or* drinks.

"We never saw a dime when we sang in church, though. All we got was lip service. *Thank you, boys. That was real swell of you to sing in our humble church. God loves you.*

"Yup, we were never paid a plug nickel from any of the churches, just nice church words. *So,* we don't sing in church anymore. That was years ago. Hardly see each other much now. We've gone our own ways."

"So, as to the question of your faith?" Florien Swain asked.

That did it. Lloyd slowed his car and pulled around to the back of the barbershop as anger moved in. He inched it along in the tracks of another car in the freshly fallen snow.

"There's really no question of my faith, Pastor! I believe in God, like most people do. I believe Jesus lived two thousand years ago right here on this earth. I believe in the Golden Rule, and I believe it should be taught more or less as part of the Ten Commandments: *do unto others as you would have done unto you.*

"Now, why is that so hard to accept? It's a religion unto itself, no strings attached, no rituals, and no sacrifices. Guess maybe it's just too damned simple. And you don't have to feed 'the kitty' every week; so decent folks can save a little money for fuel oil and for those rainy days ahead.

"As to the question of my religious affiliation, I don't need a dogma or rules that keeps me apart from God. He and I simply have a conversation."

Lloyd ended his sermon to the clergy by saying, "One belief of mine sets you and me apart. I believe with my whole heart and soul that Jesus *lived* for us, as an example. I don't believe that he *died* for us.

"Let me ask you this. What did your grandmothers do that was so terrible, so despicable, so heinous, that it would cause the death of God's only son two thousand years ago?"

CHAPTER NINETEEN

L loyd turned out of the alleyway onto the side street and rounded the corner at Vinney's tavern that stood next to his building, the barbershop. "Here we are, fellers. Got the rest of the day ahead of us." He pulled his Studebaker right in front of his shop.

The clergy sat silent, mulling over his words, and exited the car with Lloyd. As they got out, they looked up and down the street. It was quiet in the little village of Pine Nut except for one truck and two men with a long ladder stretching strings of Christmas lights across Main Street from one light pole to the other.

"I'll be right back around to open the front door for you," Lloyd said as he headed around to unlock the back door and see about the Buick parked there.

Sven turned to Florien. "I got da feeling he don't like religion. Not wit dat 'Jesus *lived* for us' nonsense. If people lived by da Golden Rule, we'd be out of a job!"

"Do tell," said Pastor Swain in a quiet voice.

The Priest continued. "Da Golden Rule *is* pretty much da basis for da Jews, Muslims, Buddhists, Indians, da Hindus, and da religion of Tao—*all* of dem. They believe fundamentally in da same tings, but you know how ornery those foreigners can be."

Swain's eyes jumped as he turned to face Reverend Pervasions. *Look who's talking about foreigners. A Norske who bailed out of his home country, went to Germany to fight in the war they lost, then changed his identity coming here as a U.S. citizen with a white collar and fake documents.*

"Yeah, those *damn* foreigners," He said with a smirk.

Now inside, Lloyd unlocked the front door.

"Come on in, boys, and take off your coats. It's warming up in here. I'll get a pot of coffee going for all of us."

Father Pervasions stepped back out of the front door and bent over to brush the snow off his shoes. "Florien, did you see who's car dat was behind da building here?"

"Indeed I did," he replied. Svendly pulled the door open all the way and was about to take a step in when he noticed a good pile of loose snow about a foot thick on the red and white barber sign right above the door. He took off his black short-brimmed hat and was about to re-enter just as the snow gave way and made a direct hit on top of his head.

He made quite a scene as he jumped back out onto the sidewalk and tried with both hands to sweep away the snow from his head and shoulders. The cold, wet white stuff went down the back of the medium-built man's thick neck.

Inside Lloyd's shop, two big black leather and wrought iron barber chairs sat looking distinct and prominent in the bland, basic rectangular room. The plaster walls were covered with off-white paint, and his ceiling, once white, now took on the familiar, dull, smoke-stained yellow. For his waiting customers, in front of the barber chairs were four small chairs that had round wooden seats with thin black swirling iron for a backing. They weren't the most comfortable sitting chairs, but they did the trick for the farmers who came to town for a cut and shave, and also for the townsfolk and businessmen who came in for a trim.

Above the chairs were two eight by ten pictures of Lloyd posing with baseball players. One was the Chicago White Sox great, "Shoeless" Joe Jackson. He was part of a traveling ball club that played against hometown teams. He played under an alias since his banishment from major league baseball. Lloyd gave him a haircut, once. They talked baseball, and Lloyd bought him a meal down at the café and never told a soul in there who he was eatin' with. He didn't want to bother old Joe with all that nonsense.

Lloyd played a little ball in his prime, too. He had a tryout with the Boston Braves, but he couldn't hit the curveball, so that was the end of that.

During the summer months, Lloyd had the radio tuned to WGN to listen to his White Sox. He lived in Chicago, a 'Southsider', as a youngster.

While he was getting the steam heat going, Sven and Florien gazed at the pictures on the wall.

"Say, Lloyd, could you tell Father Sven here who these guys are in the pictures?" Pastor Florien Swain never missed an opportunity to fire someone up.

"The first one, there, is Joe Jackson and me. He was the greatest baseball player ever, in my opinion. The great Babe Ruth patterned his swing after Joe's."

Father Sven's eyebrows lifted as he said, "I heard people talk about him. Someone told me he was as dumb as a skunk and a cheater, too. A cheater is a sinner. I guess he deserved getting' da boot from baseball. Who's dat nigger on da wall?"

"That's Mister Leroy 'Satchel' Paige, the greatest baseball pitcher who's not *allowed* to play against the *white boys* of summer, even today."

"I never understood dat sport," Sven said.

"Think of the game of baseball this way," Lloyd said. "Players start out at home. You have to get to first, second, and third base. It's at that point you have the opportunity to go home again.

Eyes darting between the two, Lloyd continued. "You call yourselves Christians, though, Sven prefers to be known as a Catholic, but, think of home plate as heaven. It's a place of bliss; first, second, and third base as the Father, Son, and Holy Ghost.

"If you can grasp that idea, then you can see that one finds a Higher Source at each base and eludes those devils—the opposing players. They, the defense, try to keep you from touching and rounding the bases, but if you do and stay ahead of the devil, you get to go home again. Baseball can be a religion unto itself. And nobody's none the wiser." Lloyd was satisfied. He'd said all there was to say on the subject of religion and on his terms.

CHAPTER TWENTY

A squatty bald man with a round face came through the doorway from the back room into the barber's parlor with two cups half full of hot, black coffee. He kept his eyes on the cups as he walked in with a grin and stepped over to the pastors to hand them each a cup.

"Hello, boys," Bishop Paul Cheney said. He stood all of five foot eight and was in his early fifties. "Nice to see you, Father Sven. Who's your friend here?"

"Bishop. Bishop Cheney!" Father Sven exclaimed as he reached and stooped to kiss his ring but stopped, realizing he was carrying coffee cups.

"It's alright, my son."

"Excuse me. Dis here's Pastor Florien Swain from da Lutheran Church here in town."

Cheney handed him the first cup of coffee and winked.

"Thank you, your Eminence," Sven said as the Bishop handed the other cup to him with half a scowl.

"Who shall be first to receive a haircut from this gracious barber?" The Bishop asked in a monotone voice.

"Why, you, of course, your Eminence!" Sven said. "You, Bishop Cheney, you are a busy man with much on your mind; I mean, many, many duties to attend to."

"If you say so," Bishop Cheney said, bowing to him. He stepped up and took his place in the barber chair. "I'd like a nice trim, Lloyd, and shave the back of my neck, would you please? Also, be sure to snip out all the hair growing in my ears. If you can, place some of it on my bald head," he said, grinning at the other two.

They chuckled to appease him. Lloyd never cracked a smile. He turned the chair to the mirror so he could keep an eye on the three of them as he trimmed the head of hair of the prominent bald man.

Lloyd shook the thick white canister on the back shelf containing the hot lather. Next, he removed a hot, moist towel from the towel dispenser next to it and placed the towel on the Bishop's neck. After a minute he removed the hot towel, lathered up the Bishop's neck, and started shaving.

Breaking the ice, Pastor Swain said, "Yup, won't be long now and it'll be Christmas. I always love this time of year. Everyone seems so jolly."

Lloyd pursed his lips and said, "Almost everyone. I gave Ed Hornsby a haircut yesterday for the funeral services. It was the most quiet and somber session I ever had. Too bad about his children, huh?" He watched the three of them for any expressions. The room was silent. "Yup," he continued, "it's a damn shame. The world is getting ugly out there." Everyone nodded, including the Bishop, and that's when Lloyd's straight edged razor sliced him. He jerked his head forward and put his hand over the wound.

"It's just a knick." Lloyd said as he grimaced. He placed a piece of wet tissue over the tiny cut, and wiped the cream off the straight razor. He pulled on the long thick strop on the wall between the large mirrors and held tight to one end of it. He passed the razor back and forth on the leather so fast it made popping noises. When he let go of it, it slapped against the wall. Looking closer at the razor, he placed his thumb and forefinger along its sides.

He thought for a moment, *Oh, what I'd like to do with this.* Lloyd re-lathered the Bishop's neck and finished the neck work. And with a final snip and running of the comb through what hair there was to run a comb through, with a flash of talc, Lloyd pulled the white sheet off of his customer, and with a shake, he rested it on the seat.

Standing behind the chair with a smile of malicious delight, clutching the long straight razor in one hand and clippers in the other, he said, "Next?"

The two ministers sheepishly declined as they followed the Bishop and ducked into the dimly lit back room, glancing over their shoulders toward Lloyd as they walked away.

Bishop Cheney reappeared at the doorway and said to Lloyd, "I'll pay you for the cut and your time as we conduct our, ah, church business around the table and discuss current policies. Naturally there will be a generous tip for you and your services."

"*Naturally*," Lloyd echoed. "And use the kerosene lantern on the table instead of the ceiling light, if you don't mind. What with the snow and wind, I wouldn't want an electrical problem this time of year."

The Bishop nodded and closed the door. Lloyd waited for a few seconds before entering the same room.

He went in, saying, "Excuse me," poured himself a cup of coffee from the percolator on the oil stove, not looking in the direction of the men in his presence. He turned and said, "The room is all yours."

He turned toward the door and stepped out to the shop, closing the door behind him. Up in his barber chair he sat with a slight grin as he opened the *Pine Nut Weekly* to the front page.

He took a sip of coffee; his mood quickly soured, still irritated with the racist remarks from Father Svendly Pervasions. It was never easy to forget the horror that bigotry caused him when he was young.

CHAPTER TWENTY-ONE

L avonne was her name. Lloyd called her Vonnie. She had black hair, but, dyed it blond. It curled under and around her ears to her neckline. She wore a thin silver necklace with a gold cross. It reminded Lavonne of her mother. She lived with her father and little brother on the south side of Chicago, just a couple of blocks from Comiskey Park near the railroad tracks, the home field of the Chicago White Sox.

Lloyd delivered the newspaper to her neighborhood before school every day. He raced through his route just to spend a few precious moments with her. Her father was a mailman. Her mother died giving birth to her younger brother Jerold.

Lavonne kept the house in order for her father and looked after baby Jerold. She looked forward to visits from the skinny newspaper kid who had a crush on her. She cared for him, too. Truth is, their feelings went beyond infatuation. They were madly in love with each other. Color be damned!

When Lloyd was seventeen, he drove to her house with the car he'd purchased from saving his nickels and dimes he'd earned from the paper route. It was a clunker, but it ran. They talked on the back porch. He father wouldn't let him in the house. He wasn't too keen on the kid, but that's not the reason he wouldn't let Lloyd in. What would the neighbors think? He was white. Lavonne was black. Life wasn't fair.

She got pregnant, and Lloyd was ready to marry her. There was the color barrier to consider, and neither of the parents wanted a marriage. When it came time for the baby to be born, she was taken to a reputable doctor near the Loop in downtown Chicago. She gave birth to a baby boy, but there were complications. She had internal bleeding and then came the God-awful blood clot. Seventeen-year-old Lavonne died. Her baby boy was given up for adoption. Lloyd wept.

CHAPTER TWENTY-TWO

The headlines read, *Hornsby Children Missing. Last seen in a late model black car, possibly a Buick, driven by a man wearing a dark overcoat and a black fedora hat, was heading west from the Hornsby farmhouse.* Smaller headlines on the front page read, *Local Farmer Hangs Himself in Pine Nut Jail. Farm boy awakens from a five-day coma.*

Another car pulled up next to Lloyd's Studebaker. It was a '41 Ford. Lloyd remembered its first owner, Clifford Maxwell. Gordon got it when his father passed away a few years ago. His mother, Inez, was first to go from consumption.

The door opened. Lloyd put his forefinger to his lips, got down off his chair, set the paper and cup of coffee on the back shelf. In a quiet voice, Gordon said, "Hey."

"Hey, Gordy, need a trim?" Lloyd asked as he made a head motion toward the back room.

"More than that. I'd like one of your specials, Lloyd, a shave, haircut, and hot towel."

"You got it."

Gordon rested himself in the chair and began his banter. "Have you been listening to the Lone Ranger lately? It seems every time he sends his sidekick, Tonto, into town to get information on the bad guys, he gets beat up."

Lloyd replied, "I suppose right after the commercial the Lone Ranger goes to town, rounds up the bad guys, and he and Tonto haul them off to jail."

"Happens all the time." Lloyd placed the sheet around Gordon, tucking it in around his shirt collar. As he did so, he leaned in and whispered, "I turned it on as they were getting themselves seated around the table."

Gordon whispered, "I got it here as fast as I could, to set it up. As I left, I saw the Buick coming up the road.

I drove the old man's car, bad battery and all," Gordon said, clapping his hands together. He would do that from time to time; he'd slap his hands together hard and rub the palms together fast and steady. It warmed up his hands, and he said it always felt refreshing and vigorous.

Lloyd whispered, "I drove as slow as I could to give you time."

He positioned the hot damp towel on his face, grabbed the straight razor and leather strap and gave it a fast stropping. It snapped and popped.

The door to the back room opened wide. Pastor Swain peered around into the front. He made quick eye contact with Lloyd, made a gesture with his hand and nodded toward the man under the towel. "A customer," Lloyd replied, startling Florien. He didn't expect him to say anything out loud. He had the look of an embarrassed chipmunk as he ducked back in and closed the door.

Sheriff Maxwell pulled the towel aside and whispered to Lloyd, "It should run a good forty-five minutes or so." He looked at his watch, 12:15.

Lloyd leaned forward. "One o'clock sounds like the perfect time for a fuse to blow on the electrical box, if need be.

"I didn't care for Florien's eulogy this morning. He inferred that you didn't know what the hell you were doing by putting Priestly in jail."

"You notice that, too? Lloyd, I'm a firm believer in the foreign word, Karma. The old boy is *gonna get his!*"

Lloyd removed the towel from the Sheriff's face and began barbering again. They could only guess as to what was being said in the back room.

CHAPTER TWENTY-THREE

"Okay, boys, I'll be brief. The cops are all over the county looking for the kids. I had a house call last night from the captain of the Highway Patrol. He found nothing, of course. After this little conversation is over, I'm heading straight to the seminary. All of the seminarians will be sent home for the holidays at the end of the classes today, along with the goddamn nuns. Women irritate *the hell* out of me.

"I've invited a few members of the LOC from around the state to attend, so there should be about thirty of us in all, getting ready for tomorrow night's activities.

"Special arrangements have been made for the transfer of the children. Also, I was told by one of our own that, if you're wondering why we are meeting here, it's because of the funeral; it makes it much more innocent looking."

"Your Eminency, if I may interject," Father Pervasions whispered as he leaned his arms on the table with his fingertips touching the bottom of the kerosene lantern in the middle of the table. It flickered as he talked. It was an eerie sight. The flame began to dance around his face, giving him a pale, ghostly look.

"I've received a letter from my contacts from Odessa, as well as Spain and Brazil, *and* a confirmation phone call from an old friend at da Vatican. Dey are ready to receive da fair-haired boy dar and send da girl on to Brazil where we'll get a tidy sum of money for her. Some prefer da boy, but my source says da Vatican wants him as an 'apostolic schoolboy' and servant at a monks retreat in da rocky hills just north of Rome. Da Nuestro Padre will be da one to indoctrinate him, shall we say, to da ways of our wishes."

"Of course," said the Bishop, "Wise decision. Those in the church should have preference over all others. He could very well make a fine priest someday."

Swain sneered at the remark.

"Now, Florien, don't get your dander up. By the way, I was hoping Flo could make an appearance this weekend, either tomorrow or maybe sometime after the ceremony. I'm sure Sven here would like to see her, too. What d'ya say, Florien, will we get some time with her?"

The Pastor half smiled. He was pleasantly surprised at the thought. Florien could make the transition to the beautiful, sexy, playful, Flo.

"How much money are we talking about?" Florien asked.

Svendly said, "Forty-four tousand and two, to you and me."

"That's the last time any of us are to mention money," the Bishop interrupted angrily. He nodded toward the door to the barbershop. The Bishop leaned in and, with a raspy angry whisper, added. "If you must know of such matters beforehand, write the question down, then rip up the paper it was written on! *Yes*, there is money involved, a lot of money. Fast money is why we're in this special sect of the LOC, not to mention the kiddies."

They nodded in agreement.

"Check on the barber again. See if anything has changed," the Bishop demanded. "I don't feel comfortable here."

He got up, opened the door, looked in, closed the door, and sat back down. "Just the same customer with Wellington boots getting a shave and haircut."

"The Sheriff wears Wellingtons," Florien remembered. The others thought nothing of it. *Even if it was, who cares?* As he situated himself back down in his chair again, a color of green emerged from the hot steam coils in the corner of the room. They turned and looked. No one said a word. They turned away from it as the Bishop twiddled his thumbs and cleared his throat before continuing.

Paul Cheney had a vision from the past. It startled him. He saw himself behind the convent. The rain was pouring down in sheets as

110

the sky turned thunderous, with lightning flashing all around. He saw himself standing over a grave, clutching a shovel, staring at a body.

He couldn't recognize the bloody mess in the grave. The lifeless soul was lying facedown in the watery death pit. The grave was filling fast with muddy waters. "That'll teach you," he said. "You sniveling *bitch*. I'll tell your parents that you ran away. You've done it before. So rest in peace, you worthless whore."

He swallowed hard, shaking the thought. It didn't seem real. *That could not have happened.* He took in a deep breath and said, "Well, maybe that's good. The ignorant, boozing Sheriff is right under our noses, right where I want him; Lloyd could vouch for that, if need be.

"Boys, I was teaching at the CC minor seminary when he was a skinny-assed high school freshman. He only lasted one year. The rector sent him packing. Poor candidate. Bad student."

Cheney couldn't remember all of his victims. Only those who gave him *extreme* pleasure. "So he's getting a haircut. Perfect. No suspicions."

Inhaling, he said, "That's about it for now. I'll have the usual rooms ready for us. You two go over the standard chant. Practice is always helpful to get the whole group frenzied to protect and preserve our clan, the world's greater society of correct and courageous men of vision." Leaning in, he continued, "You hear me, gentlemen?

"You've been in my diocese for almost a year now, Svendly, I know your background. Oh, tell Florien here how you arrived here in the Capital City Diocese."

CHAPTER TWENTY-FOUR

S vendly Pervasions smiled. Sven loved to talk, especially about himself. He started by telling of his strict upbringing as a devout Lutheran in the snow-covered mountains of Norway near the icy sea waters; how his mother prayed daily, kneeling on the hardwood floor of the living room in front of the fireplace in the tiny chalet.

"My father, Lars, was a fisherman and was gone, sometimes for weeks. My mother, Lena, was lonely and met up with other men who weren't fishermen for 'a little lovin,' as she called it. She brought dem home. My room was next to theirs. I hear tings.

"Sven," Cheney said, "Tell them about the path you took."

"Ya, I tell 'em. In da late thirties, I found myself reading *Mein Kampf* and listening to everyting I could about Adolph Hitler. I knew I had to leave my family and country to do what I could for my Führer, my excitement, my guru. I stole my mother's money, sneaked into Germany, and had papers drawn up to become a German citizen, changed my name to Stöver.

"The Red Cross had papers drawn up near da end of da war for me to be a priest. I had to pay dem, dearly."

"The Red Cross?" asked, Pastor Swain.

"Ya." Sven continued. "Dey had great sympathy toward da so called war criminals as did the Catholic Church and America's C.I.A. They drew up at least twenty-five thousand identity documents and worked closely with Odessa.

"Wait a minute," said Cheney. "Who the hell's Odessa?"

"Ya, Sven said, "Odessa, is an underground group stretching across borders who are Nazi sympathizers, like yourself, Bishop. Dey facilitated escape routes and still are; some call dem rat lines, out of Germany," He continued. "Doctor Mengele took da southern route with da help of Bishop Alois Hudal of Rome who used da monastery route through Genoa, Italy with da help of Giuseppe Siri, to Juan Peron's Argentina. Do you want me to continue with da Franciscan order and how dey helped, too, Bishop Cheney?"

"Not now," the Bishop said. "Proceed with the story."

"Well, Mengele stuffed fresh Swiss currency in his suitcase and told me of a place in Rome where dar would be much more of it for him. I was to follow a map and, should I find it, I was to send it all to him. I was fortunate in dat I *did* find it many months later via a Vatican representative.

"Da priest handed me a briefcase as we dined at a little outdoor café in Rome near da Vatican. I never saw dat man again. Dar wasn't much of the money left before I got hold of it. I kept it and lost all track of da good doctor.

Florien yawned and received a cold stare from the Bishop.

"I've had two private audiences with Pope Pius XII, a great and holy man. Do you know he didn't disapprove of da Führer's decision of erecting da concentration camps or with da Jewish question? My beloved Pope should be a saint! I remember a Catholic journalist who once asked why he did nothing about da mass killing of the Jews.

"The journalist said, 'You can stop it, you know.' Pope Pius XII responded by saying, 'My good man, Adolf Hitler was raised as a Catholic. Difficult decisions must be made in tough times. Sir, do not forget that millions of Catholics serve in the German armies. Shall I bring *them* into conflict of conscience, too?'

"Pope Pius XII introduced another great man to me, the founder of da LOC, Marcial Marciel, a Mexican priest, our father. He arrived from Mexico a week before I got there. He'd been telling certain priests, and these were his words now, 'get the prettiest and smartest fair-haired boys.' Oh God, I *love* dat man. He recruits seminarians as young as ten years old. Da rumor is this: Nuestro Padre came to ask

Pope Pius XII special permission to seek out specific seminarians sexually for relief of his physical pain. So dar you have it. Sex eases pain." He chuckled to himself, as did Bishop Cheney.

"The Legionnaires of the Christo is da future. It's *the* way to train da young, as a culture of mind-control. Marcial Marciel got it right, Opus Dei is *our* enemy.

"Oh, boys, just an aside. In Germany, there's a young seminarian in the Nazi party who served in uniform during da war. He is now in da seminary. He has an older brother who's just now becoming a priest. Anyway, he is being groomed. Perhaps in da future, there'll be a Nazi pope who *knows* of such things."

Florien didn't approve or agree with his cohort's feelings. "Excuse me for having a question, Sven, but why did you call the Bible students *damned?*"

"Oh, Florien, come on now, really! Here it is den: dey, da lousy Jehovah's Witnesses, could have stayed out of da camps. Dey had dar chance, but screwed themselves anyway. All dey had to do was sign a paper saying dey denounced dar religion or beliefs and recognize da Führer as dar leader. Da dumb shits wouldn't do it. Some got dar purple triangles, and da rest got da gas."

The Bishop put his coffee cup down, put his arms closer to the kerosene lamp, and looked at his wristwatch.

"We've been here almost forty minutes, boys. I've got a couple of items in the backseat I have to get to the seminary. I'll have a surprise for everyone at the ritual. Better take you two back to Florien's house, then I'm out of this rinky-dink town. Remember, boys, everything is set for tomorrow night." Turning to Florien, he said, "Hope to see Flo later, perhaps tonight."

CHAPTER TWENTY-FIVE

Raphael could see the anger in Will's eyes and said, "You see why your friend Gordon Maxwell needs your help, don't you? This is too big for one man to handle. Remember, too, what you saw in the hall of records? Even the thoughts of mankind are recorded. The good, the bad; whatever happens, whether it's in thought or action, it all happens."

Will couldn't take it. He was boiling over with anger, and it had to be released. He wanted to come through the wall and grab the freaks by their throats. He soared up and far away from the building, going higher and higher. He took long, deep breaths.

The men stood, grabbed their coats and slid out through the back door to the Bishop's car. Counting to three, Will reversed direction, whizzed downward, closing in fast on the back of Lloyd's barbershop next to the corner tavern.

Meanwhile, Lloyd had finished with Sheriff Maxwell and heard the back door shut. He went to the back room to shut off the recording machine. Just as the Bishop promised, he had paid Lloyd. A handful of twenty-dollar gold pieces lay on the table, which he grabbed and stashed in his pocket. As he leaned over to pull on the electric cord at the wall socket to disconnect the wire machine, a jolt of electricity bolted through his hand and there was a sudden combined thud and crashing sound.

Will slammed through the wall. Well, almost that is. As before, just his head and upper body came through. Lloyd lurched backward with the plug in his fried hand and plopped down on the hot steam coils while trying to keep his footing. His flesh burned hot. He leaped into the air and let out a bloodcurdling scream.

Gordon jumped out of the barber chair and ran in to see what the ruckus was about. Lloyd was half crazy and darting back and forth with his scorched hand and his red-hot backside. He reached for his coat, but didn't take it. Out the back door he flew. With a crazy, bewildered look, he ran around to the front of his building to his car, slipping and sliding in the snow. Lloyd jumped in and started the engine.

Gordon ran back into the barbershop to the front window in time to see Lloyd's car fishtailing in the street.

"What the hell's wrong with that boy?"

Lloyd spun out onto the street in the icy snow, fishtailing around through the alley to the back of his shop.

He was going way too fast, wherever he was going. The poor burned and confused fart whizzed fast beyond his parking spot. Out of control and going at a pretty good clip, he slammed on the brakes and turned the wheels, just missing a seventy-year-old stately elm. The car spun, and then straightened, heading right for the side of Vinney's tavern next to his shop. With his eyes as big as lemons and his mind in a state of confusion, he had his right foot pressing the gas pedal to the floor and his left foot on the brake. He couldn't stop as it slammed through the wall.

The sedan came to rest against the back of the bar rail. The apron-clad elderly bartender scooted out from behind the bar just as the car came to a stop. He and the two men seated on the stools at the bar panicked. They raced out of the front door. There were just assholes and elbows hotfooting it out of the building. The three were outside at the same time the Bishop's car rounded the corner by the tavern and turned onto Main Street.

The first one out was the town drunk, Keith Witherspoon. He almost ran into the side of the car as it drove by. Frozen in time were the blank stares of Keith, Florien Swain, and Svendly Pervasions. Keith stopped within an inch of the car as it rolled by.

Sheriff Maxwell had run from the front to the back and out the door, and all he could do was watch as Lloyd drove right past the shop, into the side of the bar. He flung open the back door and raced around the side of the building where Lloyd's car had come to rest halfway inside Vinney's bar. He found Lloyd with his hands still welded to the steering wheel, sitting, eyes wide and screaming, "My ass, my ass, my ass!"

He pried his hands off the steering wheel as Lloyd kept ranting. Holding both arms with one hand, Gordon slapped his face with the other.

With a startled look, Lloyd turned to Gordon and said, "You hit me!"

"Yes, I hit you! Now step out of the car. You have that same crazy look that Mickey had the other day. What the hell's the matter with you, for Chrissakes?"

"I got shocked and sat on the heat coils, Gordon. My butt cheeks are burnt!"

"That's it? That's *all it was* that caused you to go berserk, jump in your car, drive it around back, and slam it into the side of Vinney's tavern? Your hand got a shock and you burned *your butt,* and that's all there is to it?"

Lloyd sat as calm as he could before answering, "And I saw a ghost. Plus, I peed my pants."

CHAPTER TWENTY-SIX

"**W**here did those men come from? What the hell is going on around here?" The Bishop was tense as he drove past the three men who dashed out. No one in the backseat said a word. They were too shocked themselves.

He turned off Main Street, heading to Pastor Swain's house, where he pulled off and stopped to let them out. As he glanced into the rearview mirror, he saw Timmy Lee and Margaret Lynn huddled together between Florien and Sven. When they saw the Bishop's angry eyes in the mirror staring back at them, the Pastor and the Priest said in unison, "They're cold, Paul."

"I'll see you both tomorrow night at the seminary. By God's will, you two will be there plenty early to greet the rest and have things in order for our hallowed cleansing ritual!" he said, angry with them for feeling sorry for the two pawns who had been gagged and bound on the floor. "Many good men will be there, our brothers in sacrifice, our brothers in oneness. They'll all be there. Don't let me down, nor the Mother Church. Do *not* let the great Judge of Holiness down, lest we all will be judged in darkness!"

The ministers bowed their heads in silence as the Bishop ranted and Timmy Hornsby sobbed. Margaret smothered him in her arms. She, too, shed a tear. She was also angry and confused.

The two exited the car, and Florien escorted Sven inside. With Timmy and Margaret in the back, Paul Cheney drove out onto the cold, lonely highway heading toward the Capital City Catholic Seminary.

The road was slick and ice-covered. He held tight to the steering wheel. "Who helped you out of the rope and removed the tape from your mouths? You couldn't have done it yourselves. So now tell me, you little sinners, who did it?"

"Pastor Swain did," Timmy said as tears flowed down his red face alongside his runny nose. His little shoulders and arms were shaking hard. "It's cold on the car floor."

Something came over the Bishop just then. That old feeling came back. He felt almost like a kid again himself. That's what he liked most about having children near him; children without the presence of their parents, that is. He could feel like a kid, and at the same time have full control of them. He loved power: the power to shake their beliefs, to mold the minds of little ones. Religion was an absolute. He relished *being* that absolute power and wielding it over those in his path. Children were his preferred target.

"Come, climb over the front seat where it's warmer. I'll turn up the heat."

Timmy scrambled over first and sat next to the old man behind the wheel. Margaret with a blanket in hand, brought one leg up and over the front seat and straddled it as Timmy reached up and pulled her down. As he did, her blanket flew as she spilled over with a bounce.

The blanket draped the Bishop's hat and shoulder. He reached with his left hand to remove it, still holding the wheel with his right. As he did, he crossed the center of the road. When he turned the wheel sharply to get back into his lane, the car slid on the ice and began fishtailing.

He was petrified. Somehow, time decelerated, as if in slow motion. He turned the wheel a tad to the right. As he did, the car spun past the point of correction. It was now skimming over the ice in the opposite direction. He turned the steering wheel slowly this time, and it righted itself straight down the road.

Breathing a sigh of relief, he glanced down at the children. They huddled together with the blanket around them. His demeanor had changed.

"You terrible, little *bastard* sinners! Look what you made me do! We could all have been killed. Would you have *liked* that? What would your mother and father think about you two causing your own death and even the death of the *Bishop* of the Capital City Diocese? You should be ashamed of yourselves! You're an embarrassment to your community! Your parents don't want you anymore. You should have never been *born!*"

The scolding continued. Margaret stared straight ahead with her arm around her younger brother. At the end of his tirade, he yelled, "And may God Almighty, with Jesus at his side, strike you dead and send you both straight to Hell. Shame on you! You two are an embarrassment to the entire Catholic Church, and to the Catholic community the world over, a billion strong!"

As he finished his unrelenting madness and regained his composure, Margaret leaned forward. She wiped her nose on Timmy's sleeve, cleared her throat, and looking over at Bishop Paul Cheney saying, "We're Unitarians," and sat back in her seat for a few minutes before continuing, "and we're thirsty."

Timmy chimed in, "I gotta pee."

CHAPTER TWENTY-SEVEN

"*H* *i, ho Silver, awaaay!*" rang from Lloyd's radio.

Gordon was sitting on the second barber chair jotting down noted from the day's activities, beginning with the funeral.

From there he revisited the secret meeting, taking notes from the recording machine. He had a few more minutes to listen to, but he shut it off to write about Lloyd's escapade, ending with his burnt buns.

Lloyd had cleaned himself up at the washbasin in the back room and changed his clothes. He always had a change of clothes or two, especially white shirts. He looked sharp, and his customers appreciated that. On this day, however, he didn't care about his white shirts or anything else. Lloyd had never been so confused in his life; after all, he'd just seen a ghost. He came out of the back room looking as good as he could under the circumstances.

"How you doin,' pardner?" Maxwell asked.

Lloyd was clutching a pillow he had grabbed from the back room, climbed up, placed it on the first barber chair, settled in with his left leg dangling over his armrest, and said, "I'm so confused I couldn't pound a nail through a mud puddle." He squirmed; the scalding his butt cheeks took was fresh and blistering. His right hand was bandaged.

Gordon remarked, "You'll have to call your insurance company. I have no idea what you're going to tell them."

"I know. I know," he said. "Leave me alone," he said, almost growling.

Gordon snickered and continued penning his report.

Keith Witherspoon opened the door, staggered in, and sat down on the first chair against the wall. His faded black and green-checkered wool shirt was half-tucked into his trousers and half out. His upper teeth were long gone and so was his razor.

"Boys," he confided, sitting there with his right forearm resting on his right knee. "I've been on a five-day toot and I want to make a proclamation." Gesturing with his left hand, he spoke. "Today, I swear off drinkin'. I ain't kidding this time, Sheriff. I know I spent many a time at your hotel at the other end of town. You always treated me fair and gave me a good hot meal the next day. I don't forget stuff like that. You're a good man, but I got to come clean here and now. From this day forward, I quit drinking." His arm slid off his leg, and he almost fell to the floor.

Gordon heard that same story a hundred times, a hundred different ways. He was too busy jotting down notes and trying to concentrate. Lloyd, however, was intrigued. "Go on, Keith, continue."

"Like I was sayin.' I ain't gonna touch another drop, so help me, Hannah!"

"Why's that?" Lloyd asked.

"Well, God all fishhooks. There I was, mindin' my own business just talkin' with the boys next door at Vinney's tavern there, havin' a bump and a beer, rollin' the dice, playin' ship-captain-and-crew with the guys," he said, pointing toward Vinney's with a finger. "We was talking about that pretty nurse I danced with the other night, Pam Darling, and jokin' with one another about which one of us stood a chance with her." Keith paused and rubbed his hand over his five-day growth of stubble before he proceeded. "I was talkin' to old Frank Telfore, the beekeeper, sitting next to me, and I says, 'I'll hold her tonight for you if'n you hold her for me tomorrow night.'

"Well, old Frank got to coughin' and laughin' so hard he had beer comin' out of both nostrils. It was the damnedest thing you ever saw. Then a'course I started laughin' *and that's* when the shit hit the fan!

"Your car crashed right through the wall, and came to rest against the bar railing. I tell you, we were nothing but steppin' and fetchin' for the door, and before you could say *yellow slippery buggers*, I was nose to nose with the side of a big black car. I ain't ever seen such a sight in all my born days, Lloyd. *By God*, it was somethin'! Yes sir, I quit the booze for good this time."

Lloyd's ears were bright red now, and his face flushed with embarrassment.

"But that ain't what I'm here to tell you boys."

Gordon's ears perked up at Keith's last remark.

"Why's that?" the Sheriff asked. He uncrossed his legs, set the paper and pen down, and encouraged him to finish his story.

"Well, I don't know how to say it, but I was the first one out the door, and my feet never stopped movin' till I was in the street. I stopped dead in my tracks as that big old black car, er, Buick, passed right under my nose. It was so close I could almost smell yesterday's fart lingering inside the door! A half a step further and I would have been road-kill."

"That's it? That's all you had to tell us?" the Sheriff snapped.

"No, *hell* no, Sheriff! A'course there's more to it. When I stopped out there, I saw three men. One was Pastor Swain a'sittin' in the back-seat with that Norwegian priest, and I don't know who was drivin', but he was a short little bald-headed fart, dressed in black."

Lloyd snickered and turned to Gordon. They gave a nod to one another and returned to Keith and his story.

"Yes, sir, the Priest and Pastor Swain just sort of turned to me with a blank stare, and I had no choice but to stand there and stare right back. There's something else, too."

"*Damn* it, Keith!" Gordon pleaded as he shifted his weight from cheek to cheek.

"Well, at first I doubted my own eyes, but the more I remember, and the more time I had to think about it, the more positive I am about what I saw. Between the two pastors and on the floor was a blanket with two big bumps in it. As the car came by and, just as I stopped there and looked in, two heads were coming out from under the blanket."

"Two heads? Two heads of what?" Gordon demanded.

"Well sir, I'll tell you. It was a little boy and a girl, maybe the ones everybody's been lookin' for. I knew'd the first one was a girl 'cause I saw pigtails."

"The Hornsby kids!" the Sheriff shouted as he leaped from the barber chair. "Which way was he headed? Never mind. He's *got* to be goin' there! I had asked Ashton Plenn, the captain of the Highway Patrol, go to his house specifically! *Damn it to hell!*"

Sheriff Maxwell flew out of the door, running to his '41 Ford. He jumped in and cranked the engine. It spit and sputtered as he sped off to the other end of town to his office to get his official squad car the village of Pine Nut had bought for him to perform his duties. He wanted to radio Zaugs, then cussed out loud because the village of Pine Nut thought it was too much money to spend on a two-way radio. *Just so Gordy could talk to Mickey back at the Sheriff's office from our new squad car we bought him.* Assholes.

***

Bishop Cheney came out of a gas station with three bottles of Coke, three bags of Red Dot potato chips, and a handful of Hershey bars. He sat back in the driver's seat and looked over at the kids as they huddled together on the floor. He instructed, "Alright, you two heathens, you can get up now. Uncle Billy has a treat for the both of you."

Timmy and Margaret looked at each other as they hurried to sit on the seat again, still covering themselves with the blanket.

"You two, sit up straight and be sorry for your sins as you say your prayers before you partake in food," he said in a stern voice.

The children sat up straight and bowed their heads in silence. Then Margaret said, "Thank you, God, for protecting us and keeping us in your heart, and please tell Mommy and Daddy that we'll be home before long. Amen."

The Bishop laughed loud and long. He took a sip of Coke and hiccupped. When he did, his false teeth came halfway out of his mouth.

Timmy jumped. He'd never seen false teeth before and teeth hanging from the end of this man's tongue scared the bejeezus out of him.

128

He must be the devil, Timmy thought.

Paul Cheney re-adjusted his dentures and handed the kids the Cokes, chips and candy bars. They hadn't eaten since he had fed them leftovers from his five o'clock supper the day before. Margaret spoke up, "My dad calls these male Hershey bars."

"Male?" the Bishop questioned. "Why male?"

"Cause they got nuts," she said.

They inhaled the chips and candy bars in no time and finished drinking their Cokes at the same time he did. Timmy opened his mouth and presented one of the longest and loudest belches ever.

Margaret laughed so hard she had tears coming out of the corners of her eyes. Oddly enough, the Bishop was silent and showed no emotion. He just started the engine, backed out of the empty lot next to the gas station, and headed out onto the highway toward the seminary.

"I gotta pee," Timmy said, holding his hands between his legs and pulling his knees together.

"Me, too," Margaret said.

"Why didn't you two say something sooner?"

"I did," Timmy whispered.

"Here, take this Coke bottle, climb in the backseat and use it to urinate in."

Timmy pushed the blanket aside and climbed over to the backseat. He put the bottle down on the floor and unzipped his pants, while Cheney kept his eyes glued to the rearview mirror, adjusting it so that he could watch Timmy's every move.

It took some doing, but Timmy managed to get it all in the bottle without spilling a drop. When he was finished, he placed the Coke bottle between his knees and zipped his pants. As he did so, the bottle slipped. Timmy was successful in reaching it before it spilled out onto the floor. He picked it up and placed it on the back of the front seat, holding it there for the Bishop.

Cheney reached for the bottle with his right hand, knocking it from side to side. Some of the urine splashed out onto the Bishop. It splattered on side of his face, neck, and into his ear canal.

He rolled down his window and threw the bottle out onto the highway. After wiping off the fresh urine with his handkerchief, he placed it back in his pocket and continued down the road as if nothing happened.

Embarrassed and afraid of what the Bishop might do or say, Timmy remained in the back and lay down on the seat. Paul Cheney looked to Margaret and she at him. She thought, *What would Ingrid Bergman do in this situation? What would she say?* Helen Hornsby had taken little Margaret to an Ingrid Bergman's "The Bells of St. Mary," and she was captivated by Bergman's character and tried to emulate the actress.

"I've decided to wait," Margaret said in her most grown-up voice. "I'll use a ladies' powder room when one becomes available."

Cheney, already taking a huge chance at being seen with the children, couldn't trust her to go by herself.

Up ahead was an old cheese factory run by a fellow Legionnaire. He could talk with the cheesemaker about the upcoming ritual at the seminary. Cheney pulled in.

Holding tight to their hands, he stepped to the front door and pulled it open. He had an unnaturally strong grip and their hands were hurting. He was oblivious to their pain as they made their way inside.

Inside, there was a large window where visitors could watch the cheese makers transform the whitish milky whey into cheese curds in the long steel vats. No one was there. There were two doors, one on each side of the window. One led into the factory and the other to a washroom. He opened the washroom door and stepped inside with the kids.

"Here you go, sweetie. Uncle Billy and Timmy will stay right here while you do your business."

"I don't think so!" Margaret said emphatically. "You'll wait outside this *door*. I'm going to *freshen up*. This is one place where there's a natural separation between man and woman."

Margaret pulled free from the Bishop's grip, folded her arms and stood firm, staring at him, and said emphatically, "What would your grandmother think of you?"

Cheney begrudgingly obeyed and, with Timmy in tow, backed out as she slammed the door shut and locked it.

CHAPTER TWENTY-EIGHT

Gordon was seated at his desk talking on the phone with the captain of the Highway Patrol. Outside, next to the '41 Ford, his new police car sat with the hood up while the local mechanic was replacing the dead battery.

"Ashton, I want you to put out an All Points Bulletin on Bishop Cheney. He's driving a new black Buick—*What's that*—yes, Bishop Paul Cheney—*I know, I know* you were at his house last night, but listen, *will you?* I have a man here in Pine Nut and he says he saw the two kids in the backseat of his car not more than ten minutes ago; a boy and a girl—*yes, it could the Hornsbys.* In fact, I'm damned sure of it. You don't think *they belong to him, do you?* Look, I don't know why the *Bishop*—Just *listen!* I think maybe he's on Highway 14 headin' toward the seminary, if he's not already there."

Ashton replied, "The Bishop is a good man, Gordon, besides the seminary is out of your jurisdiction. I'll pass this on to the CC police. Heard you were in the hospital. What was that all about? Been nippin' the brandy again?"

Frustrated, Gordon slammed the receiver down on the phone cradle.

"Fuck! I'll bet a dime to a sack of nuts the word won't go out until it's too late.

"Goddamn it. *Goddamn* it!"

He could feel in the pit of his stomach the hurt and pain of those kids. Something ached even deeper, right to his soul. He seemed to be tapping into the long-ago-buried pain from that same seminary.

He picked up the cell keys from his desk and threw them as hard as he could. They zoomed across the room and smacked against the back wall, just missing a framed picture of President Harry S. Truman before dropping to the floor. He began gnawing on a fingernail as he paced the jailhouse floor. The more he paced, the emptier he felt, becoming void of all emotion until he felt like a hollow empty shell.

He put his elbows on the table and cradled his forehead with both hands. His mind was in search of what to do next, how to save those kids, yet in his mind, it was his younger self up against those men in black.

"Goddamn those religious self-righteous bastards!" He could no longer control his emotions as he let out his anger, frustration, and humiliation of years gone by.

He took his checkered red and blue handkerchief from his back pocket, wiped his eyes, and blew his nose so hard he made a snorting sound. It reminded him of the kind of snort an elk would make, and he half laughed out loud at the thought of it.

Stuffing the kerchief in his back pocket, he reached down to the bottom right drawer, pushing the rolled up newspapers aside and fetched his bottle. He set it down on the desk and looked at the label: Five Star Brandy.

Gordon hadn't had a drop of alcohol since the night he got stinking drunk at home and woke to find Will in front of the mirror in his bedroom. He unscrewed the cap and brought the bottle to his lips, paused, took a swig, then sniffed the sweet, addicting smell of brandy. He stole another alluring whiff, and raised it up as in a toast. Setting the bottle back down on the desk, he screwed the cap back on; laid it back in the drawer, and pushed it shut, stepped outside and spit it out.

Back in his chair, he ran his fingers through his reddish hair front to back, remembering it had felt much thicker not that long ago. He took another deep, comforting breath and exhaled.

He wanted to go to the seminary, even if it was out his jurisdiction. But, how? That was the question.

Ashton Plenn hadn't been much help. Worse yet, his new squad car sat outside now for over an hour, worthless while it was being attended to. His personal car couldn't be trusted on the highway. Seconds turned to minutes. The phone rang. It was Ashton again.

"Yup. Seems you were right after all. We think he was heading to Capital City and beyond. I've got an eyewitness. He told me he saw the Bishop alone in the car about fifteen miles on the other side of Capital City. He may be headed for Boston, maybe New York City."

Gordon could do nothing but sit it out and wait for the search warrants and subpoenas he'd asked for and promised to get, from Capital City DA's office, and the Attorney General.

His thoughts took him back again to the seminary, remembering fellow seminarian Ashton Plenn. He was a senior when Gordon was a freshman; a real goody-two-shoes kind of creep. Eddy Lord, stocky strong hulk, had him pinned up against the wall in the gymnasium one time when Ashton told on him for smoking in the boys' room. Eddy was about to rearrange his dental work when Father Frank came in and pulled them apart.

Ashton, tall and blond, played football as a wide receiver, but managed to drop the ball in the end zone too many times. Father Frank, who was also the basketball coach, said that Plenn couldn't find a cow's teat with both hands.

He'd rat on his classmates at the drop of a hat. No one heard of him talking nice about girls. As far as Gordon knew, he never dated. He always thought there was something fishy about that, *a weird duck,* if you asked him.

Where the hell is Zaugs? Gordon pulled himself out of the seminary and drew his chair closer to the desk. He never left the office without at least posting a note, usually. He got back on the phone.

"Lloyd, are you busy?"

"Not now. I was just heading up the street for a bite at the café. What's up?"

"If you wouldn't mind, could you order me a toasted cheese sandwich and a chocolate malt for a chaser and bring the recorder by?"

"I'll do that for you, Sheriff. It shouldn't take but a half hour, at most."

"Perfect. I'll be right here in my office waiting."

***

Snow was falling on that December day in nineteen forty-nine. Mickey Zaugbaum was driving along Main Street, listening and humming to Gene Autry's new song, *Rudolph the Red-Nosed Reindeer*, and glancing over to the passenger seat at the camera Gordon had purchased.

He pulled up in front of the Sheriff's office and shut off the engine as the song ended. He grabbed the camera and looked up in the rearview mirror to see Lloyd coming to a stop behind him. Lloyd got out of his damaged car carrying a white paper bag and met Mickey as they both started for the jailhouse door.

Gordon was standing with the phone receiver in hand after talking to the Hornsbys as the two of them marched across the sidewalk and up the steps. Hanging up the phone, he said, "I'm glad you two are here. I'm hungry."

"I didn't bring no food," Mickey said, watching the Sheriff as he hung up the phone.

Gordon's eyes rolled as Lloyd handed him his lunch, and set it and himself down at the Sheriff's desk.

Lloyd said, "It's on me," and walked back down the steps to his car.

"Heard you bumped into Vinney's." Lloyd turned and gave Mickey the middle finger.

Inside the office, Gordon wolfed down the toasted cheese and slurped his way to the bottom of the ice-cold chocolate malt. He was looking over the invoice the mechanic had placed on the doorknob to his office. Finished, he sat back in his chair and let out a loud belch.

"Whoops!" He got up and walked to the back of the room to retrieve the keys he'd flung earlier.

Deputy Zaugbaum just sat and watched the Sheriff. He had great admiration for his boss when he wasn't drinking.

He watched the Sheriff sit back down and pull from the top drawer the manila folder holding the photos that Ms. Darling gave him earlier. He opened it. Spreading them on the desk again, Mickey leaned over the desk as they both eyed the pictures. Zaug's eyes darted from one picture to another and another and another.

"Ain't it something? I wonder who those men could be, don't you?" Mickey said without looking away from the photos.

The face and consternated look of Oliver Hardy appeared in Gordon's mind as his eyebrows rose. "That's the whole *idea*, Mickey."

Mickey kept his eyes on the photos and asked, "Where's the one with the boy holding the prick; you know, the one where you can't see the man's face."

"It's here someplace." Gordon shuffled the pictures all around, searching for it, but he couldn't find it.

"Anyway, where've you been? There was no note. You almost always let me know where you're going."

Zaugs lifted his hands off the table and stood straight. "I went to the church basement, grabbed all the pies and other goodies that I could carry, and took 'em home to the kids and the old lady. After half of a pumpkin pie, a cup of Joe, and a pee, I cruised the hospital parking lot." He continued and lied a little. "Ole Doc Bullock couldn't get his car started, so I stopped, got the jumper cables out of the trunk, and gave him a jump start. He was acting all fidgety and said he was in a big hurry at first, but after I got his car started, he got in and asked me to sit there with him for a while. He was asking about you; concerned, you might say. He says he thought you should still be in the hospital with your mouth wired shut."

He could sense the cold stare from the Sheriff.

"Well, that's what he *thought* and that's what he *said*!"

"Does it *look* like my jaw is broken?" asked Gordon.

"No, it sure doesn't. Tell me again how that happened, wouldya?" the deputy said as he walked to the front of the desk and leaned into it.

"Like I said before, Mickey, I must have been sleep-walking and ran right into the brick wall next to my bed."

"Oh, yeah," said Mickey as he leaned in and tapped his forefinger on the desk. *My ass,* he thought.

Gordon looked up at him and asked, "By the way, did you get a few snapshots of the Padre and Pastor?"

"Never got the chance, boss," Mickey said looking away. "Question. Lloyd ever cut William's hair that you know of?"

Gordon replied, "I asked him about that. Lloyd has never seen the kid. Anyway, Pa cut his hair and his own."

Shaking his head, Mickey said, "Listen, I think maybe I'll drive down to the café and do some snooping, see what the folks are talking about."

"Go, but be back by half past. Hopefully, we'll get some calls about the Bishop and the Hornsby kids. I've got a hunch; you and I are going to be busy for the next day or two at least. Get geared up for it, okay?"

"You can count on me. By the way, who was on the phone when Lloyd and I came in?" Mickey asked.

"Ed Hornsby. I called to see how they were doing and told him a little else, since there really isn't anything I *can* tell him, not just yet, anyway."

He wanted to catch all the fish in the pond, and the Bishop was just one guppy.

Gordon stood and walked Mickey to the front door and stood there watching Mickey as he made a U-turn with his car and headed down the street to the café. He sat back down, pulled out the photos again. One photo was facedown, the one he'd been looking for. He picked it up and placed it in front of him. He reached back in the desk for a magnifying glass, and placed it over the picture. He thought, at first, that it was an odd-shaped tattoo.

Could be a birthmark, he thought. He'd seen birthmarks on people before, but he couldn't put a particular one with the owner. He tucked it in his shirt pocket and put the rest back in the manila folder, which he placed back in the drawer.

He'd seen that mark on someone, but who? He picked up the receiver and was ready to call Plenn, but then he placed it back on the cradle, grabbed his coat and hat, and headed down to the barbershop to pick up his new magnetaphone. Gordon drove slowly through town, looking for Mickey's car at the café, but he didn't find it on the street.

"Lloyd, you forgot to bring me the magnetaphone."

"No, that's not true," Lloyd interrupted as he got up off his favorite barber chair.

"It's in the car."

"But why didn't you bring it when you brought the food?"

Lloyd stammered a little. "Well, I wasn't sure I should have because of Mickey being there, that's all."

Gordon tilted his head as spoke.

". . . and he wasn't with you when you brought it over."

"I hear your concerns," Gordon said, hiding his most recent thoughts.

He could feel a change in his young new deputy in the last couple of days, yet he couldn't put a finger on it. He felt he couldn't tell him everything, not yet at least. There were questions that needed to be answered. It was for that reason he hadn't told Zaugs about what he was up to that morning. It was also the reason why he didn't say anything to him about telephoning and requesting the Attorney General's office to have multiple warrants issued for arrests and the state police alerted for backup to serve those warrants.

It was a tough sell, but he had gotten a verbal okay from the Attorney General himself. He wrote down all of it; from the meeting in the back room to Lloyd coming unglued and Keith Witherspoon's seeing the kids in the Bishop's car. He had covered it all and didn't advise Mickey of a goddamned thing.

So much to do, so little time. His chest was pounding as he paced the office floor, but as for Mr. Five Star, he never entered his mind.

CHAPTER TWENTY-NINE

Anne slouched on the couch, drained. She laid her head on one armrest, folded her arms, closed her eyes, and drifted off.

Two young people, very much in—lust, were sitting at a small round table outside a quaint sidewalk café. She, an American with hazel eyes, auburn hair and long legs, peered deep into the dark eyes of a thick, tall, handsome Italian. The tables surrounding them were filled with people making small talk. Flitting about was a male waiter dressed in black with a white apron tied around his waist.

It was a warm and lazy afternoon in Rome, as couples, arm-in-arm, strolled the nearby sidewalk. Pigeons gathered, pecking at scraps dropped by the patrons. Two doves cooed under the table of the lovers.

They sat leaning across the little wrought iron table kissing, ripping pieces of bread, dipping it into their wine and serving each other, sucking on the thumb and forefinger of the other as they did so. The doves cooed and pecked at wine-soaked orts the lovebirds dropped to the ground.

The Italian moved his chair closer to his lover's. They embraced, hugging, kissing, and caressing, oblivious to the rest of the world. He kissed her bare shoulder, all the way down to her hand, sucking each of her fingertips. As he did, he slid off his chair to a kneeling position in front of his American lover. When she slipped off her sandals, he leaned down and kissed the top of each foot, sucking each toe.

He put one hand on her lower leg, partly for balance and to caress her warm, smooth calf. As he nudged her leg out from under the table, she turned her body to allow him full access to both legs as he kissed his way up her ankles to her calves.

The Italian stud, drunk with passion, kissed and licked his way to the backside of her knees, caressing the warm, smooth flesh as he worked his way toward her tender and inviting thighs. She sat contented, running her fingers through his long black hair with one hand, sipping her glass of red wine with the other.

He continued kissing every inch of her hot passionate flesh, making his way deep into her lustful pulsating loins. The aroused woman set her glass of wine down and held his head with both hands as he disappeared beneath her flowered skirt. Flushed, she quivered as she felt a rumbling deep down inside of her writhing body, as if Madame Pele was about to let loose a mountain of hot shooting lava.

He burrowed deeper between her legs. She arched back, looking skyward, and pulled his head closer, tighter. She began licking her dry, parched lips. Her body began to shudder. She reached and pulled her lover's face up to meet hers. His hands were firm, yet gentle, as he massaged her inner thighs.

Their lips met, and their tongues explored new territory at the little table outside the sidewalk café in Rome. She began to moan, and another moan, another, and another as they became one in trembling body and mind, tongues in light battle, hands caressing, petting each other's bodies until she shook wildly and uncontrollably, reaching a climactic peak.

Her last long melodious moan echoing through the nearby streets startled the birds. They scattered as the sun shone a bright white light all around.

As the light ebbed and color began to reappear, the scene had changed. The dark-haired lover was gone, leaving his glowing lover alone at the table. Gone, too, were the bottle of wine and the hard round loaf of bread. Instead, a single red rose lay across the table as a waiter stood before it.

She found herself reading the newspaper, taking a long drag from a cigarette, and exhaling into the air above. The headlines read, *American Nurse Asks Pope to Marry. Pope Says Si to Amore!* Next to the column explaining the romance and upcoming wedding of Pope Pious XII to Nurse Anne was a color picture of the elderly Pope wearing his Papal headdress and clutching his staff. It was a headshot of him smiling a thin-faced toothless smile and sporting several days of stubble.

"Oh, God!" Anne said as she blinked the sleep out of her eyes, getting herself up to a sitting position on the couch in the nurses' lounge. "Why do my dreams always, *always* end up like that?"

"Excuse me," the orderly said. "I'm sorry I woke you, but there's a phone call from the barber in town. He asked that you bring a book to him; a Madame Helena Blavatsky?"

"She's regarded as the mother of modern spirituality," Anne replied, brushing the sleep from her eyes. "Thanks."

The orderly continued. "After *something* happened this morning, he said he is curious about other possibilities beyond man's power? Something like that, anyway."

"Got it," she said in a stiff voice. Thanks!" *It's possible that he wanted to know more about the afterlife. Or maybe he saw a ghost,* Anne thought, as she drove to the café. Whatever, she was hungry. She needed a change of food *and scenery and job,* she thought, driving down the main street of this tiny village of Pine Nut. A town she was ready to leave.

After stepping into the café, she stood at the door scouting the long narrow room with a u-shaped counter of ten stools, and on one side three booths lined the wall. She was hoping to find a little corner booth just to be alone with her thoughts, have the chef salad in peace and quiet with no interruptions for a change, a place to unwind, and a place to just think.

"Hey, Anne! Over here!"

It was Pam Darling, waving her hand from side to side. She was sitting in the last booth, the corner booth, with Kathryn Knee, the schoolteacher.

Oh, crap. Yet, *Why were they there, together no less?*

It wasn't long before the three of them began to talk nonstop through several cups of coffee, and they still had plenty to say. Some of the old farmers sitting on stools nearby got up and moved to the other side of the counter, away from the animated conversation booming from the corner booth.

The customers at the café came and went. All but one: Mickey Zaugbaum. He was answering and sidestepping question after question from the local patrons. He got up from his stool at the front of the counter and moved to a stool near the ladies in the booth. He turned to them and winked.

As they watched him make his move, Ms. Darling whispered, "We have to go somewhere so we can continue our conversation in private, he's *weird*."

Mickey began to say something to them, but his eyes were set on Pam Darling as she leaned forward with her voluptuous chest resting on her folded arms on the table. His mouth was open, ready for the words to come out, but the sight of her lily whites kept him frozen. All of a sudden, the six-foot-four waitress had had it with his ogling, grabbed him by his collar, pulled him halfway over the counter, and said, "Pay up, little buddy!"

He put the crumpled piece of paper he had in his hand back in his pocket. *Damn.*

"What's wrong with him?" Kat asked out loud.

"Lloyd has a back room. Maybe we could talk there," Anne suggested as they got up to pay their bill and leave.

CHAPTER THIRTY

"Here's the key, ladies. It's becoming a busy little place here," Lloyd said, setting the key on the table. "When you're finished, just turn off the kerosene lamp, lock the door behind you, and push the key under it. I've got a spare at home."

"You're a doll for driving over here," Pam said as she patted his cheek and pinched it. Flustered, he blushed and ducked out the back door with the thick book on Madame Blavatsky's autobiography under his arm and damn near slipped on a patch of ice as he made his way around the front end of his damaged Studebaker.

Anne looked at her watch. "Oh, my God!" With an angelic smile, she continued, "For the first time in my life, I have this sudden urge to become ill." She stepped into the barbershop behind the second chair to the phone and called the hospital. She told the receptionist that she was awfully sick, had a terrible headache. In fact, she thought it was the beginning of the flu bug and didn't want to expose her patients, so she thought it best if she didn't come in to work at all.

Kathryn added kerosene to the lamp and lit it. The light was off in the barbershop, and the door to it was closed. They sat around the table, the same table as the clergy had used just hours earlier. Anne looked at her watch. *Four o'clock,* she thought, *and it'll be pitch dark in an hour or so.*

Anne said, "Winter solstice is nigh, ladies, maybe we should be riding brooms."

"Here's the skivey," Anne said, looking into Kathryn's eyes, pausing just long enough for her to say, "Call me Kat."

"Here's the skivey, Kat," she continued. "Will's dad had almost whipped him to death last week. He survived; you saw him at the hospital, and he's feeling better. In fact, his scars have healed and he's eating solids already. He's an amazing kid, almost supernatural."

Pam opened her purse and placed several photos in front of Kat. "Pam and I discovered some pretty scary pictures of young boys with men."

"Oh, my God!" Kat exclaimed.

"Now, let me explain a few things here. When Pam and I are through telling you what we know, we want your input," she explained to Kat.

Both Anne and Pam shared some of what they knew as well as what they didn't know. They told her about the color changes in Will's room; Will's miraculous healing; his friendship with Sheriff Gordon Maxwell, and the Sheriff's broken jaw healing; to Dr. Bullock and his photos of naked men with children.

Pam told of her experiences with Trent Bullock and the latest episode with him at his house and what she discovered in his basement. She went on to say that they had presented all of that info to Sheriff Maxwell.

"What can we do?" Kat asked.

"That's the million-dollar question," Anne said as she pulled out a pack of cigarettes and offered them to the others. Pam Darling shook her head no.

Kat said, "I'm a teacher, ladies, and in the contract I signed, I'm not to smoke or drink in public within a ten-mile radius of the school." She smiled, took one, reached into her purse and pulled out a shiny metal flask. "Speaking of drinking in public," she said as she poured a shot in the deep one-ounce cap she had unscrewed from the top of the flask. The three of them slammed down one shot each, then she put it back in her purse.

"For medicinal purposes," Kat said.

There was a noise outside. A car was crawling up the alley and stopped near the back door. They sat motionless, holding their collective breath, and after a few moments, the car rumbled away. With that, they looked at each other in silence. A minute later, there was a light rap on the door.

"Uh-oh." Pam said in a fast, hurried whisper. There was a pause, then another rap-rap-rap on the door.

"Open up. It's the Sheriff," the voice said.

Anne dimmed the lantern's light and whispered, "What if it's not him?" There was silence. No one moved a muscle. It wasn't long before they heard footsteps moving away from the door, a car door opening and closing, and a car easing away.

***

Maxwell drove back to his office. There on the desk was a crumpled piece of paper. He peered down to it as his eyes darted from the phone to the piece of paper and back.

What the hell? The note read, "Something's come up. I'm out of here. Please understand."

He thought things over. *There's a joker in the deck.*

CHAPTER THIRTY-ONE

The ladies were hashing things over. "The way Bullock was acting today, I sense something big is going on, and I want to know about it," Anne said as if she were spitting the words out. Pam nodded.

"First, Sheriff Maxwell winds up in the hospital just a couple of days after Will was brought in. He arrested Will's old man, and then he hung himself while the deputy was in charge. The Bishop from Capital City was here this morning, and *not for the funeral.* Somebody saw him getting a haircut here at Lloyd's place."

Pam chimed in, saying, "Then, the bastard was seen driving Pastor Swain and Reverend Pervasions to Swain's house sometime after the funeral."

"Something's up. So, what do you think?" Anne asked, nodding toward Kat.

"I don't know," said Kat, "but when I saw that man in front of the house, I just knew he didn't belong there, and then the children were gone. He took those innocent children and my heart broke. I feel so damned guilty. I should've run faster. I could've done *something* to keep them safe." Kat broke down sobbing.

There was another knock on the door, a sound of a key turning the lock. The door made a creaking noise as it opened slowly. The women froze in place.

"We have to talk." Gordon joined them at the table.

They told Gordon what the town's folks were discussing at the café. Gordon filled them in the best he could.

He pulled a folded envelope from his shirt pocket saying, "This is the last letter that my buddy William wrote the night before he was taken to the hospital. It's several pages long. I won't read it all to you now, but, I will say this," he cleared his throat and began. "I can only imagine the torture and cruelty this kid had to take to survive this long. His pa has been whipping him since he was at least eight years old. How he lived this long is nothing short of a miracle."

"Couldn't you stop it, Sheriff?" asked Kat.

"I did everything I could, under the law and then some. But, there are no laws protecting children. I'm sure you've seen parents bat their kids around like they were nothing more than small buckets of shit. They're yelled at, ridiculed and worked half to death and yet, that's just the way it is. Some kids have good parents, some don't. What'ya going to do? It's legal and this is the way our society is. I'm a Sheriff. I wear a badge and I swore to uphold the law and protect the citizens and yet, there is *so little* that I can do to prevent child cruelty. There ain't a good law against it."

"Beating a child is not legal, Sheriff," Kat replied.

Gordon shot a glance her way then stared down at the envelope in front of him. "He battered his wife, too, and I can't tell you how many times I visited the Priestly farm, arrested the old man, put him in the clinker, yet I had to release him. The clergy stood by the old man, the judge was easy on him, his lawyer never charged him much of anything and in the end, I, somehow, looked like the bad guy for taking him away from the farm and *arresting the sonofabitch*!"

Gordon took a breath. His hands shook. "We don't have much time, here so let's get to it." He flipped a black and white photo on the table along with his magnifying glass. "Any of you know what it is? The mark, I'm talking about."

Pam said, "That's one of the photos I got from Bullock." Her mind was racing. Flashes of rape zipped by. She blocked it out once again.

The other two took their turns examining the photo, but didn't know what the mark was.

"Ms. Darling, do you remember this? Is it a birthmark? Did the other pictures you see show the faces of men?"

"It looks somehow familiar, but I can't place it. Many showed faces, but I didn't recognize them, Sheriff. I'm sorry but I was so nervous. They're still where I found them, at Bullock's house. Oh, and another thing. Doctor Bullock told me he was going out of town this weekend."

He filled them in what he knew from the notes he got from Will and what he had learned from the magnetaphone of the meeting at midday. He told them he'd been looking for Mickey, but couldn't find him. The ladies said that he was at the café when they were there less than an hour ago, answering questions and making an ass out of himself and didn't even acknowledge their presence until the end.

Gordon listened. He also told them of the LOC and of the meeting at the Capital City Catholic seminary tomorrow night.

"I knew it! That's the sneaky meeting that Butthead Bullock is going to. I want to be there for that," said Pam Darling.

"I'm in," said Nurse Anne.

" No. You ladies are not going anywhere. I've orchestrated something that's never been done around these parts before. We'll have to see how it plays out."

"You going to the seminary tonight, Sheriff?" the Nurse asked.

"Later," he said. "I've got a couple of things I'm working on and sorting out, but, yes, I'll be there at least by tomorrow. Now, mum's the word, ladies. We didn't have this conversation, did we?"

"Somehow, I don't think school is going to be open for the next couple of days," Mrs. Knee said.

Nurse Anne glanced toward Pam, saying, "Two nurses from the hospital will be absent for the next couple of days."

Pam agreed. "I'll call in after we've finished here."

"Bring back Timmy and Margaret," Kat pleaded.

"Timmy and Margaret are foremost on my mind," he said. "Just between you and me, I think they're warm, been fed, and in a nice warm bed tonight, all by themselves."

He wasn't sure about any of it, but he didn't want to alarm the ladies.

CHAPTER THIRTY-TWO

Raphael and William were sitting on the barber chairs listening that night. William turned to his angel and asked, "Why am I still here? I should have been dead, Ralphy."

"Every child is your concern, William. That's why we are here. This all began with your very first letter to Sheriff Maxwell. *You* are the one these children have been waiting for."

Will nodded saying, "I guess so."

Raphael extended his arms and hands, raised them to the heavens, and said, "Let the good times roll."

"The Sheriff needs a little direction," Will stated.

Raphael lowered his arms, turned to William, and with a thundering, teaching voice said, "Tend to his needs, be helpful in all ways for the sake of the children."

Will stood in awe and respect for archangel Raphael. There was no need for thanks or praise. It was a time to act.

It was pitch dark when William hovered over Trent Bullock's house. Sheriff Maxwell was putting the third and final chest into the trunk of his squad car. Will descended, opened the door, got in, and set himself down in the passenger seat, invisible to the Sheriff, and turned on the radio. A mystery drama was playing, and an eerie voice rang out, "*Only the shadow knows.*"

The Sheriff drove back to his office, unable to turn off the radio that somehow just started playing. *I'll have to get that fixed, too,* he thought, *new cars ain't what they used to be.*

He unloaded the evidence from the trunk of the squad car and placed it in the first cell down the hall, along with the magnetaphone. He shut the door and locked it as Will hovered over the Sheriff's office.

After pacing the floor, he reached for the bottom drawer and pulled out the brandy. *God,* he thought, *I don't want to go back to that place.* He unscrewed the cap and set it down on the desk, reached back in the drawer, and pulled out a shot glass. Around the outer edges was a hand-painted Hawaiian girl wearing only a grass skirt. With her arms out-stretched, she wore the most inviting smile as if to say, "*Come to the islands and play.*"

A school friend from the seminary sent it to Gordon from Pearl Harbor. He got it in the mail on Saturday, December 6, 1941. Sunday morning, his friend, Eddy Lord, was gone. He was stationed on the Battleship Arizona where he worked in the engine room. He was never found.

Gordon pulled out a well-worn notepad and scanned the pages, flipping them over until he got to the end. On the remaining blank pages, he began filling out the last report of the day's activities.

Will was proud of him. There the poor guy sat with an open bottle of brandy, working on a case big enough for the New York Police Department, and he appeared to be doing it all alone.

He wrote and, as he did so, he would stop, as if someone were dictating to him. Then he would look in that same direction, waiting for the next round of words to come. Three notepads and the better part of two hours had gone by. It was long past midnight as he sat back in his chair and dozed off.

Will remembered Raphael's words, "God-Thought" as he watched from high over the jailhouse building and made an attempt to penetrate the walls. He closed his eyes and moved in. Much to his surprise, he made it complete and whole and was standing next to the gun cabinet where the Sheriff kept the key to the jail cell.

Coming out of the catnap, Gordon peered through his eyelids. He saw green. It was all around the cabinet in the hall and now against the far wall. Gordon yawned and stretched. Half kidding, he said to himself, "You still here, Will?"

On a side street in Capital City, inside an old faux brick front motel that had seen its better days ...

"Yes, I know Priestly was the one who applied the makeup on the kids so no one would recognize them, not even their parents. That's how good he was. He even changed their clothing and the color of their shoes. The police never had a clue. He wasn't an intellectual giant by any stretch of the imagination; we're all aware of that. Anyway, he's gone now, and we need to recruit someone to take his place. I have one in mind, but it'll require a sum of money to keep him quiet, at least for now," Swain explained to Sven.

"Yah? Who would dat be?" asked Sven.

"Someone who feels like he's underpaid and gets no respect. One who knows police work, how they go about searching for those of us who desire contact with kids, what clues they look for, things like that. Fortunately for us, we have moles in uniform and white collars, and we have had conversations with a particular guy about the LOC."

Sven broke in. "Dat's good. You do good work, Florian. We must always protect our clan. Just to let you know more dan what I should tell you, da bulk of da payment will be in gold coins. It will arrive at da seminary after da safe voyage of da two children to Rome and Brazil. Half da money will be received after they reach Rome, the udder half when da girl arrives in da Cardinal's quarters in Sao Paolo."

"Why there?" questioned Florian.

"Da girl is to go on to Siam, which is her final destination. Brazil is just a ploy. There's much more money in Bangkok den Sao Poalo."

"Let's get something straight here, Sven. I'm in this particular group of the LOC, not for the Pope and certainly not for a *religion*. Like Doc Bullock, I'm in it for the teaching tradition only! That tradition has been around from Aristotle to Alexander the Great, great men, greater teachers, great warriors, and conquerors all.

"The teacher should be the one to initiate the intellectual *and* sexual stimuli with the student. For full cooperation and loyalty, the teacher must be able to mold the student to his likeness, and the student must submit his very being, up to and including his soul, to his instructor. All rich and intelligent life must be taught exactly this way! Therefore, we *are* the way. Your Bishop recognizes that. We are an off-shoot of the *Legionnaires of the Cristo,* and I don't give a tinker's damn about the fucking Pope.

"Op*us Dei* then and *Opus Dei* now, and it shall be that way!"

Sven broke in saying, "Catholicism played a major role in that era, did it not Pastor Swain?"

"Touché." The pastor paused a moment. "Although I don't know what it had to do with God, if anything, except that it continued the teaching that the weak must submit to the powerful. It wasn't to be a godly interference, to be sure.

"As you know, Sven, deep down in the bowels of the Vatican, are the secret ties. It goes farther back in time than two thousand years, does it not, Svendly? It's thousands of years old and tied to the taking of wealth from families, the wealth that comes from power and greed, which produced something not made in the heavens. Isn't that so, Father Pervasions?

"And what about the scrolls that were found in those earthen jars a couple of years ago? Are they not written by some of the same authors as the Bible?"

"Yah, of course, whatever you say," Sven said with an expressionless face.

"I must be going back to my room now to prepare for tomorrow night's meeting. It's been a most interesting conversation. I'm sure you have da right man for da job. I'll see what da Bishop has to say about distributing money for a replacement. Good night."

Svendly nodded to Florian and closed the door of the motel room.

Back at his house, a half hour before his new acquaintance appeared, Trent Bullock found himself shaking uncontrollably. Reaching into his bag, he grabbed a long narrow rubber hose and a syringe. He rolled up his left sleeve, tied the quarter inch rubber hose around his bicep before getting out a small blue vial, tipping it upside-down to insert the syringe, and pulled the plunger back.

"What's he doing, Ralphy?" asked Will.

"They call it, 'self-medication.'"

CHAPTER THIRTY-THREE

Florien Swain stood gazing at the mirror attached to the front door of the small room of the antiquated motel just outside Capital City.

"Are you a man, Florien Swain?" he asked the image in the mirror. "Are you? Show me what you're made of."

This is the same routine he would go through over and over ever since his undoing by his mother. Some say he cross-dressed after being shell-shocked in World War I, yet others thought he'd been doing it his entire life. He went out of his head during combat. Some say he never quite got over it. He left part of himself on the battlefield. Maybe.

He would lose all connections with his daily activities; all his troubles would disappear when he became *her*. All the tension, all the humiliation, all hurt went away when Flo arrived.

When the women of his parish hugged him, it made him feel nauseous. He felt comfortable only in the company of men.

Florien found extreme pleasure in hugging children. It didn't matter if it was a boy or a girl. In his excitement, he felt the rush of blood running through his loins, which was what he enjoyed the most about having control over the children. When he was younger, he had a fondness for weak men and an occasional weak young woman. He hadn't had sex with a woman for over fifteen years. The last time was with the fifteen-year-old, Pam Darling. As time went by, however, he learned how to handle men, any man who desired the company of Flo, that is.

He could handle children with increasing ease. It created a kind of drunken euphoria for him. He had them, literally, in his hands. He gave them orders, and they obeyed. He loved that. When he hugged them, he would massage their backs and arms. If he met no resistance, he went further, dropping his hands down to the buttocks and bringing his hands around to the front of boys, girls, men; he didn't care. If there was no resistance, he would keep going and remove the necessary clothing until he gratified himself.

After the interlude, he gave his victims a special blessing along with a warning. He promised them a special place in heaven with Jesus and the angels *if* they remained silent. *Our little secret.* If the children were to tell their parents about the incident, he told them that he would have God come down from heaven and strike their parents dead. God would know they were bad children and see all the bad things they ever did. God would kill them and their grandparents, aunts, and uncles, and force the children go to hell for eternity.

The sexually abused children remained silent, destroyed, innocence forever gone.

He raped innocent children in every township, and he'd been ordained a Lutheran minister for over twenty-three years. That's a lot of hurt children who wound up as adult children with damaged childhoods that carried over into their dysfunctional daily lives. Others committed suicide. They were the lucky ones.

More than once he and his wife were escorted out of town in the middle of the night with a shotgun barrel staring him in the face. His wife, Rose, remained in denial. She believed in the power of prayer. Praying would make it all better, and his need for sexual gratification with children would go away. His exploits with children pushed her over the brink. She slashed her wrists at age twenty-nine.

Dressing up in women's clothing began for him long before his entry into World War I. His mother, Marcella, encouraged him to do it by sitting him down on the bench seat next to her in front of her makeup stand in her bedroom. She applied makeup to herself and then on her darling doe-eyed little boy. He liked to be close to his mother. She pampered him. He became her bedtime playmate.

His father was away much of the time. As a traveling salesman, he sold sports equipment to schools. His mother was left alone to raise the child. She hungered for affection. Each night his father was away on business, she had young Florien keep her company and sleep with her.

"Come, Florien. Protect me tonight, while your father is away. I so need your manliness and your warm hugs to help me feel safe." Marcella would read passages from the Bible to him while playing dress-up.

Marcella would don a long nightgown and dress Florien in a skimpy short one. He watched as she removed her dress. His eyes were fixed on the girdle with the long clips on the bottom that attached to the nylon stockings with the dark seam down the back. She stripped to her girdle, brassiere, and panties.

Marcella removed the bra one strap at a time, burlesque style. She would put a finger over her smiling lips and wink at him, then went about unhinging it from the back and taking it off with her breasts heaving as if they were honoring their freedom.

Marcella would hold each breast, pushing them up and together, and rubbed on body cream as she watched herself in the mirror. She removed her girdle, then her panties, shifting her body weight from one foot to the other as she turned herself one way, then the other, admiring her mirrored image. She slipped on her nightgown; then it was little Florien's turn.

He craved her attention, and he got it. The attention he received over the years was like an aphrodisiac. He'd be dizzy with pleasure and excitement during those evening rituals.

They would kneel at the side of the bed for the evening prayer, then he would jump to his feet and lunge forward onto the bed, pouncing and giggling as he rolled and rolled. His mother would to try and catch him.

Eventually, they would slip under the covers. There she rolled to her side and pull him next to her as he laid with his backside to her front. She caressed his body until he fell asleep.

The ritual began to change. As they applied makeup in the mirror, she handed him a little gift box one night. It was his very own makeup kit. Thereafter, he applied it to his face as she did to hers. They removed their clothing and Marcella embraced him in front of the mirror, watching as they caressed each other.

One night his mother gave him one of her long, inviting kisses. As she did so, he rubbed and caressed her legs and held tight to her warm buttocks. While staring at the mirror, he became aroused. His penis grew long and stiff against her legs yet, when he looked at his mother's smiling face, it also felt alienating. It was a strange feeling, yet somehow erotic.

Each night when his father was away, he was in his mother's bed. He liked the strange exotic feeling. One night, Marcella massaged him with an orchid-scented body cream. She dabbed it on as she caressed his scrotum and penis. He became much more aroused this time. She laid much closer to him, almost resting her head on his ear.

She felt his erection throbbing in her hand and did not stop. The reality of it hit young Florien. This time he was so excited he couldn't breathe. He kept his eyes closed and never moved a muscle. He was in a panic. What would his mother think if he let her know that what she was doing made him feel excited? *This is not right, is it?*

She held his shaft again, this time with a firm grip. He closed his eyes and exhaled slowly. His little boy body was tight, frozen with fear and excitement. He couldn't let his mother know. What would she say? Florien didn't understand the fear. What was happening was beyond thought and speech.

He stayed silent and motionless for what seemed an eternity. Squeezing tighter, she rubbed his penis up and down, faster and faster. He felt pressure building in his body. It felt as if lightning was shooting through his body as momentum built. His body trembled. He couldn't help it. Florien experienced his first erupting ejaculation. And it came from his mother's hand.

The next morning Marcella talked to Florien at the breakfast table. She told him that what happened the night before, what they did, what she did, was to be kept a secret, especially from his stern father. She smiled, leaned across the small table and kissed his cheek.

Nothing more was said about the incident. They went on as if nothing had changed. That little routine in the evenings remained ongoing. Yet, something did happen. There was a huge change, a life-altering experience for Florien. He had feelings so new, so different, yet he couldn't explain it or talk to anyone, especially his mother about it.

He thought of his father during those times. He missed him. Florien fantasized about being with his father. He wanted to be held in his arms, to feel his warmth and smell his aftershave. He felt his father had abandoned him and his mother.

From that day on, he was taught the art of denial. They never spoke a word of their new activities, however perverse, however exciting— not to each other, not to anyone. It was, as she said, *their special, little secret.* Not yet ten years of age, and she taught him sexual behaviors, perverted as they were between mother and son.

That night forward, he never experienced the simple gratifying pleasure from a sex act with another partner. Any sex act was accompanied by guilt, shame, fear and something pathetically odd, silence. There was never any discussion about it, as if it never happened. Fear, guilt, and shame piled upon each other at the same time as sexual arousal and ejaculation.

He loved it. He hated it. Florien became bitter toward his father for leaving him and his mother alone so much of the time. He blamed his father for his mother's sins. He blamed him for his own sins.

Over the years, those special times with his mother became orgy events. Before his twelfth birthday, he'd already been introduced to intercourse, oral sex and sodomy. Marcella had made her only child a sex slave.

The sexual contact eventually ended. It was his decision. He stayed in his own room by his own reasoning and performed in front of his own bedroom mirror on and by himself.

Marcella grieved for the loss of his youthfulness. And hers. She seduced her son and raped him, again and again and again. For years.

CHAPTER THIRTY-FOUR

B ack in the tiny motel room, the forty-nine-year-old stood in front of the small mirror in an old dress that his mother had worn, applying lipstick and rouge the same way his mother had taught him all those years ago.

After finishing applying his makeup, he reached into his suitcase and pulled out a hatbox, set it on the nightstand, and removed the lid. There, in the box, was a brown-haired wig made from his mother's hair. He placed the shoulder-length wig on his head, walked back to the mirror, and adjusted it until he felt it was perfect.

It was then that he became a she. Flo reached for the perfume bottle in a feminine way. She sprayed under her dress, on her genitals, squirted mist on her wrists, rubbing them together. Flo pursed her lips in the mirror, applying the lipstick as her mother had taught him.

There was a rap at the door. She put the perfume bottle down as her pulse began to rise, placed the hatbox back in the suitcase, and slid it under the bed. She looked around the room to make sure nothing was out of place, and she padded to the door and unlocked it.

"Uncle Billy, I've been expecting you. Do come in. Let me take your hat and coat. My, you look handsome tonight, you little devil, you."

Flo took his coat and hat and placed them neatly in the little closet next to the washbasin. On the dresser she had placed a half pint of brandy and two glasses. She poured two fingers in each glass and handed one to her Uncle Billy. He was shivering from the cold winter night, took the glass and held it up. They clanged the glasses together. "Salute."

He downed it in one gulp.

"Another, if you will, Flo. God, you look inviting tonight," he said.

"Oh, you're a sweetheart for saying that." She poured his glass half full. "Here you are, my precious," she said as she sat on the edge of the bed and crossed her legs. As she did so, she lifted the dress high above her knees, exposing her freshly shaven legs, hoping for a warm response. He watched her before stepping over and sitting down on the chair next to Flo as she sipped her brandy.

"I've been under a great deal of strain these past few days. I need a little respect for all those tedious duties," he sighed peering at her freshly shaven thighs under the dress and taking another gulp. "You may call me Billy. No need for the uncle tonight, thank you," he said, winking as he unfastened his white collar.

"God, you wouldn't believe what the past week has been like for me. Those damned kids. Thank God I had help. An old friend from the past dropped in for a couple of days."

Though puzzled, she let the last comment drop, saying, "It must have been absolutely brutal for you. I just don't know how you manage; I really don't."

Flo made the first move and got up to pour herself a second glass, bringing the bottle over to the nightstand and adding to Billy's drink. She set the bottle down and kissed his shiny bald head.

With the glass of brandy in one hand, he put his arm around her and, extended it under and between her legs to the genitals and hung on.

He held fast to Flo's scrotum and penis as he lifted his head up to receive a kiss on the lips from her. She obliged and nestled her cheek on his and set her drink down. Billy moved his hand away as she sat on the bed again with her legs spread wide and rested her head and shoulders on the wall directly behind it.

"I can't stay but a short while," Billy sighed, as he leaned and massaged her loins. "I love it when there's no underwear."

"Mm," she said. "I never want these moments to end."

166

"God understands." Billy continued as he jerked Flo's penis up and down, up and down.

Aroused, she moved to the edge of the bed to make it easier for him. Billy continued caressing Flo's hardness as Marcella had caressed it in the past, massaging and working his way up and around his hard circumcised male member and back down to his testicles.

The light from the table lamp flickered and went out.

"Oh, what beautiful timing," Flo said, surprised. "Come on up and lay next to me."

Billy dragged himself up and laid his body next to hers. Flo unzipped his trousers and reached in. They began stroking one another as they lay in silence in the darkened motel room. Try as she might, it was no use. Billy's penis was small and limp. It stayed that way.

The light flickered again under the clear lampshade on the night-stand, beginning to emit a light green glow. The color deepened to a dark green and grew brighter and brighter. They lay motionless as the lightbulb made a hissing sound.

The light grew brighter and brighter still.

"My God! How much brighter can it get?" Billy asked.

Flo reached down behind the bed to the light cord. Struggling, she said, "I can't unplug the damn thing."

"It must be a sign. I should be getting back to thinking about tomorrow. The children have been at the seminary for a few hours now. Big day planned," he continued as he tucked his shirt in, and redid his belt, and zipped up his fly.

Flo handed him his coat and hat.

"Oh, I was looking forward to this night as much as tomorrow night," she sighed.

"Now, now, there will be other nights, more opportunities. I'll see to it," he said with a pained expression reaching up and patting her cheek. He pulled on his coat and hat and reached for his glass. It was almost empty. He raised it to his lips, grabbed Flo's crotch with the other, looked into her eyes, and said, "To good health and happy days," and drank the last drop.

Flo watched through the tiny window as Bishop Paul Cheney ambled into the big black Buick, backed away, and merged onto the highway. The taillights dimmed and faded until there was no light at all.

She removed her wig and put it on the nightstand, fumbled for the light, found it, unplugged it and sat down. The light didn't blink; it dimmed for a while before going out.

Flo sat on the edge of the bed and put her hand out where her Billy had laid next to her. Her eyes welled with tears.

***

The rest of the night was quiet throughout the region from Capital City to the tiny sleepy village of Pine Nut forty some miles away. Roughly six hundred people there were fast asleep and in the dream state of their lives, but not so for Ed and Helen Hornsby. They were up, staring at two empty beds. Candles were lit and prayers were said for the safe return of the missing children.

CHAPTER THIRTY-FIVE

"**I** believe Capital City will be a good fit for you, Mister Zaugbaum," Trent Bullock said.

Mickey replied, "I've always had an interest in the college atmosphere where students gather from across the country and around the world to learn from the masters.

"What I intend to do is to learn as much as I can from you and the society. It has a rich and noble history, and I'd like to help in any way I can. And thanks again for having me here at your house, Doctor.

"Gordon Maxwell's days as a Sheriff are numbered. Christ. He's drunk more than he's sober. One day he'll be gone and I'll have his badge. We should have a smooth operation."

Trent nodded. "Sounds good. Yes, it is a noble cause, and I like the enthusiasm you have, young man. You came to us highly recommended. I enjoy your company, Mr. Zaugbaum."

The drive to the seminary was roughly an hour from Pine Nut. The morning started off fair enough, with clear skies and mild weather. The fresh snow was like a white blanket covering the rows of alfalfa and cornfields. The drive was smooth with no other vehicles ahead or in the rearview mirror as they made their way on the two-lane highway toward destiny.

"Look—over there in the field, on your left, Doc. There's a buck and three doe," Deputy Zaugbaum said as he pointed. They were pushing their noses deep into the snow and nibbling on corncobs missed by the combines when the corn was cut and chopped for silage for the farm animals. The magnificent stag stood a few feet from the other three and watched the passing auto. The doe continued their search for fresh food, looking up at the car, then back to their meal of the day.

"Looks like maybe a sixteen pointer or more," Mickey said, trying to count the tines on his antlers. "Wow, the deer hunters missed a real trophy, I'm here to tell you."

"Question for you, Mr. Zaugbaum. What separates you from Mr. Maxwell?

"Ah," Mickey answered. "I like tradition and fraternal orders. The pageantry of pomp and circumstance arouses my sense of passion. He, on the other hand, is set in his ways and looks to the past through rose-colored glasses. He has no ambition other than one day he wants to go fishing and never come home."

Bullock smiled. "I'll treat you to a pound of fresh squeaky curd."

They stood looking through the pane of glass at the big vat of cheese and the old man wearing a white shirt and pants with a white cap to match. The thick, heavyset man had a long rake and was pushing and pulling at the solid, yellow chunks that lay below the milky white whey in the tank.

Knowing what they wanted, the cheesemaker sank a big hand in and filled a small waxed paper bag with the fresh curd. He pulled out another handful and another as the milky fluid dripped from his hands. The cheese maker opened the door.

Otto Strickler was in his mid-seventies, a hard working strong German, still with a heavy accent from the mother country. "Here you go, boys, just as fresh as can be. You know about tonight, yah? Say, by da way, Cheney was here yesterday afternoon. I didn't get a chance to talk wit him, but he was here. I see him from da house. He was holdin' onto two kids," Strickler said with a stern face and nod.

"Tonight," Bullock agreed.

"I'll be dar," Otto Strickler said as he closed the door to his factory and picked up the long-handled rake and went back to the business of making cheese.

"Fresh warm cheese curds," Mickey said as they climbed back into the car. Neither said a word about the cheesemaker's statement about the Bishop or the children. It was as if there were an elephant with them in the Oldsmobile, yet they pretended it wasn't there.

Mickey spoke, trying to get a reaction from the doctor. "This curd is so good, and it's almost as if it came down from heaven." There was just silence from the doctor, except for an SBD. The car stunk to high heaven. Mickey wanted to roll down the window and stick his head out into the cold, oncoming wind.

Sitting still wasn't easy for the Mick. They took a handful each and popped a couple of cheese curds into their mouths at about the same time.

Mickey tried everything he could to get his mind off the grotesque, rotten smell. "I'm not a man of many questions, but I'm new to this. Police work is okay, but in that small town, frankly, I'm bored to death. I've been covering for the alcoholic Sheriff for a few months, and already, I've had it! By the way, does the cheesemaker have dementia or something? Why did he speak of the Bishop with two kids? I mean, he may know you, but he didn't know me from Adam-saw-a-fox."

"Mr. Strickler is a strong, hard-working, loyal member of the LOC and has been for a long, long time. The problem is getting out of hand. I'll have to speak to the others about him. He'll have to be removed."

"How?"

"Too many questions."

Mickey wanted an answer, not a reprimand.

The glare of the sun was magnificent as it mirrored off the white snow-covered fields. A forest of trees in the rolling hills protected the white fields. Ahead stood bright red barns and white farmhouses as if from a Norman Rockwell painting. It was so still; there wasn't a breath of wind in the air. Dark clouds loomed in the distance.

"Do I wear what I have on?" Mickey asked. The thought came to him so fast it surprised him.

"No, we'll have robes and headgear over our clothing. The priests will have similar garments on along with the postulate hats. It's akin to the Ku Klux Klan outfits. In fact, it's the same except for the emblems. They have their rites. We have ours.

"The Bishop is the leader. He'll be the one with a long staff with the white bone and crystals. Some say it was taken from the skull of St. Augustine of Hippo, a Pope from the early church. He helped establish the doctrine of Original sin."

"What a guy," Mickey said. "Catholics never cease to amaze me. I said something negative about them in front of Maxwell and he all but come unglued."

"At any rate," Dr. Bullock continued, smiling, "He'll lead us into the secret ritual room. You may also have a suit and tie waiting for you. We'll see," the doctor said. "Just one other thing. That mustache will have to be shaved the minute you get to the Seminary. We have certain standards."

His heart began to pound a little harder, a little faster. Mickey tapped his fingers on the armrest of the passenger door as he thought of Gordon sitting alone at the jailhouse wondering where the hell he was.

CHAPTER THIRTY-SIX

Margaret Lynn lay awake resting on a small bed. She felt something warm by her foot. She rubbed her eyes with the palms of her hands and sat up. At the other end of the bed, she could see the same crop of hair she knew so well. Tugging on the blanket, it came down past Timmy's forehead to his chin. She smiled and lay back down, clutching the blanket.

They were being held on the top floor in a corner room with two windows. The door had been locked from the hallway. The ceiling was painted off-white and the walls had a coat of stale light green paint with a white baseboard running along the floor. The windows had iced up, but the rising sun was melting it from the bottom up.

She rolled out of bed and tiptoed on the ice-cold hardwood floor to the end of the bed and pulled the metal cover from the white porcelain pot on the floor. She turned fast and sat on the cold rim, shivering, as the tinkling became a gushing stream. She reached for the toilet paper. In a flash, she was back under the covers of the warm bed.

"Wake up, Timmy, wake up," she whispered. He rolled over onto his tummy and pulled the top blanket over his head. She took it off of him.

"Go away!" he said, coming out of a deep sleep. Timmy sat up and looked around the room until his eyes rested on Margaret. Tears welled, and he began to sob.

There was a rap on the door. It opened just enough so a hand could place a metal tray on the floor and push it forward. The door closed and was locked again.

Margaret jumped out of bed, picked up the tray, and set it next to Timmy on the sheet-covered thin mattress.

In no time at all the sugarless oatmeal, toast, strawberries, and a half glass of milk was shared and consumed. Margaret lifted the plate off the bed and saw the time on the alarm clock on the floor. Seven a.m.

There were two white envelopes taped to the underside of the tray. Margaret opened one. The lettering was printed in large letters. She read it aloud.

Did you say your prayers before eating? If you did not, God will punish you, for you've started the day with sin. Pray now for your parents' souls. Pray to Jesus, Mary, and Joseph all day. Prepare yourselves for a long journey, for as Jesus fled to Egypt as a small boy, you, too, shall flee across the seas. Remain silent. Your voices shall not be louder than a whisper or you will be silenced with tape across thy mouth and thy hands bound with cloth. As sinners, you must suffer the consequences. For, as Jesus said, "Then suffer all ye children unto me." Jesus will surely punish you forever, and you'll be damned to hell and never see your parents again.
This is the Word of God!"

Timmy and Margaret leaned together, wrapping their arms around each other.

Margaret said, "Don't worry, Timmy. I'm your older sister, and it's my responsibility to get us out of this place."

Timmy wiped his running nose on his sleeve and walked quickly to the farthest corner window. He pushed up the bottom half as far as he could. Still sobbing, he looked out at the quiet winter scene below and just stood there for a while. Then he opened his trousers, and leaned forward as close as he could against the outer screen.

"What are you doing, Timmy?"

"Peeing."

There was another rap on the door. Timmy scrambled back to the bed. The door opened, and in walked a nun. She was dressed in black from head to toe. Her head and face wrapped with white rubber from her forehead, to her thick eyebrows, around the sides, and under her chin.

Margaret noticed a faint outline of a mustache on her white upper lip, and so did Timmy. She must have weighed close to 300 pounds. To the children, she looked like a giant black pumpkin with a pink scrunched face covered with wild eyebrows. In her hands she held an empty chamber pot. With a huff and puff, she bent down, placed it at the foot end of the bed, and removed the other one.

The nun said in a deep gruff voice, "Stay where you are. I'll be right back." She waddled out of the door with full chamber pot in hand. She wobbled back in with a suitcase and set it down. Picking up the empty food tray, she stopped for a moment and peered at the children through her glasses that rested on the tip of her chubby little nose. She said a short prayer and made an outward sign of the cross toward each of them. To the kids, she resembled an ugly fairytale ogre. They were afraid of the black blob that had invaded their room.

"Did you see the handkerchief up her sleeve?" Timmy asked, finally able to speak.

"I saw it," Margaret answered. "Daddy was right about Catholics. They're cultish."

"They scare me," Timmy said, "They ain't nothing like the people who come to our Sunday meetings at home." He sat silent for a moment before asking, "What's in the suitcase?"

They scrambled off the bed and opened it. They found it packed full of clothing. Margaret was curious and searched through the suitcase, looking for something, anything she might be able to use. Tucked deep in a small side pouch she felt something familiar. She pulled out a pencil.

"What are we going to do?" Timmy asked.

"What would little Orphan Annie do?" she answered, trying to get his mind off the nightmarish situation they were in. They sat back on the bed and thought over all the radio episodes of the program that they could remember.

Margaret grabbed the pencil, and they crawled under the bed. On the white baseboard, she wrote names. Bishop (Uncle Billy) Cheney's name, Pastor Swain, and Father Pervasions, She also wrote the names of the good people they knew, people like William, Mrs. Knee, her parents' names, as well as Fibber McGee and Molly.

"Why did you write Fibber McGee?" Timmy asked.

"You laugh at Fibber when he opens his closet door, and so do I," she answered.

She also wrote down the month, December, and the year, 1949, on the baseboard behind the cot.

I'd like to write something, if that's okay with you."

She gave the pencil to Timmy and he wrote: *PS. To Helen and Edward Hornsby, my mommy and daddy, I luv you very much and I will never every give you up, your son, Timothy Lee Hornsby.*

Still under the bed, he gave the pencil to Margaret as he laid his face down on the floor and sobbed. She wrote a phrase from her great Grandma Jenny that Margaret would never forget. She loved to be with children more than with those her own age, it seemed. Margaret continued writing:

"My Grandma Jenny is a Catholic, too. She would not like you for what you are doing to us. She would say to you, "Let go of those kids before I take a switch after you! You can either skedaddle down the dingo or go and piss up a rope!"

CHAPTER THIRTY-SEVEN

Will stood in front of the mirror in his hospital room, gazing at his hair. He pushed the comb front to back on the sides and on top, making a slight swirl at the top of his forehead. He also pulled a few strands down to his eyebrows and off to one side. He turned his head from side to side, stopping each time to admire the new look. He peered straight ahead at himself and cheerfully exclaimed, "God, I can't wait till tomorrow. I get better looking every day!" Grinning at himself in the mirror, he continued, "Tonight . . .". At that moment, a corner of the room turned green, as Raphael appeared.

"Hey, Ralphy," Will said as he beamed. Raphael nodded.

"Top of the morning, pal," he continued. "Are you ready for the big event tonight? They're having a big cleansing ritual and planning on taking the Hornsby kids off to Rome and God knows where else."

"You're on your own on this one," Raphael stated.

William stood silent for the longest time, still holding the comb. He didn't know how to respond. He uttered in a quiet monotone voice, "What do you mean? I thought the two of us would be there tonight."

"Whatever happens tonight is not angel business. It's not in my line of work, so to speak. We come to help in the way of guidance, healing, and love. If you call us for support in any of those arenas, we'll be there for you. We have given you the tools you need. Use them. It won't be long before it's time for you to go home."

"Home?" questioned Will. "Which way home?"

His pa was dead and buried, and his ma was in the hospital.

Where do I belong? Should I go to the Light when this whole mess is over, back home to God's house?

"Ralphy, you just told me it wouldn't be long." Will was frozen in thought.

He was thinking of Raphael's' words. *All you have to do is think of me.* He was confused.

"That's still true, William, just think of me and I'll be there. As you know, I am there, always."

Raphael moved to the corner and faded away. Will stepped back to the bed and sat on the edge. He flung the comb at the mirror. It'd been a long time since he'd felt alone. He put his head in his hands, and for the first time since he was nine years old, he wept.

CHAPTER THIRTY-EIGHT

At the Sheriff's Office, Gordon Maxwell was placing the receiver back on the hook. Talking with the Attorney General made him breathe easier. He was told that the arrangements and coordination of the upcoming event was progressing smoothly and he wished the best for him.

He finished his paperwork, put it in a manila folder, placed it in the desk drawer in front of him, and locked it. He pulled open the bottom drawer, brought out the old bottle of brandy, and set it on the desk. Gordon stood, not taking his eyes off the bottle, and began talking and walking.

"We've been friends for several years now, Mr. Five-Star. We haven't always seen eye to eye. I have to tell you something now. You may not like what I have to say to you.

"Oh, sure, you and I got together when my wife left. You were the only one who cared, or so I thought. You let me sleep at night and forget what happened to me at the seminary. Without you, I'd toss and turn, but you helped me get the sleep I needed.

"At first, you took away my troubles, made me laugh, and have fun. We had a great time together. Somewhere along the line, the laughter stopped. I *needed* you more than wanted you.

"In the hospital, I had time to think about you and what you did for me, and also what you *did*n't do for me. You see, the last couple of years, you've clouded my mind. You began playing tricks on me, Mr.

Five-Star, and that wasn't nice. I have to hand it to you; you're a tough *mother*.

You're a master at deceit; you're cunning and sly. I had plans, ideas, cases to solve, people to attend to, good folks, and, of course, the kid, but you kept getting in the way.

"It was you who kept me from helping Will before it was too late. No. I take that back. I don't want you to think you had that kind of power over my thoughts and actions. Not anymore. No, Mister Five-Star, it was me. *I* was the weak one. I'll accept the blame. But somehow I got a reprieve. I don't know how, and I don't know why.

"How Will appeared in my room that fateful morning when I busted my jaw and broke my nose, I don't know. I don't even know if what he talks about is real or not. I don't know if it's you I'm hearing or angels. You got me all confused!

"One thing I *do* know. Everything I do now, I do it sober. I'm sober now, and I like it that way. I look forward to mornings, now. No hangover and no fogginess in the brain. That old empty feeling is gone, so I'm putting you away. Just wanted you to know where I stand with you. No hard feelings."

Gordon Maxwell walked back to the desk, put the bottle back in the drawer before stepping to the gun cabinet. He turned the key, pulled out a Remington 12-gauge shotgun, and placed it on his desk. He took out his black leather gun belt, strapped it on, and slapped the loaded Walther P-38 revolver into the holster and two loaded clips in his gun belt. He touched it again reminding himself that it was a gift from a seminary friend, Bobby Spadaro. He got it in the mail two days after his death.

He picked up the shotgun, went outside to his squad car, and put the Remington and a box of shotgun shells in the trunk, closed it, and climbed into the driver's seat.

***

Driving the new '49 Ford squad car out of Pine Nut, he decided at the last minute to turn off Main Street and cruise by the Zaugbaum house.

Mick's car sat in the driveway, covered with snow. A little farther up the road was the hospital. He glanced over to it with Will on his mind. He drove up the street and rounded the corner to Doctor Trent Bullock's house. He slowed as he reached his house and eased to a stop while looking at the front porch.

He studied the place, searching for answers. It was right in front of his eyes. Two sets of footprints in the freshly fallen snow tracked down the steps, across the sidewalk to where the snow outlined a car. One set of tracks stopped at the edge of the sidewalk, while the other set tracked around the car to the street side at the driver's door.

Gordon eased down the road. He wished he'd made more contact with Ashton Plenn, the captain of the Highway Patrol. The next second, however, he recanted that wish as he slammed on the brakes and skidded to a stop on the little neighborhood side street. He sat there gazing straight ahead as his face developed an ironic smile.

"I'll be a sonofabitch."

He turned the radio on and tuned in to a country gospel song. As the Carter family sang, Gordon sang along.

"Where were you when God handed out singing voices?"

He bolted straight up and clamped hard onto the steering wheel. Will materialized in the front seat.

"Jeezuz. You scared the hell out of me! Were you in the backseat?"

"Nope. When you gonna believe in angels, God, and me?"

There was no response from the Sheriff, and not another word was spoken until he pulled up in front of the hospital.

Gordon reached for the keys, shut the engine off, and lunged to grab Will's neck. All he got was a handful of air.

"See what I mean?" Gordon yelled. "It ain't you! It's me! I'm seeing things. I'm hearing things. It's the booze. I still got the goddamn DTs."

CHAPTER THIRTY-NINE

He jumped out of the car as William stayed put. Gordon Maxwell flew up the stairs with the holstered gun flapping at his side, two steps at a time. He raced inside and down the hall to Will's room.

Huffing and puffing, he pushed the door open. There, was William, standing, combing his hair in front of the mirror, pulling it down and off to one side of his forehead.

Will saw his reflection in the mirror and said, "Hi, Sheriff. Can we go now? Nurse Anne gave me these new britches, a flannel shirt, and street shoes with Santa Claus socks. She said it was an early Christmas present. By the way, it was me in the squad car. You're just not a believer yet."

"I . . . oh, hell." Sheriff Maxwell said. "You'll just get in the way!"

"I might, but not in *your* way. I wouldn't miss this for the world."

"I'll wait," Gordon said, "I don't know what I'm waiting *for*, but I'll wait."

"I was there, in your office when you talked to Mr. Five-Star, too. I think you're going to make it, pal, I really do."

Still confused and rankled, Gordon said, "You talk about the past; what do you know of the future?"

Will squinted as he looked at the Sheriff. "Okay, Mr. Nonbeliever, I'll bet you a nickel to a candy bar that out on the highway, on a curve, there'll be a deer standing in the middle of the road. You'll slam on the brakes, stop within a few feet of the frightened animal, scaring the hell out of you. It'll be the biggest eighteen-point buck you ever saw. How do you like them apples?"

CHAPTER FORTY

It was quiet in the car as Gordon drove the snowy scenic route toward their destination, taking in the beauty of the snow-covered pine trees that dotted the white rolling landscape. It was almost breathtaking the way the sun shone down on the icy snow crystals resting on the bows of the branches.

As he drove on, looking at the gleaming sights, he spotted a red-tailed hawk resting atop a telephone pole.

"Up there," Gordon said. The hawk stood guard, overlooking his territory. He turned his attention from the majestic red-tailed hawk back to the curvy road and glanced at the speedometer as the telephone poles streaked by.

He was approaching sixty-three miles an hour heading into the curve. He let his foot off the gas pedal and reached for the radio knob. As he did, he noticed a brown, four-legged animal in the middle of the road. In a panic, he slammed on the brakes as the car fishtailed and skidded hundreds of feet over the ice and snow patches.

Right in front of Sheriff Maxwell's squad car stood the biggest deer he'd ever seen. "Ho-lee brick shithouse, look at the rack on that stag! It must be at least an eighteen-point buck!"

Will began laughing out loud. "And you might see it again, you just never know about them things, huh, you old fart." Will said. "I've been to a place called the Hall of Records."

Silence reigned in the car leaving the impressive stag in the rear-view mirror. Gordon drove a little slower and never took a hand off the steering wheel the rest of the way. William broke the quietness several miles down the road. "You owe me a candy bar."

"Oh, you'll get your candy bar." Gordon thought that Will had a concussion or something, though. He talks about the craziest things sometimes.

"I'm nuts, remember?" Will replied.

Gordon didn't respond. He kept playing the scene over and over again, pressing hard on the brake pedal, the deer getting closer and closer. He could still hear the blood curdling halted screeching of the tires on the occasional dry pavement as they fast approached the defenseless stag.

"Where do you think the Hornsby kids are?" Will asked. Gordon didn't answer.

As he drove toward destiny, his thoughts took him back to the weekends when the seminarians were allowed to go home. The suitcase was packed and by his side as he sat on the top step in his blue suit where he waited impatiently for his parents. He'd spot them as they made their way in from the main entrance. Before the old light grey Plymouth came to a complete stop, he bounded down the steps of that huge red-bricked building with suitcase in hand and into the backseat chattering on and on to his folks about everything that he had learned and done that week . . . most of it anyway.

He couldn't tell them about the rumors on his floor about some of the priests. He didn't know how. Priests were like gods so they could do no wrong. But there was a persistent rumor that hanky-panky was going on.

After the first Christmas break the twins, Allen and Kip never returned, an old story now. When his father backhanded him, he split his lip. His ear hurt, too, but he didn't say anything about it to his father. Years later, at the induction center, a doctor discovered he had a punctured eardrum. It kept him out of World War II.

Revisiting the past was becoming a daily routine. He shook his head as he drove, trying to shake a vision from his days gone by, only to be confronted with another image.

He could remember the confrontation he had with the rector about Father Smiley and Father Long. The rector was a fat man, not old, not young. Obese. His white shirt never stayed beneath the black pants and shirt. Everyone at the school felt sorry for the small chair he sat on. Father Dittmar had black, thinning hair. He was easy to talk to, but noncommittal. No one knew where he stood on any subject.

Gordon approached him about Smiley and Long after the twins told him what happened to them up at the lake. That led to his first trip to the secret room and subsequent humiliation with the younger Father Cheney as the leader.

He tried Father Dittmar once again when his roommate, Charlie Schlimgin, told him that both priests, also violated him in the seminary. He couldn't remember where exactly, but he thought it happened below the kitchen. He recalled taking short steps on wooden planks. It was a small, dark room underground. The two priests blindfolded him in his room, and they led him to it.

There, they shared wine and got him drunk. They stripped him naked and performed fellatio on him. They forced him to do it to them while they took pictures. Gordon reported this to the rector, Father Dittmar. Charlie Schlimgin was last seen in front of the school the next morning waiting for his parents. He never returned. That incident also was the reason for Gordon's second and final trip to the secret room.

He drifted back to that night in the seminary where he was once again in that same ugly secret room, humiliated, sitting naked, and tied to the same cold, brown wooden chair in front of all the men in black. It was a sick kind of ceremony, and he was the sacrificial lamb.

CHAPTER FORTY-ONE

He shook his head to shake the thought and glanced over at William. He looked so innocent. Gordon could almost see a glow around him as he sat there with his eyes closed, looking so content, a look he'd rarely seen in him.

He slowed and turned onto a dirt road lined with small fir trees. School-aged children had neatly planted the seedlings years ago. President Roosevelt's CCC program funded the tree plantings.

He drove back into the pines, between the neat and straight rows, for close to a mile before coming to a stop.

"The kids, Sheriff. Where are they?" Will asked.

"In a warm place. Frightened, I'm sure, but warm." He shook the cobwebs from his thoughts.

"I gotta go. I need to baptize a tree," Gordon said, as he ducked behind a pine and let the yellow roaring stream flow. As he was empty-ing his bladder, his mind shifted to a dark night at the seminary in the secret room. He held a secret even from himself for all these years. It was a dark episode in his brief seminarian life.

Paul Cheney was a young priest then. He began making himself more important than the others and became the unofficial head of a small group of Opus Dei priests at the seminary.

Gordon was again tied to the chair on the makeshift stage, naked at the age of fourteen, feeling helpless, afraid, angry, humiliated, and ashamed. Just thinking about it after all these years brought back the hurt. He thought of slashing his wrists, hanging himself, anything to

189

get away from Cheney and the seminary. He felt the same fear and angst he had twenty years ago.

In the chair, he was soaking wet with the padre's urine dripping from his head, face, and the rest of his naked body as the group of men in black laughed at him. He wanted to die. That was the second time that Cheney pissed on him, and it would be the last time.

Gordon stared in disbelief as another vision shot through him like a shard of glass. He thought of the Hornsby kids and the seminary.

He doubted Bishop Paul Cheney would sexually harm the two children. He liked to humiliate children, goad them, embarrass them, but he never did anything sexual with children that Maxwell *knew* of. The Bishop liked to have others do the dirty work. He watched. Most times he was impotent.

He recalled a time when the nuns were away on a retreat one weekend, leaving their house, which was across the little lane next to the seminary, empty. All the students went home except for two seniors and himself. They had to stay back as punishment. The two seniors were supposedly caught cheating on their exams. They didn't, though. They glanced at them as they passed the time. They had finished before the rest of the class.

Gordon had to stay back because he refused to write a one-hundred-word essay on the aardvark. The priest thought Gordon was talking too loud during biology class. There was always chatter going, but on that day, at that time, he didn't say a word. The teacher looked up from his book and picked out someone to be the scapegoat and he chose Gordon.

He was pissed. He explained to the young priest that he hadn't said a word to anyone, but the priest became indignant. They exchanged words. The student and teacher matched wits, both too stubborn to back down.

Gordon refused to accept responsibility for something he hadn't done and told the priest to "strive to be a better teacher and stop bothering the students." For that, he was hauled down to the principal's office. Even there he held his ground with Father Dittmar.

On that Saturday morning, in his street clothes, he was in the gym with a bag of basketballs practicing one-handed jump shots and lay-ups. The two seniors walked onto the floor wearing their basketball uniforms and gym shoes. They took turns playing a little one-on-one; Gordon beat both of them.

They finished up the day by playing two-on-one.

They showered, dressed, and walked out of the gym to the cafeteria. With the nuns gone, they hadn't eaten all day. They ambled into the kitchen and found a variety package of sliced meats, salami, ham, and roast beef in the fridge. One found a loaf of bread and lopped off a few slices for the others. They inhaled the food.

The seniors were Bobby Spadaro and Edwin Lord.

Bobby was a tall lanky Italian kid from Kenosha, a factory town on the shores of Lake Michigan seven miles north of the Illinois border. He always had the coolest-looking clothes and never had a hair out of place.

His parents ran a popular Italian restaurant in downtown Kenosha. Some said his Papa was a Mafioso boss.

The other senior, Edwin Lord, another Wisconsinite, came from a small town of five hundred people, near the Wisconsin River. He was a stocky guy, muscular with thick arms, had long reddish-brown hair about the same shade of red as Gordon's, and he had freckles. He was the kind of guy everyone wanted as a friend, especially if you ever got in trouble with someone big and ugly. No one messed with him.

Eddy was the name he preferred. Ashton Plenn found that out when he kidded him one too many times about the name Edwin. There was nothing *wrong* with the name, but it seemed there was *always* something wrong with Ashton. He could act angelic, but he was really a whiny sonofabitch. The guys called him 'the perfect asshole.' He delighted in a weird way at being known for his perfection.

Eddy all but squeezed the life out of him one day in the gym. Ashton got a little too cute, as he called out to Eddy, "Oh Edwin," he said in a granny's voice, "it's time for you to take your cod liver oil. Come to your grandmother, Edwin, and sit on my lap, my poor little Edwin."

Eddy's body had years of hard farm work embedded in his muscles. His grip was so strong, he lifted him right off the floor while clutching his throat. Ashton kicked and squirmed.

Eddy was holding him high off the floor when the gym teacher, Father Frank, saw what was happening and rushed to the two boys. "Put him down, Mr. Lord. Let him go." When Ashton's feet were back on the floor, he collapsed and started to bawl. All the guys ran down there and watched Ashton Plenn cry like a baby.

Bobby rummaged through the cabinets in the kitchen and came across a gallon jug of wine. He pushed it aside and found a bottle, a pint bottle with a label. He grabbed the bottle out of the cabinet and read the label—Five Star brandy.

CHAPTER FORTY-TWO

They went up to the top floor, the freshman floor, and all the way to the end of the hallway. There at the end of the hallway was a window. Directly across from it was the nuns' house that the students laughingly referred to as the nunnery.

Little did they know that that evening would be a life-altering experience.

Bobby pulled a pack of Lucky Strikes out of his jacket pocket and passed it around as they each took a cigarette. He lit the match for the three. They sat on the floor talking, smoking, and passing the bottle around.

That night, a big, four-door black sedan rolled up in front of the nuns' house. Two men emerged from the auto and walked up to the front door. The shorter of the two got out a key from his pants pocket, and they went inside. The first-floor lights flashed on, then a few minutes later, the upstairs lights shown through the window shades.

The shadow of the man who had opened the front door appeared near a window and pulled the curtains open. He lifted the window and stuck his head out. He stood there with his arms resting on the sill as he peered at the seminary building. He looked it up and down and all around before turning around and tending to whatever business he had at the nuns' house.

The boys glanced at each other, not saying a word, but paying close attention to the men who entered the vacant red brick house.

Both men went out the front door again and to the back of the car to the trunk. They stood for a moment and looked around and at the seminary building again, as if they were up to no good. They pulled and tugged at something wrapped in a blanket. They looked at one another, then shoved it back down in the trunk, got in the car and drove it around to the back of the convent, out of sight from the boys' view.

That's when Gordon got the idea of getting a telescope from the science room. "This kid's got some smarts," Eddy said.

Bobby had placed it on its tripod in front of the hallway window and zoomed in on the house across the lane. With a few minor adjustments, it was in focus. They took turns peeking into the telescope for a close-up view of the activities across the way.

"What do you think's in the trunk, guys?" Eddy asked.

"Hard to say, but my gut tells me something bad," Gordon responded, "like a body."

Bobby had first watch. "There's graves back there, you know. Wooden white crosses on nameless graves. They say it's for old priests who kicked the bucket, here. I don't know if it's true or not."

"Geez. This place is screwy," Gordon whispered. Eddy chuckled and took a drag from his cigarette.

As Bobby peered through the lens, nothing was happening. They sat and passed around the bottle again before Bobby and Eddy recalled ghost stories they had heard from the upperclassmen.

"Is it true? About what's buried in the yard?" Gordon asked.

"It's not good; I'll say that." Bobby said.

"There was talk of late-night grave-digging parties. Some of the students say they saw skeletons coming up and out of the graves as they dug."

"You're shittin' me," Gordon said. The hair on the back of his neck stood out.

It ain't no shit," Eddy said, chiming in. "Select students had to dig the graves for the deceased priests the night before the burial rites. They weren't allowed at the services, though." Eddy took another sip from the bottle.

194

"So if the dead really did come up what would be the purpose?" Gordon asked.

Bobby thought for a second as he peered through the scope and said, "Maybe they were—I don't know, begging?" Bobby moved the telescope a tad.

"Hey, there's movement," he said. He watched as the two men roughhoused. "They're screwing around with each other." Stunned, he grabbed the other two by their shirtsleeves.

"It's Father Cheney! The little bald sonofabitch is pulling the other guy's chain!"

The others pushed Bobby aside and took turns to see for themselves.

Eddy said, "What a piss ant! He teaches the ethics class, for chris-sake! He told us that if one's mind had anything other than good thoughts stirring about, then those thoughts were sinful, requiring confession. The clown is a walking contradiction."

At first they laughed. The laughter died soon as they viewed the naked two–man show. After the chain-pulling incident, the two ran naked like silly little children, chasing each other from room to room.

The running soon became a romp as they wrapped their arms around each other in full embrace near the upstairs open window.

They didn't need a telescope to see what was going on. The taller of the two men slipped down and out of sight, leaving Father Paul Cheney standing.

Minutes later, he stood and the two walked away, cheek to cheek.

A light went on in another bedroom down the hallway. The two again appeared where the boys could see them.

Cheney climbed onto the bed on all fours and positioned himself sideways on his knees and elbows like a dog peering back over his shoulder to his partner. The taller and much younger man rubbed something on his penis and in the area of Cheney's ass. He stood at the side of the bed with his hands on Paul Cheney's hips and entered him from the rear.

CHAPTER FORTY-THREE

G ordon had learned what he knew of homosexuality from snide remarks and references from his uncles and cousins, but until that
night he'd never given it much thought. This particular night found
him and his new friends seeing something far out of the ordinary *and*
it involved at least one member of the clergy who preached against
such behavior. Yet, there he stood, naked as a jaybird, fondling another man's privates.

What they were doing appeared unnatural, nauseating, yet somehow they found watching it to be strangely exotic. They never admit-
ted it, though. They didn't know how.

"Do you think what we're doing and what they're doing is a sin?"
Bobby asked. Gordon looked at Eddy Lord for an answer.

Eddy thought for a moment before saying, "Well, Father Cheney
there says that anything sexual is pretty much a sin. Even sex between a
married couple is a sin unless they're trying to have a baby. He taught
that in ethics class.

"Sex isn't any different from all the other teachings around here.
Whether you watch it, think it, or participate in it, sex is sin, and it's
wrong, and you go to hell for it no matter what, *unless* you confess
it." Eddy crushed his cigarette out on the windowsill and looked at
Gordon for his opinion.

"I don't know," he said, "I got in deep shit when I told Father
Dittmar about what happened to the twins and my roommate. Sure,

Father Long and Smiley were shipped off to parishes, but were they punished?

"The twins and my roommate are gone. They got screwed big time. How did they deal with what happened to them? Where are they? If they're home, who do they talk to about it? Fuck. The priests won't be arrested. I know they won't.

"But, I kinda think what people do is their own business as long nobody gets hurt. I mean does God go around with a clipboard checking our thoughts? Do you think he takes a shower with us to see if we pull our puds or not? If he does, and He judges us on that, then God's a pervert, too. So everybody I know goes straight to hell and that's that."

Eddy and Bobby were rolling with laughter. "God in the shower with a clipboard," one of them said and the laughter started all over again.

After a couple of minutes, Bobby sat against the wall, resting his arms on his knees. "I caught my mother and father having sex on the living room floor one night. The way they were positioned, head to foot, well, let's just say, they weren't trying to produce a younger brother for me. Guess they're goin' to hell, too. If having sex is a sin and it feels so good, yet at the same time it's so bad for you that you have to confess your sins to a priest who has the same feelings, then what's the point? Why can't we just talk to God about it?"

They all came to the same conclusion.

Bobby lit another cigarette and said, "Everything we've been taught all these years, all that our parents have been taught, all of it just went right out this fucking window tonight.

"When we die, we die. And at that point, God, if there is a God, will have to sort all this shit out. I say from here on in, TNWO. There's No Way Out."

Gordon Maxwell, Eddy Lord, and Bobby Spadaro vowed to each other that they'd never say a word about that night to anyone.

What was in the trunk? Why did they drive the car to the back? What'd they do for an hour before the boys saw them again?

They kept their vow of silence. Feelings needed to be stuffed and forgotten. That's how things were taught. The boys stuffed it, but they never, ever, ever forgot about it.

Eddy stopped going to Mass in the chapel at school and, for that, he was kicked out three weeks before graduating. He enlisted in the Navy, got a GED, and became an engineering mechanic assigned to the USS Arizona.

He sailed the seas, and he loved it. The warm breezes of the scenic South Pacific kept his life balanced as the trade winds blew. The freedom of travel is what he cherished, as well as the people of the islands of the South Pacific.

He was stationed at Pearl Harbor until he met his fate in the engine room the morning of December seventh, nineteen forty-one.

Bobby Spadaro graduated from CC Seminary and was drafted into the Army. He was assigned to the First Infantry Division in Europe during World War II. He never got a scratch during three years of fierce fighting.

One night soon after getting home, he climbed into his parents' new Cadillac convertible, drove out of the city limits of Kenosha, and headed west to Eddy Lord's house near the Wisconsin River. With the top down, cruising Highway 130, he had the gas pedal flat against the floor as he crossed the river bridge where the stop sign was nailed onto the face of a hundred-foot rocky cliff on the edge of the blacktop. They say the speedometer froze at 120 mph.

Nobody ever knew why. No one could say for sure that it was a suicide. In his shirt pocket the coroner found a piece of paper with scribbling that appeared to be letters of the alphabet: TNWO.

Gordon knew. He knew what it meant for his friend Bobby—there was no way out. Gordon had lost two good friends inside of five years.

CHAPTER FORTY-FOUR

H e finished, zipped, took out his kerchief, and blew his nose. As he did years ago, Gordon stuffed his feelings one more time.

"We must be close to the seminary." Will said. You okay, boss?"

Gordon answered as he stuffed the kerchief back in his pocket, "Shaking out some cobwebs. Yeah. We're close, and at the end of these last rows of pines to the east is the outer grounds of the seminary." Pointing, he said, "See out where the ball diamond is and the football field sits? Up from there is the main building with the tall white steeple, just at the top of the hill."

"I see it, but are you all right, Sheriff?" Will asked again, as he peered through the trees.

"Gettin' better."

"I see the steeple," Will said, trying to change his buddy's somber mood. He bounded through the trees to the edge of the pines. There was a hayfield covered with snow. Beyond that he could see the backstop of the ball diamond. It wasn't more than a half a mile away to the back door of the seminary building from where they were. Gordon followed.

"We used to sneak over here for bullshit sessions and cigarettes."

Gordon grinned, saying, "Father Frank taught algebra, civics class, and was also the gym teacher. He'd come out here with us around Halloween time, and we'd share hair-raising ghost stories. Occasionally, he'd hand out little cigars. I think they were called cheroots.

"Boy, we thought we were big shots, all of us puffing on those damned cigars. That priest was one of the nicest guys you'd ever hope to meet. He didn't hang with the rest of the priests. He was the kind of priest whom parents wanted to invite to for dinner, you know what I mean?"

"So, what became of him?" Will asked.

"Don't know. He took a parish in a small farming community in south-central Wisconsin somewhere, and we never heard of him again. His name was Francis David Kenyon, but we called him Father Good Guy around the other priests. He preferred to be called Frank. Not Father Frank, mind you, just Frank, like he was just one of the guys.

"He graduated from the seminary, became a sportswriter, and married. As the story goes, he and his young bride were riding bicycles one day on a sidewalk when she lost control and went onto the grass. When she tried to get back onto the sidewalk, she lost control of the bicycle and hit her head on a low branch of a big old oak tree.

"She must have hit it just right because it snapped her neck and she died, just like that. Snap—and it was all over. So he became a priest. Frank stuck up for us once in awhile, but he always said his hands were tied. It's not run exactly like a democracy, you know."

Just like in those days gone by, Gordon Maxwell gathered rocks and placed them in a tight circle. Will helped by collecting dry twigs and branches lying about on the ground protected from the snow by the bows of branches.

Enough was collected to build a nice little fire in a small clearing within steps of the squad car. Gordon unholstered his side-arm and placed it in the trunk, temporarily, next to the shotgun, blanket and the picnic basket he had filled with bologna sandwiches.

After taking a bite of his sandwich, looking out toward the seminary, the Sheriff said, "I hadn't counted on the hills being full of snow. We'll be making tracks from here to there and back again."

William looked at the Sheriff, then up toward the steeple on top of the seminary and said, "You know, I have a gut feeling that tonight might be just right for night flight."

Gordon paused between bites, glanced over at Will on the other side of the fire ring, and asked, "What the hell is night flight?"

CHAPTER FORTY-FIVE

The kids dragged themselves out from underneath the bed. Someone was at the door. They froze. A key turned. A nun appeared at the doorway and stepped in, went straight to the suitcase, and pulled it onto the bed. Another nun came in behind her and pushed the door shut.

The nuns opened the suitcase and examined the contents. There were sets of dresses, pants, wigs, and men's toupees. Also, there were several sets of shoes and socks. One nun pulled out a paper bag and the contents were dumped onto the pillow. It consisted of two small jars of shoe polish, a comb, hairbrush, and a small leather-bound makeup kit.

"Looks like it's all here," one said to the other, then slipped out into the hallway, but glanced back in saying, "I'll be across the way. Meet me there when you're finished."

The stout nun picked up the brown, brunette, and red wigs and placed them on Margaret.

"I'd much prefer to be a brunette, like Ingrid Bergman." Margaret sighed. "I think she'd approve."

So, Margaret became a brunette. The nun slipped a dress over her head and had her try on a pair of saddle shoes, plaid stockings, and a brown knit sweater. The final touch was makeup; ruby red lipstick, rouge on her cheeks, eye shadow, and mascara.

Timmy was dressed as a girl child with adult makeup, including red lipstick, and wore a chiffon dress and brown pumps with white stockings. When the nun finished, she put the rest of the contents into the suitcase, hugged them, and left the room, locking the door behind her. Timmy and Margaret stood facing each other, staring at their clothes.

"She smells like that stuff in daddy's bathroom, the bottle with the ship on it." They sat on the edge of the bed together and held hands.

Timmy wiped his nose on the sleeve of his new blouse a couple of times, before turning to Margaret. "I miss my daddy."

"I know." Margaret said, nodding in agreement.

Down below, on the grounds around the seminary, the golden brown leaves were falling from the tall oaks and majestic silver maples onto the freshly fallen snow. A nun walked along, toting a suitcase almost at a trot toward the red brick house with green shutters. She bounded up the steps as the door opened for her and disappeared inside. Bending down, she set the suitcase on the floor, pulled her black gown up and over her head and headdress, and pulled it all off.

There he stood wearing his dress slacks, white shirt, and freshly shaven face. "It's a helluva lot easier without the pillows stuffed under that robe," he said.

"You did your job well," agreed the doctor. "They'll look nothing like the kids the police are looking for. You're going to enjoy the activities."

"I can't wait," Zaugbaum said, "I'm looking forward to this evening's event."

CHAPTER FORTY-SIX

"Mind if I smoke?" asked Nurse Anne.

"Oh, go ahead," Kat said. "Might as well stink to high heaven tonight. I've never done anything like this before in my entire life and what's funny about it is, I don't have the slightest idea of what the hell we're doing!"

"I don't, either," Anne remarked, "but *goddamn it*, we're going to do whatever it is that we do, if it's the *last* goddamn thing we do!"

Pam Darling was in the front seat of the coffee-colored Ford. She looked back at Anne through the rearview mirror, then over at Kat as she drove along the highway toward Capital City Catholic seminary grounds.

"We want to get there after sunset," Pam said. She glanced down at her wristwatch for the time, "And it looks like we will; hopefully no one will see us. I've been there with Trent around this time of day. We'll have no problem getting in through the kitchen. It just so happens I have another key that he thought he misplaced. I've got almost a dozen of them, various keys, various rooms, hotels, etc."

"I'm a little worried about the car," Kat said. "It's all I have left from my husband, Lee; the car and the two-thousand-dollar life insurance policy he left me when his plane went down over the Mediterranean in the spring of forty-three."

"Don't worry, Kat, it'll be safe here. We'll park near the back entrance in a little place even the priests haven't discovered yet," Pam whispered as she directed Kat off the main road and onto a narrow dirt road leading to the back entrance of the seminary. She prayed the car would be safe.

After parking the four-door sedan behind the corrugated metal coal shed, Pam said, "Follow me, girls," and directed the other two toward a small, white hardwood door near it. It had a windowpane no bigger than a small picture frame. She peeked in, looking for movement, seeing no one, unlocked the door with Trent's key and opened it. The lights were off. They stepped in and quietly closed the door.

"We're in," Pam whispered. "The nuns do the cooking here. They're away until the semester break is over and the students return. Of course, there are a few priests here, but like the Sheriff said, there's going to be lots of men here tonight."

Kat Knee whispered, "I'm here for one reason. I want to find those kids, come hell or high water!"

"Just be concerned with staying out of sight from the priests. The good ones are where they should be, out tormenting and otherwise bothering the good people at the local parishes," Pam said as she looked around.

Anne said, "Good point. If they were behaving at all, they wouldn't be hiding out in a seminary this time of year."

Kat stood silent for a few seconds and scanned the dark room. She could make out a large-handled meat-carving knife on a thick wooden table. She picked it up. "Now, I'm a God-fearing Christian, don't get me wrong, but if any of them harm one of my schoolchildren, there's going to be balls flying everywhere!"

Anne grimaced at the thought of flying, bloody testicles. "Give me the knife, Kat. Pam and I are better qualified."

Her hands were shaking. Kat handed it over.

Relieved, Anne put the knife back on the table, asking, "Where do you think we should be looking?"

"I'm guessing they're in a dorm room somewhere upstairs. The top two are dorms where the boys stay during classes. They're in one of those rooms. The first floor is all classrooms," Pam said.

Anne put a finger to her lips. "Listen!"

They stood frozen as they held their breath. In the distance, they could hear footsteps echoing along the marble hallway. They were getting louder and the voices closer.

"Now what?" Kat asked nervously.

"The wine cellar," whispered Pam, motioning with her arm.

The three tiptoed around the long rectangle table to a small solid wooden door near the coolers that led down to a cellar. Pam opened it. The door was not more than four feet in height. They had to duck as they stepped down the creaky old wooden steps to a dark, musty room.

At the bottom of the stairs, Pam stood and looked up to a small ledge at the side of the steps, felt around through the cobwebs, and found a candle. Alongside it was a box of wooden matches. She struck one on the side of the box and lit the candle as they huddled close at the bottom of the steps. They followed a narrow path on the dirt floor and stumbled upon three wooden casks of wine and two three-legged stools.

The hallway door opened to the kitchen, and the light went on. They could see the slivers of light shining from the bottom and sides of the little door at the top of the steps and heard the voices of two men.

"Who's the new man with Doc Bullock?" one asked.

"The deputy Sheriff from Pine Nut," the other answered.

The gals glanced at each other in disbelief.

"He's at the nuns' house with the doctor. The two of them will be taking the kids to the train station for the midnight run to New York. That's where they'll be getting on a plane toward morning, going to Rome with the Italian priest."

"How much money is there in child smuggling to the Vatican these days?" one asked.

"Depends on their age and gender. Either way, this time there's big money on these two because they're going to the head of a the new group, the Legionnaires of the Christo. That's the word, anyway. He gets his pick of the litter, the fair-haired boy. The other is going to a Monsignor in Brazil. Somebody said upwards of a million bucks this time, all in gold coins; paid by a cardinal, one of the Holy See, and a friend of the Bishop and Padre Pervasions. Nuestro Padre gets the boy.

"Who is the *he* that you're talking about?"

"I've heard his name only once. Father Marcial Maciel Degollado. The head of the LOC."

It was silent a few seconds before the first voice asked, "How do you know this new guy, the deputy Sheriff, can be trusted?"

The second voice answered, "Bullock said he was okay. We needed a replacement. The one we had for the past few years hung himself. The doctor trusts him and so does the Bishop, and that's good enough for me."

They were stunned. Why is Zaugbaum in cahoots with Dr. Bullock's gang? It certainly would answer the question why Mickey was missing and Gordon couldn't find him. They were more intent now than ever before to find the kids and get them out.

"We've got to tell the Sheriff!" Kat whispered.

"I'm sure he knows. I mean, I hope he knows," Anne said, trying to keep herself and the others calm.

CHAPTER FORTY-SEVEN

Pam rummaged, found another candle, and lit it. She handed one to Anne as the voices and footsteps left the kitchen. She stepped to a small wooden cabinet, pushing aside another stool. She opened the door and discovered long dark, hooded robes and shoes.

"I think we have our wardrobe for tonight's coming-out party," she whispered, as she grabbed the clothing and laid the keys nearby. They were monk robes and smelled as if they'd been there for some time fomenting along with the wine. With the candle, she bent lower and peered into the cabinet.

"Aha!" She pulled a bottle of brandy and a manila envelope out of the cabinet.

Anne took the bottle as Pam handed her candle to Kat. Kat held it close as Pam opened the envelope and pulled out the contents. She placed the eight-by-ten glossy pictures on the stool and picked up one as the three leaned in with the candles to get a closer look.

"Oh my God!" Kat exclaimed as she rushed her hand to her mouth to silence herself. It was a photo of a man standing naked with a huge, lengthy, fat erection. There was another man in the picture, and they were holding hands. Pam placed it back in the envelope, then eased it back out and looked at it again saying, "Look at his side."

"I see it," Anne said. "It's the same guy Sheriff Maxwell showed us!" she exclaimed.

Pam paused, swallowed hard, and in a measured tone said, "I-I know that man."

Anne and Kat gave her a side-glance.

"And, yes, I've been down here, too," Pam said.

"Let's see the others," Kat said, still eyeing Pam.

Anne picked up the next photo as Pam put the first one away. It was a picture of two men standing where the girls were. Their faces weren't in the picture, just the two men shown from the chest down holding each other's peckers.

"I don't believe this!" Kat said.

Anne handed that one to Pam. She put it back in the envelope and picked out another. The next photo was of two men also aroused and facing the camera.

"Damn," Anne said, and handing it back to Pam. "All the pictures were taken here, in this little wine cellar, right where we stand."

"If the kitchen is used by the nuns, surely they've been down here?"

No one said a word; they just shrugged.

"It's organized religion," answered Pam, "What can I say? Anyway, who's got the time?"

"It's almost five-thirty," Kat said, glancing at her wristwatch.

Anne unscrewed the top of the brandy bottle and said, "We wait or we look for the kids now. What's it going to be, ladies?"

There were more voices. Several men were conversing and they heard one say, "I hear maybe three dozen are going to be here tonight."

Anne, touched the bottle to her lips, took a swig and whispered, "We wait."

Pam took the bottle and said, "I agree." She took a long pull from it and passed it to Kat. She took a sip, coughed, wiped her lips, and took another before handing it back to Anne.

"Let's see those photos again. So tell me, Pam, who's the guy with the birthmark on his side?"

Pam looked at Anne and Kat. "I'll tell you this, and I want you to swear on a stack of Bibles you've never heard it from me."

Anne looked at Kat, who was looking back at her. "We swear," they said in unison.

"Dr. Bullock and I, ah, Trent was having sex with me at his house. It was a time when I was just a naïve candy striper at the hospital. It was my birthday, and he talked me into having sex with him while another man was in the room. We were in bed on top of the sheets humping like there was no tomorrow and this guy, well, he stood in front the dresser and watched us through the mirror as he masturbated. He had a big, well, you saw the picture."

"That's disgusting!" Kat said in a hurried voice. "What else did he do?"

Anne eyed Kat, shook her head, and chuckled.

Pam continued, "That's all he did. He just stood facing the mirror, watching us diddle around as he played with his big bad self."

Anne turned back to Pam Darling and said to her, "So you recognize him? Who is this dirtbag who watched that night?"

"It was, uh, damn. He's a big shot somewhere. I can't think of it now. But I'll know him when I see him."

CHAPTER FORTY-EIGHT

"**I**'ve got it figured out, Sheriff, you old dog, you. Tonight you're going to be Santa Claus."

"Perfect," Gordon said with a snarl. "And I suppose you're going to be Rudolph the red-nosed reindeer."

"Something like that."

They sat in silence around the campfire as the sun set behind them. The clouds had covered the sky, and it felt warmer. As the evening progressed, the clouds thickened as fog began to settle in.

"It's going to get soupy tonight, Will. The visibility will be low and lower yet by midnight, but it'll help cover us for the crackdown later on. Will, I've ordered the Capitol City police to move in, on the seminary on the front side at eight-thirty sharp. It'll be about that time that I'll be confronting the bastards in the room.

"I wanted my deputy to be there with me tonight. I told him how I wanted it done. But, I hadn't got any firm commitments from Capital City when he just up and disappeared. I'm going to need all the help I can get tonight, so if you could pry one of your angel friends loose, I'll take him."

He shook his head, downed the last of the cola, and gobbled up the rest of his bologna sandwich.

"I'm not sure how things are going to work tonight either," said Will. "You know how Santa flies through the sky on Christmas Eve? You're gonna find out how he does that."

The night air was getting chilly for the two. Gordon got behind the wheel of his squad car and started the engine with Will in the passenger seat. He leaned over, turned on the radio, and found the station broadcasting the Bob Hope specials. They listened to his rapid-fire jokes, but tonight, Gordon wasn't laughing. They kept an eye on the back entrance to the cold eerie brick building up on the hill.

Though the fog was getting thick, they could see headlights streaming up the hill to the ghostly, red brick building. Will turned to Gordon, "You have an idea of how you're going to find Timmy and Margaret?"

He glanced to Will and said in a monotone voice, "I won't have to find them, Will. They'll be at the ceremony. In fact, the two of them will be on the stage, set up in that damned room. The same room the Bishop and the priests had their fun with me when I was your age."

Pressing the steering wheel, leaning back, and taking a deep breath, he continued, "No, I won't have to look for them. I just want to be *in* the room when the lights go on. I want to see the faces of those sons-a-bitches in attendance. I want to personally pull off the headdresses and the robes and look each one in the face. I want the reporter from the *Capital City Gazette* right there taking pictures of each one of them, too. You worked hard on this and damned near paid for it with your life! Yes, Will, I want it for you *and* for me. It's a little payback time tonight, and by God or by hell, it's going to be a night to remember for a long, long time."

Will sighed. His thoughts were on the kids.

CHAPTER FORTY-NINE

"**D**o you believe in Santa Claus?" Margaret asked Timmy.

"Yup. I talked to him at a department store in Capital City, once."

"Also," Margaret continued, "you remember what William told us? Just call on our angels, and they'll be right there to help us out." Margaret was thinking about the night the Bishop's friend entered their room. Her thoughts were incomplete. Moments of time were missing.

"He tied us up and put that bad tasting tape over our mouths, which hurt. He and the Bishop made us feel bad, and Bishop Cheney didn't always feed us much, neither."

"So, he's in trouble with God, huh?" Timmy asked.

"I think so," Margaret answered. "And with Santa Claus."

"You shouldn't go round hurting kids like us," Timmy continued. "Like Mrs. Knee said, "All children have the right to feel safe and loved at all times."

Timmy felt a little braver as Margaret helped ease the fear in his heart.

"I bet she gets after the Bishop when we tell her what he did to us, huh? And I bet Daddy will want to whoop the bad man good!"

"How do you like being dressed up like a girl?" Margaret asked, changing the subject.

"It feels stupid. I don't like it. I don't like lipstick. It tastes icky. I just want to be with Mommy and Daddy." Timmy closed his eyes, pressed his hands together near his heart, and prayed.

"Please, angels, help my sister and me to be with Mommy and Daddy tonight. We don't like to play dress-up no more, and we don't like the angry Bishop or Pastor Swain or Reverend Sven too much, neither, and especially Father Burke, that friend of Bishop Cheney, the one who made us feel bad. We think they should be spanked and sent to their rooms with no food or radio for a week. Amen."

"You know what I think, Timmy? I think it's okay to ask Santa for help, too. You never know." She mused, "You just never know this time of year."

They laid on the bed holding hands for comfort and drifted off to sleep after saying their bedtime prayers. "Now I lay me down to sleep with a sack of peanuts at my feet, should I die before I wake, I pray my soul my Lord will take. Amen."

CHAPTER FIFTY

The ladies stood at the bottom of the steps wearing the hooded garb they found in the cabinet. The shoes were not shoes at all, but were Mukluks. They were way over ankle high with leather soles and heavy wool about three sizes too big.

"If this all works out," Pam asked, "are you going to go right on teaching, Kat?"

"Guess so," she said. "Since my husband was killed over the Mediterranean, I don't have a lot of money. I may write about this, though, if we get out of here *alive*."

"Yeah," Nurse Anne said clenching her jaw, "Somebody should write about this shit, the fucked-up pedophiles, those twinkle-toed rump-riders." She took one final swig from the bottle and passed it around. Looking at her wristwatch, she started for the steps, whispering, "It's eight-thirty, girls. Let's go get 'em."

***

As the Legionnaires gathered in the hallway at the front entrance, men in the white albs handed out the ceremonial black robes and headgear to those in attendance. They gave the instructions to the men as they placed the robes over their clothing.

Florien Swain was in a white robe. "We'll go over our lines before we go in and will recite each line three times, repeating after me. Ready?"

"We offer up the children to the City of the Damned."

They all chimed in and chanted three times, *"We offer up the children to the City of the Damned."*

Bishop Paul Cheney appeared before the group and led them in the rest of the chants. Also in attendance were Dr. Trent Bullock, Reverend Svendly Pervasions, Pastor Florien Swain, Deputy Mickey Zaugbaum, and the cheese factory owner, Otto Strickler. With them were five former Nazis who had been guards at Auschwitz and Dachau and now were insurance salesmen from Ames, Iowa and Lincoln, Nebraska. They fled Germany at the end of the war and were living and doing business under assumed names.

Then, there were four priests, members of the LOC, who taught at the seminary, and priests from other diocese. Along with them were close to twenty other men who weren't clergy. Among them were elementary teachers, Boy Scout leaders, and state legislators who were on the take.

The legislators took money from the others to ensure no bills would pass that contained language protecting children. In all, there were almost three dozen members of the local splinter group of The Legionnaires of the Christo in attendance that night.

"We offer up the children to the City of the Damned," echoed through the halls.

"That sounded fine, gentlemen. This time, stomp a foot on the floor twice after we say it. Again. *We offer up the children to the City of the Damned.*"

The eerie verse echoed. The vibrations rumbled through the halls from the stomping feet. It was like electrical pulses bolting through the veins and arteries of a sick, cancerous body searching for the valve to a cold, cold heart.

"Our loving God will wash the blood from our hands."

"Very good, all you Legionnaires. I want you all to remember your vows of silence and also remind you of the great tradition that's being preserved here that's been handed down to men like us for thousands of years. *We are* the guardians of hope. Gentlemen, the Reich shall rise again.

"In fact, I've been told there's one young German priest who is being groomed. He was a Hitler youth, a Nazi soldier and, God willing, someday he'll be the Pope. He'll serve us well into the next century.

"We'll not be defeated, for it is God's will that we succeed and gain strength to do the right thing, the Christian way of keeping traditions alive for all future generations to come. We are but a handful of men here tonight, but we're one handful of a thousand other handfuls throughout the world, and we will not give up our will, nor will we succumb to indifference. We'll wear this gown of truth, for God Almighty is on our side. We'll spread our way to the rest of the world, for one day all corners of this planet will become hallowed grounds. Christian pedophilia will bud and blossom.

"We cannot fail. For this, we ask God to strengthen our side and our cause. Now follow the glorious White headdress and gowns all ye of the black robes of the Red Cross of Valor. March on, all you Legionnaires of the Cristo, march on!" Cheney's commanding voice blended now with the rest.

They chanted and paraded along the hallway toward the classrooms. Bishop Cheney turned right, then left, and walked them into another hallway. They zigged and zagged, then another right on the opposite side of the building heading back in the direction from which they had started. He opened a small, unassuming door, the entrance to the secret, unsacred ceremonial room.

The singing commenced with, *"Onward Christian soldiers—marching off to war, with the cross of Jesus going on before. Christ, the raised master, leads against the foe; foreword into battle; see his banners!*

CHAPTER FIFTY-ONE

They sang all five verses as they stood in front of their chairs and finished by singing the third verse again. *Like a mighty army moves the Church of God; brother, we are treading where the Saints have trod. We are not divided, all one body we, in a hope and doctrine, in charity.* They ended with the refrain, *Onward Christian soldiers, marching off to war, with the cross of Jesus going on before.*"

Some of the white robed men were strategically stationed across the room as guards. Two were at the front entrance, on each side of the doorway, inside, and one on the outside. One each on the side walls of the room and one stood at the stage setting where two empty chairs were positioned, facing the crowd. The one on the stage motioned for the rest to be seated. As they did so, one white robed man at the near side of the room turned off the lights. The only glow now came from the one lightbulb that hung down above the two chairs.

All was deathly quiet for several minutes. There was a faint odor of the recent use of incense in the closed, window-less, sterile brick room.

The Bishop sat in the first chair of a set of three closest to the stage, clutching his long staff in his hand. On his right side sat Reverend Pervasions, and Pastor Swain was on his left. In the middle of the front row behind those three sat Dr. Trent Bullock, Otto Strickler, and Deputy Mickey Zaugbaum. The rest were all black robed with the pointed headgear and sheets over their faces with two holes for their eyes.

There was a light tap on the door. One of the white robes next to the door opened it and whispered to the men in robes to enter and sit in the vacant seats in the back row. They shuffled into the darkness with their hands outstretched, searching for the seats. The guard closed the door. All was silent again.

Bishop Cheney held tight to his staff. He closed his eyes and said a silent prayer; *Forgive me, my Lord and my God, for I have forsaken you. Forgive me my sins and cleanse my soul.* He took a deep breath and, as he exhaled, stood, turned and faced the group, raised the staff high, driving it twice to the floor.

The men responded, "We offer up the children to the City of the Damned."

He slammed the staff down hard two more times and continued leading the rest by saying, "Our loving God will wash the blood from our hands."

The chanting continued three more times, and again it was quiet as the Bishop sat down.

Dr. Bullock let out another SBD. Those around him did all they could do to keep from gagging. Even the Bishop had a hard time sitting still. He twitched his nose in disgust.

Zaugbaum managed only by holding his breath as long as he could until the horrific smell subsided. He couldn't help but wonder what his former friend, Gordon, was doing and where he was. *Hope he don't shoot me.*

***

Will looked to the one true person he could trust, the one who cared for those without a voice. "It's time."

Gordon took a deep breath and let it out as he ran both of his hands through his hair a couple of times before looking at Will. "It ain't going to hurt, is it?" he said, playing along with his new plot.

"Naw," Will said. "It'll be a walk in the woods. Have faith in me while we fly up and over the seminary. I'll do the rest. No screaming!"

"Oh, don't say that. Don't say screaming. You didn't have to say—screaming."

A faint green and yellow glow appeared in the dying embers. It grew larger and brighter as Raphael appeared and stepped out of the green.

Sheriff Maxwell stood straight up and froze in place. His eyes rolled back, and he fell flat on his back in the snow.

"He's going to be a problem," Raphael said.

"He'll be my responsibility," Will responded, as he slapped the Sheriff's cheeks. He helped the beleaguered Sheriff to his feet.

"Hey, Ralphy," Will said, "The last time I saw you, you said you wouldn't be here, tonight. What happened?"

"I'll be blunt. The Boss overruled me and suggested I guide you."

Gordon brushed as much snow off as he could while adjusting to the glowing stranger standing in front of him. He closed his eyes and reopened them, but the winged one was still there.

"Uh, good evening," he managed to squeak out. "I heard a lot about you from William here. I'll be alright, trust me."

Still in a foggy daze, Gordon said that he was willing to go along with plans set forth for the evening.

"To help you, Gordon Maxwell," Raphael replied, "In a few minutes you won't see me again. However, I will be with Will. I won't leave you, but you won't see me. It's best that way."

Gordon stood there with eyes and mouth wide open, trying to listen and comprehend at the same time. He closed his mouth, swallowed hard, and spoke, "Yes, sir."

"As William stated earlier, you will be Santa Claus. When you're aloft, you are to make no noise. You just do as Will instructs. When you do talk, you'll be addressing those in attendance over there on the hill. They'll hear your voice as the voice of Santa Claus."

"This is too much." Gordon slouched.

"Get used to it now or fate will step in and change the course of the future," Raphael said in stern voice.

Gordon snapped to attention. "Yes, *Sir!*"

"Now be off with the two of you, and do what's right for the world. The children's fate depends on you tonight, not just the two children on your mind, but for all children. It's your charge to do something positive tonight. Do it for the innocent silent ones, the oppressed and abused children." Raphael stepped back into the embers, becoming colors of yellow and green, then faded away.

"You've worked long and hard for this night, my friend," Will said.

"And you, William, have been waiting all of your life," Gordon responded.

"I'm but a messenger serving my Lord, Sheriff. Suffering will happen to me no more. Now we're off to the seminary. Excuse me; *Santa* is going to the seminary. No yelling. No shouting. Got that, Sheriff?"

Will stepped behind him and lifted him high, floating slowly at first, then sped faster, skimming over the treetops.

If this is the DTs, I'd have quit drinking a long time ago. If this is a dream, so be it. If it's part of an element from beyond this world controlling this, then God help me. I'm in your hands.

"Relax and enjoy the flight," Will said as he held the Sheriff with one arm, then the other, hoping he wouldn't drop him.

The fog was so thick it could be cut it with a knife. "It's hard to see. Are you there, Will?"

"I'm the one holding you up," he answered.

"Oh, Lord, have mercy." Then in a startled voice, Gordon said, "I forgot my gun! It's in the car!"

"You won't need it, trust me. When those guys see you, the last thing they'll think of is a gun. Now hush it!"

Will began singing. *"Dashing through the snow, oer the fields we go, laughing all the way."*

"I ain't laughing, Will!" Gordon said.

CHAPTER FIFTY-TWO

One man in a satin, white, hooded robe, stood behind the stage in front of a small door, like the kind meant for an attic or crawl space. It opened, and out through the door came another man in white with the two children, dressed in women's clothing and wigs. They were led blindfolded with a towrope, up the makeshift steps at the side of the stage, to the chairs facing the men. Each child's hands' were bound behind them and their mouths gagged with cloth tied behind their heads.

There was a dark quiet in the room, and the soft sobs from the children could be heard all the way to the back. They were placed in the chairs, and tied to them. The man in the white robe whispered to them in a stern voice, "Say nothing now, not a word, if you want to stay alive to see your parents."

Their little bodies shook as their sobbing became louder.

In the last row in the three seats nearest to the door, one in a thick dark robe whispered to those on either side.

Suddenly there were two heavy hands on the shoulder of the one speaking. He bent forward and whispered, "Quiet, men. The fun is just about to start."

Kat nodded and felt the pressure lift off her shoulder, much too scared to say a word. They breathed a sigh of relief.

The Bishop stood raising his staff again and with a strong and sturdy voice proclaimed, "All you sons of the mighty Legionnaires of the Cristo, rise as we proclaim together."

Down came the staff, *hard* to the floor twice, and he led them with, *"Now is the time to set the seal of fate upon our arms, upon our chests."* The attendees repeated the chant, and again he slammed the staff on the floor twice and said, "It is written in stone that we prevail *Onward, Christian soldiers, for the ships set sail."* He and the others echoed the refrain two more times.

Trent Bullock leaned to Zaugbaum, saying, "You must be commended for your makeup job on the kids."

Will, invisible, floated Gordon high to the ceiling as they skimmed along the hallways and set him down, around the corner, out of sight from the secret doorway, as the chanting echoed in the halls.

"Shh," Will motioned toward the door. "I'll distract him." Gordon nodded, to *whom* and *where* he nodded, he wasn't sure.

Still invisible, Will knelt in front of the guard and quickly tied his shoelaces together. At that point, Gordon stepped around the corner, walking briskly toward the guarded door. The man in robes tried to take a step forward but stumbled to the floor.

Gordon disposed of the hooded doorman by tying, gagging, and strapping him to the toilet bowl facedown in the boys' room just a few doors down. "Guard *this*, you ugly fucker," Gordon whispered in his ear as he kicked his ass hard several times with his Wellington boots.

He glanced in the mirror in the washroom. Santa Claus winked at him. He winked back. He looked at his wristwatch. Eight thirty-eight. "Showtime."

He re-ascended to the top of the ceiling, moving into the hallway. At that moment, the front door of the seminary opened, and the Capital City Police appeared in the entryway, listening for voices that would lead them to the secret room.

Several found their way around the hallways, moving closer to the secret ceremonial room leaving the rest of the officers waiting outside at the paddy wagon. There were seventeen police cars lined up from the driveway entrance all the way to the front of the building.

"Looks like you'll get your wish," Will whispered. "Now, close your eyes. We're going inside, and I'll set you down between the children, but wait until I give you the signal before talking."

Gordon nodded.

William took three deep breaths and let them out as he began his God-Thought. *Lord, don't let me get stuck.* As he exhaled the first time, he smelled the faint scent of roses, as if Mother Mary were present. He breathed in two more times, and passed through the wall with ease.

Gordon Maxwell opened his eyes as he floated in above the door. He looked down upon the thirty-plus men in attendance as he drifted toward the stage. It was pitch black, high up above the lone lightbulb over the children's heads.

The Bishop had finished his chant and was speaking to the assembled group standing in front of the stage facing the Legionnaires.

"And how great the men of the mighty Legionnaires are! Now I have but one more statement and a final warning for the children. He turned to the children tied to the chairs on the stage, saying, "You two, who are privileged to be sitting here upon the stage with this select group of empowered men of noble integrity, listen well. You're about to embark on a special journey."

Gordon descended. "Now," whispered William, "speak your truth!"

In a flash, Santa was standing tall between the two defenseless children and said in a loud cheery voice, "*Merry Christmas,* one and all!"

There was much commotion as the lightbulb above the two children went out. The room went pitch black for an instant as Santa Claus began glowing bright red. Shock vibrated through the hooded men in the room. His red suit was pulsating; his white beard as bright as a thousand watt spotlight, and his face was a hot whitish-pink.

He put his hands on the shoulders of the two children and, as he did so, their hands were freed from the ties and the cloth fell away from their mouths. The room went silent for a moment. Timmy and Margaret leaped from the chairs and held tight to Santa's legs as he bellowed, "Now, nobody move! Santa has a few words of good cheer for all of you."

The room stayed silent, and they returned to their seats, including the stunned Bishop. They didn't understand what was happening. They were awe-struck. Hypnotized. The men obeyed out of fear.

"Just as the Bishop said, there's one more thing to say to these children, and it should be stated this way; I'm sorry! "Now say it! Stay seated and say it, you cowardly ignorant fools. *Say it!*" Santa demanded. "Say, 'I'm sorry we hurt you.'"

The stunned group began talking loudly. "*Quiet! All of you,* or you'll get no presents from me this year!"

Again the room fell silent. Bishop Cheney stood and stepped up to the front of the stage with staff in hand and asked in a loud voice, "Who are you?"

"Children know me far and wide! They've known me for centuries. As Bishop Paul, aka, Uncle Billy, Cheney, you, of all people, *don't* know who I *am?*"

The Bishop replied, "I do *not* know who you are! If you're of this earth, I do not know you, Sir. And if you're from spirit, then you did not come from God. You are the devil's work. Perhaps you are Satan's right hand or, worse yet, Satan himself. You must leave this holy building at once!"

He took the staff, removed the skull with the white crystals, and let it fall to the floor. What remained was a long, sharp, pointed end of the staff. He took aim at Santa Claus. With a heave, he thrust it forward. Just inches from Maxwell's heart, Will stepped out of his body and grabbed the staff as it touched Santa's red suit, and hurled it high into the ceiling and it stuck.

Hysteria and chaos erupted. The hooded group turned into a wild mob leaping from their seats and bolting toward the narrow entrance. Stumbling and tripping over the chairs and themselves as they went, they tossed their headgear aside. While rushing the door, it gave way as the men continued to shout and fight while trying to flee from the madness that confronted them.

CHAPTER FIFTY-THREE

G ordon stood with the children as he watched the chaos unfold in front of him. Patting their heads while bending down, he said, "Come. Hang on tight. We are going for a ride."

Will stepped behind the Santa suit, and in a flash, they were out of the building and streaking through the starlit sky above the fog.

In what seemed like a split second, Santa and his two little friends were standing in Ed and Helen's living room, next to the Christmas tree.

"I've got one more surprise for you," Santa said as he turned on the tree lights. "I'll awake your mommy and daddy."

Santa flew up the stairs to the Hornsbys' bedroom. They were fast asleep. He looked at the clock. It was nine p.m. *Perfect* he thought, and tapped Mr. Hornsby on the shoulder and said, "Ed, you have a gift under the tree, hurry!" and floated through the bedroom window.

Mr. Hornsby looked at the clock and kissed his wife on the cheek. "What's up, hon?" Helen asked.

"I had a dream. I dreamt that Santa Claus woke me up, said something, then flew out through the window and disappeared."

She saw a faint glow of colored lights down the stairwell. "I thought you turned the tree lights off," Helen whispered.

Ed blinked the sleep out of his eyes, "I did."

She threw back the covers, and they scurried down the hallway, bolting down the stairs, stopping for a brief second, glancing at the multicolored lights in the living room. They continued down the steps. There, sitting under the tree, were Timmy and Margaret.

"Mommy, Daddy," they said in unison with arms outstretched.

Ed and Helen rushed to their children, hugging and kissing them, locked in a tight embrace.

"You're *home*. Oh, thank you, God, thank you angels for being here and for hearing our prayers. Thank you, thank you, thank you, for answered prayers."

"Thank you, God, for Santa," Margaret whispered to herself.

CHAPTER FIFTY-FOUR

The calamity had spilled out into the hallway by the time Sheriff Maxwell returned. The Capital City Police were caught off guard as the throng of men smashed through the doors during the melee. The officers assigned to watch the entrance to the secret room and hallways were thrown against the far wall as the door blasted off its hinges, as thirty half-crazed men rushed to get out.

The officers outside the front entrance heard the disturbance and raced to the aid of their fellow officers inside. When they opened the double doors, a flood of robed men stampeded their way out of the building. The officers found themselves being run over by the charging throng of men in black and white as they fled the building.

Kathryn, Anne, and Pam huddled together in the nearest corner by their seats as the chaos ensued.

"Look. By the stage," Anne blurted out. The other two turned their attention to the small door behind the stage. Four others followed the Bishop as they slipped through the small, unguarded door.

"Here we go," Anne said as her heart pounded, and took off hugging the wall in the opposite direction of the mass of fleeing black and white robes.

After taking a few steps into the small walkway, they saw the five they were following, stepping fast, single file at a fast pace, heading down the narrow, crude corridor lined with kerosene lamps along the way. The walls and flooring were constructed of stone and odd-sized thick brown brick, unlike the rest of the red brick seminary. It was a passageway, to be sure, and where it led they would soon find out.

The men never looked back as they hurried along the crude, musty corridor. They came to a dead end. The Bishop grabbed at a thick, knotted rope draped from the short ceiling and wrapped around a metal vertical bar, on one side of the wall. He undid the rope from the metal bar, and he and two others pulled down with all their might.

The ladies stood with their backs against the wall, trying not to be seen. They were successful as the five looked back to see if they were being followed, saw no one, and pulled on the rope again. As they did so, the end of the wall gave way. It opened outward from the top and came down as they eased the rope upwards through their hands. In a minute, it laid flat on the ground as the men scurried over it like rats fleeing a sinking ship.

A moment later, the women followed. When they got to the exit, they found themselves near the back entrance to the seminary near the convent and a hundred feet or so down from the kitchen entrance and coal shed.

Dozens of cars were scattered around the grounds. The five robed men hurried toward the kitchen door, where a black-robed man stood waving frantically.

The ladies, in the brown monk's robes, followed at a distance, hugging the wall of the Seminary as they shuffled silently along the building.

At the door, they took a quick peek in the window as the men removed their headgear. They were huddled in a circle. One of the men spoke. "I'll take Doc and Reverend Pervasions with me to the wine cellar until the heat dies down."

"A good idea," the Bishop said. "Swain and I will go and get the hell out of here for a few days. Deputy Zaugbaum, come with us. We'll need you for protection in case there's any trouble. Surely the police will be here soon if they aren't already."

Mickey nodded in agreement, and they stepped out of the back door. In the darkness, they peered out at the mass of autos parked helter-skelter.

Pondering their next move, the ladies had huddled near the closest car. Out of sight, yet they were within earshot of the other three.

Mickey spoke first. "So how often does Santa Claus visit the seminary?"

"Will you *shut up*?" Swain bellowed, "The Bishop is *thinking*!"

Paul Cheney, looking perplexed, said, "It was planned! That entire episode in there was an obvious evil plan to keep us from continuing the ceremony. I must admit it was a clever plot to be sure. The one in red is a devious man with the agility of a circus acrobat. He was on to us. But how? Whoever it is must have the children now."

"Agreed," said Swain, wringing his hands, "but what do we do in the meantime? It's *terribly* foggy, and we need to get away from here, now!"

Searching the sea of randomly parked cars, the Bishop found his Buick, but it was boxed in. "Damn it! See if someone left the keys in their car and we'll take that one," Mickey said in a hurried voice as he started opening car doors.

They rummaged in vain through the autos. The ladies were crouching low. The Bishop saw the futility in their search and said, "This will get us nowhere. We'll take my car later after some of these vehicles are gone. Quick, follow me to the wine cellar!"

The three went inside and joined the others. There the six of them stood in the candlelit cellar listening to the muffled sounds from upstairs. The ladies slipped back into the kitchen where Kathryn reached up from the butcher-block table and pulled down an iron skillet from the vertical notched bar overhead that held the cooking utensils. The other two shot a glance at her as she held it with both hands.

"Just in case," she whispered.

CHAPTER FIFTY-FIVE

William stood in spirit form, aglow in green and yellow from the top center of the pitched roof. He wasn't alone. Next to him stood his angel friend, Archangel Raphael, wearing light green corduroy jeans and a collarless silvery white shirt with the sleeves rolled halfway up to the elbows. They watched the craziness unfold from above.

The first group of the Legionnaires to make it outside the front door paused for a split second, shocked to find a paddy wagon and all the police and squad cars waiting for them. The wave of men in robes behind them continued running out past the doors, knocking the men down the steps and running them over as they scattered in all directions.

The police grabbed as many of the fleeing men as they could, thumping them with nightsticks and flinging them into the waiting paddy wagon. They caught others, whacking as many as they could get their hands on.

Those who escaped the police, ran for their cars around the back of the long brick building, slipping and sliding in the icy snow in hopes that they would reach their autos and escape the chaos and *Santa Claus*.

"Is this where the Sheriff rounds up the bad guys?"

"We have your friend standing at the end of the seminary building, next to the big dumpster, at the corner down from the kitchen. There's a wooden step stool there. He'll single-handedly take care of half these men. With him is a reporter from the *Capital City Gazette*.

He's taking pictures of him, who, by the way, is wearing his uniform and not a Santa suit."

Off in the distance, there were more squad cars with red lights swirling on the dashboards arriving at the seminary grounds.

"How is all of this going to turn out, Raphael?"

"The events will unfold as the free will of mankind is used by the dysfunctional use of man's intelligence," said Raphael.

"And that means?" asked Will.

"It means, they'll screw things up for themselves," Raphael said, "As they say on the radio, *stay tuned.*"

The Sheriff was busy grabbing the fleeing freaks, in their mad dash to get to their autos to freedom. He would leap out of the foggy shadow of the dumpster, grab one and two at a time, and thrust them toward the steps. As their weight and Gordon's strength pulled them toward the dumpster, they had no choice but to follow. When they reached the top step, Gordon heaved them airborne.

The photographer clicked, and the camera flashed as the men sailed up, then down into the hollow metal container, screaming as they flew and groaning after hitting the hard metal floor where the cold stench of rotting leafy vegetables, sauces, gravy, potatoes, and old rotting meat covered the floor.

Between customers, Gordon turned to the photographer and asked where he came from.

"My mother; but that's not important right now."

Turning serious, he answered, "I was in one of the squad cars tonight as a ride-along and brought the camera for a few shots if needed. Quite a night, huh, Sheriff?" He aimed and took a quick shot of the Sheriff as he threw another one in the dumpster. "And what's that they say about Santa Claus, anyway?"

Gordon shook his head and slid his hands along his thighs wiping them and catching his breath, saying, "I ain't heard that one."

He lied. He never acknowledged that series of events of Santa in the secret room to any authority, except in jest.

"I'm looking for the Bishop and a few others," he said to the reporter. "If you get a shot of him running, you'll have the big cheese to chew on for awhile!"

"He's here tonight?" the stunned photographer questioned.

Gordon nodded in the affirmative as he wiped sweat from his brow. "As my friend would say, 'Yuppers.'"

"No! That can't be! I refuse to believe that. I *know* that man. I've had many a conversation with him. I've dined with him at the Men's Breakfast Club here in town. He's a man of the cloth and performing wonderfully as the head of many hundreds of good and decent families here. He's raking in a *lot* of money for the diocese. He's incapable of hurting others. It just isn't in his heart! You must be mistaken, Sheriff Maxwell. Why, he wouldn't hurt a flea!"

That angered Gordon. He peered in the direction of the reporter and two robed men who were running at top speed toward the back of the seminary. He took one big step around him as he ducked, thinking the Sheriff was about to take a punch at him. He grabbed the two runners by the throat, one in each hand, and yelled, "Join the party!" He slammed their heads together and dispatched them to the bottom of the dumpster.

"Naw, the Bishop wouldn't hurt a flea." Gordon wiped his hands on his pants again as he caught his breath. "A child now and again, piss on a junior seminarian while he's being buggered by another priest, but *never* a goddamn flea!"

CHAPTER FIFTY-SIX

"**N**ow what?" Pam whispered. They thought for a moment before Anne squinted and produced a devilish grin as she nodded to Kat. She tiptoed to the door that led down to the wine cellar. She stood there for a moment in silence. She rapped on the door. The men were startled. When she reached for the knob and opened the door a crack, the men froze in place, too scared to even blow out the candles.

Anne turned and nodded to the other two, brought her attention back to the dark stairwell, and whispered in a low raspy tone, "Come, gentlemen. Up. Hurry. I'll take you to safety."

They stood, eyeing each other as they waited for a reaction. One breathed, and in a quick voice asked, "Who the *hell* is that?"

The Bishop's eyes were darting from one man to the other and back. "Wait," he whispered. "Lawrence? Lawrence Burke, is that you?"

Anne looked to the others with surprise and raised her shoulders with arms out and palms up, not knowing what to say.

"It ain't the goddamn Easter Bunny," she continued in the low raspy voice. "The place is crawling with cops. Come. One at a time, as I call for you. Hurry! The cops are coming in all directions. Come, so I can get you out of here!"

Bishop Cheney glanced and nodded toward the first man.

"You go. Lawrence Burke is a friend of mine. He's been staying at my house. He'll show you a safe way out. Go now."

The voice upstairs rang out. "There's no time to lose!"

"Lawrence," Cheney questioned, "When did you get here? I didn't see you earlier."

In a quiet, yet raspy whisper, the voice replied, "Got stuck in a snow bank. You know how I drive. I just arrived as the ceremony began."

The Bishop nudged the hesitant man toward the wooden steps. "That's Lawrence Burke, all right. He's a terrible driver."

Clutching tight the handle of the iron skillet she was holding over her head, Kat positioned herself back and to the side of the door hinges. Pam stooped behind Kat. Anne adjusted her hood downward. As the door creaked open, she saw his face.

"Come on, dummy. Hurry up," she whispered in a husky voice. His eyes followed her. Holding onto the doorknob with one hand, he pushed the door all the way open. In his other hand, he held a snub nose .38 special and aimed, point blank, at the back of Anne's head. She didn't see the gun as she turned and started walking toward the main doorway to the kitchen from the cafeteria. He took two steps toward her to catch up as Kathryn Knee stepped out from behind the open door, took short fast steps toward the man with the gun, and brought the heavy iron skillet down fast and hard meeting the flesh and bone, making a quick hollow thud.

He crumpled to the floor, covered in a heap of robes. The gun fell from his hand, bounced on the floor, and came to rest under the kitchen's butcher-block table. The three grabbed the injured man, dragging him to the meat locker, opened the thick, heavy wooden door, and pushed him into the far corner, backed out, shut the door behind them and turned the metal latch, locking it.

"One down, five to go," Anne said, wiping her hands on her musty brown robe.

The ladies didn't see the man watching them from the top of the cellar. He slipped back down the steps and told the others, "He's gone. Wait for my signal, then follow me. I'm going up there to see if we can all get out of here, together."

With a candle to light the way, he went back up to the open door. With his headgear already removed, he put his hand up shoulder-high and waved a white kerchief wrapped around his Smith and Wesson.

He put the candle close to his face as he stepped up on the floor from the top step.

The ladies were back in position behind the open door; Kat again raised the iron skillet high over her head. Anne reached around the door, pulled him by his collar, and jerked him toward her. They were face to face. Pam closed the door.

He put a finger to his lips, and whispered, "I'm here to pull in the big fish. Help me get to my car." He nodded with his head. "Those guys don't know it, but I'm going to drive them out of here and right to police headquarters." Again with his finger to his lips he nodded and whispered, "Not a sound, now."

Anne hesitated for the longest time before shrugging in compliance. She put a finger to her upper lip as she stared at Mickey. He shrugged. Kat lowered the iron skillet and went to the back entrance with Pam. Anne stayed behind, to the side of the cellar entrance.

Zaugbaum backed down a couple steps and motioned the four to come up with him. They followed the deputy up and out of the kitchen. Mickey knew where Swain's car was and pointed to it not far from Dr. Bullock's Oldsmobile. They, too, were boxed in, and time was running out. Pastor Swain and Father Pervasions, however, spotted Svendly's car. With his, they could make it out of the parking area. Mickey hotwired another car, started the engine, and turned the headlights on.

Bishop Cheney hopped in behind the steering wheel. Doc Bullock, who was behind Zaugbaum, had found a car with the keys still in the ignition. He would follow as soon as he could get it moved. Bullock's Olds was now available for service. Mickey still had the keys.

The fog was as thick as soup. The visibility was awful. He waited for them before rolling the car onto the driveway. The Bishop followed. Swain and Pervasions were right behind. Zaugbaum crept along. It seemed forever just to get even a few yards down the dirt road at the back entrance. He stopped a couple of times while keeping the others in sight in the rearview mirror. He stomped the brake as a dark figure stepped in front of his headlights.

Mickey's chin banged on the steering wheel. The next thing he knew, he saw a man aiming point blank at him in the thick fog.

"Halt right there, *Mister*!"

The dark stranger took two quick steps to the driver's door, pulled it open, and with a flashlight, shined it on Mickey's face while pressing something hard and cold against his left temple.

"You *sonofabitch*!" Gordon Maxwell roared.

"Take it *easy*," Zaugbaum pleaded. Talking fast, he continued. "I'm on your side. I tried to hand off a note to the ladies back at the Pine Nut Café for you, but I never got the chance. It was all worked out with the Capital City Police and me. I got the names of everyone at the ceremony tonight. You missed it!"

Gordon stood silent for a second before noticing the following cars edging closer. "Get in," Zaugs ordered, "We almost have this thing under control. Don't blow it!" Gordon hesitated, but opened the back door, slid in, and laid low.

"I'm right behind you," he said nudging the back of Mickey's head. Zaugbaum put Bullock's black Olds manual transmission into first gear, eased out the clutch, and began moving again down the driveway toward the back road.

"If all goes as planned, Boss, the other three cars will follow me right to the police station. None of them have ever been there before. It's so damned foggy they won't know where they are until I lead them right smack dab in front of the station. How do you like them apples? Oh, and one more thing, Gordon, stop pointing. It's not polite. I don't like it when people point their fingers."

***

Gordon glanced at his right hand as he clenched his fist, realizing that he left his gun in his squad car out in the pines. He shook his head in disgust as he looked behind him to watch the parade of cars following behind.

"Christ, I-I wasn't sure . . ."

"I know, but that's the way the lieutenant wanted it. They wanted me to move 'inside,' so to speak. The key to this whole thing working out was to gain the confidence of Doc Bullock. It wasn't easy. I gained his confidence through Pastor Swain. Hell, even the Bishop likes me," Zaugs said, grinning.

"That ain't saying much," Maxwell mumbled.

"Hey, you missed him!" Zaugs said with a shot, looking in the rearview mirror, trying to find Gordon's eyes.

"Missed who?" he asked.

"Santa Claus! That's who. You missed the merry old gnome himself! He came down through the chimney, ah, into the room somehow and stood right between the Hornsby kids. What a sight! I don't know how, who, or what, but the old red-suited, white- bearded man appeared in the nick of time and flew away with the two kids hugging his legs as he they sailed right through the ceiling!"

Gordon smiled briefly before saying, "No way!"

"Yeah, way! The most amazing thing I'd ever seen!"

Gordon peered over the front seat and asked, "How are you going to write it up in your report?"

Bullock's car was blocked front and back. He slipped the car in reverse. He backed up so fast, it slammed into the car behind him, pushing it into the one behind it. He jammed it in first gear, popped the clutch, and jerked the car forward toward the car in front of him, ramming it into the seminary near the kitchen door. He backed it up again, driving forward, veering around the broken car in front, and sped out onto the icy pavement slipping, sliding, and fishtailing past the coal bin before coming to a rolling stop.

The ladies were knocked for a loop as they sat on the kitchen floor by the wall. They jumped up to see his car swerving away from the building just as the engine died. A round sphere of green light appeared in the sky and they watched it hover over the car. Bullock couldn't get the engine to turn over. He tried and tried, but it wouldn't start. In a panic, he jumped from the car and ran back into the kitchen as the girls took cover under the butcher-block table.

Trent Bullock ran from one end of the kitchen to the other in a panic. He stopped at the cellar door and bounded down the steps. Missing a plank, he lost his balance, tumbling headfirst into the wall, knocking himself out. The gals got out from underneath the table and pushed it up against the front of the door, sealing it shut.

"Two down, three to go," Pam said as each shook the other's hand.

"Who're the other three?" Kat asked.

"Asshole Swain, the squatty little potty-mouthed Bishop, and the mysterious Norwegian, slash, German, slash, ex-Nazi, slash, Vatican child smuggler, Svendly-boy," Anne responded.

Kat held out a large knife. "Ever wonder what a castration would sound like without anesthetic?" She stared toward the cellar door.

"Probably something along the lines of wild pig squeals, I'd guess," Anne responded. "We better check on the clown in the cooler."

They unlatched the lock and opened the heavy meat locker door, and there he was, sitting with his arms folded around himself, shaking, shuddering, and crying. They pulled him out and dragged him to the table, which was now in front of the cellar door, and tied him to one of the metal table legs. Pam rummaged through the drawers and came upon the potato bin.

She grabbed a big Idaho and shoved it into his mouth, saying, "That'll keep the silly shit quiet. He won't be a bother any time soon. The big boys he'll be rooming with will find him to be a cute pleasurable sex object up at the big house."

A part of Pam's memory returned. "That's what happens when an officer of the law becomes one of the bad guys. Revenge can be an awful, disgusting sight, huh, sad boy?" She said tickling his little chinny chin-chin.

"Won't you have fun taking showers with the big squirrelly burleys, who'll call you sweetheart, you little pussycat you?"

Ashton Plenn sat with a huge knot and a trickle of blood on his pounding head. He shivered and shook with a potato stuffed in his mouth. Crying uncontrollably, he half gagged as tears rolled down the back of his throat.

CHAPTER FIFTY-SEVEN

As the deputy was making his way down the back road, Gordon told him to turn toward the city, then pull over and stop.

"I want to make sure the Bishop doesn't get any thoughts of leaving us behind," he said. Mickey pulled over and waited for Bishop Cheney, who was creeping along the winding pathway down to the back road to the lead car.

"I don't see Doc's car yet. Just Swain's car behind the Bishop," Mickey said.

"Yup. But one way or another, we got him. He won't go far," Gordon said. "Here he comes now. Good. All he has to do is turn in our direction. Turn on your red light."

"This ain't my car," Mickey said. "I borrowed it a few minutes ago." They watched the car the Bishop had as it idled at the end of the driveway. Then, it happened! All of a sudden, his car lurched forward, turning in the opposite direction; he sped up the dirt road away from the commandeered lead car, and away from Capital City.

"That sonofabitch!" Mickey said as he spun the car around in hot pursuit. "He's making a run for it!"

As they tore through the countryside on the little dirt road that dark foggy night, Sheriff Maxwell barked, "Slow down! Not more than a half-mile there's a curve and a little one-lane bridge crossing Cruesson's slough. It narrows, and I don't want us flying through the air. Christ, we can't even see his taillights anymore in this soupy shit."

But, Mickey didn't want to slow down. He was getting good traction with the sand meeting the tires. He knew for sure he could go at least sixty miles an hour with his driving skills, but he followed orders. After all, like the Sheriff said, it was difficult to see . . . anything. He tried using the bright lights, dim lights, and then just the running lights. It didn't matter what he did, they couldn't see ten feet in front of the car. All of a sudden, lights appeared on the road, heading straight for them. It was too late to slam on the brakes, so Mickey whipped the wheel to the right, narrowly missing the oncoming car.

"Was that him?" Mickey asked.

"Not sure. Be careful! We're coming to the curve now. The bridge is just ahead," Gordon warned as he white knuckled the armrest and braced his left hand on the dashboard.

"Jesus, would you look at the fog now! Must be from the slough." Mickey eased off the gas.

Just then, they came upon taillights. Mickey slammed on the brakes, fishtailing, stopping inches from the rear of the steaming auto. He kept the engine running with the headlights on high beam as they exited the car.

In the thick fog and icy road, they walked carefully to it. They could see and hear steam hissing from the remains of the radiator that used to be at the front end of the vehicle, but was now lodged somewhere in the middle of the mangled metal remains. As they peered at the vehicle, they realized it had come to a crashing halt after hitting the right side of the steel bridge abutment head-on.

The auto had plowed into it so hard that it sheared through the front of the car on the driver's side and stopped with the girder planted where the backseat had been.

Mickey held out the flashlight he took from the glove compartment. The driver's door was open, and the hood of the vehicle was nowhere to be seen. The abutment had made a long, deep U-shape indentation in the auto.

Mickey turned and stopped at the door on the driver's side. As he did, he slipped and fell hard, but somehow managed to hang on tight to the flashlight. While he lay there, he smelled a foul odor next to his head. It was a pungent aroma; sweet and yet like body sweat. He shown the light at it and gave out a loud moan. Gordon slipped around the side of the car to see what had happened.

"Oh my God!" he exclaimed as he helped Mickey to his feet. He kept the light pointed to the ground.

"It's an arm," he said as he shivered, looking at it. "It was severed at the shoulder. He must've sailed right through the windshield and kissed the bridge."

He flashed his light inside the car to the front seat, smelling a hint of perfume. The top of the steering wheel was broken off, and the windshield was smashed out, leaving glass both inside and outside the bent metal that used to be a sedan. As he pointed the light around to the rearview mirror, there was steam coming off an elongated, yellowish flesh-colored hollow chunk of ribbed meat that hung from the mirror attachment. It looked like a throat pipe. Blood was dripping from it down to the edge of the seat and onto the bent-up floorboard. Mickey turned the light away from the car toward the bridge.

"I don't really want to look up there."

"I do," Gordon said as he took the flashlight from his deputy and walked up in front of the mangled mess. He shined the light up from the car to the right side of the road, then to a nearby tree. It was bare of all its leaves, but the tree seemed to have something hanging from a branch. He ambled toward it, stepping with care through the snow as he went. As he did so, he shined his light on his footing and the tree.

"Just his pants, I think. Wait, so is the hood. Can you believe it? They're both up there. The hood is lodged in the crotch of the tree and his shredded pants are just hanging from a small branch."

Gordon said nothing as he walked back to the car around to the driver side and looked into the car, pointing the light to the floor.

"He sure left in a hurry. His shoes are still here on the floor, Mickey."

Directing the light at the speedometer, he pointed out to Mickey that the speedometer needle stopped at eighty-five mph.

Gordon moved ahead to the middle of the bridge, looking for the body. He shined his light up, down, and all around. He paused and leaned on the rail of the bridge to shine a light down to the flowing stream below. As he did, he placed his right hand on the rail and felt something warm and slippery. It was a wet and bloody swatch of cloth. Looking down at it, he removed his hand from the rail, which was now covered with warm thick blood. He wiped it on his pant leg as he leaned farther over the rail while Mickey approached the bridge.

"Oh, God!"

Gordon flashed the light right below the bridge. He and Mickey stared at the grotesque sight for a minute or more. Their eyes followed the beam of light from the clothing hooked on a broken metal bar that once was attached to the top and bottom rail. The thick metal rod was broken off from the rail. A chunk of white satin cloth was attached to it. The rod held the Bishop by his right arm with the rest of the ornate robe curled and folded under his chin.

His bare body dangled below. His eyes were half open, yet he looked peaceful as his naked body swayed from side to side, dripping blood and other bodily fluids into the water below. The impact had been so sudden, so strong that his body split open from the bottom of his spine to the upper portion of his chest cavity.

The body heat against the cold, chilly night gave off a wavy steam. As he dangled from the bridge, the two men watched as his warm steamy intestines sagged and began unfolding down toward the flowing stream of water beneath the bridge.

"Jeez," Zaugbaum said with a sick feeling. He ran to the other side of the bridge and heaved his own guts out to the cold, flowing waters below.

Gordon had many emotions running through his body, along with too many years of bad memories. He turned the light away and walked back, holding Mickey steady as they made their way to the borrowed Oldsmobile. He sat his queasy deputy in the passenger seat. He stepped around the car and got behind the wheel. Pausing, he shook his head as if the shaking would clear his thoughts. He eased the car around, away from the crumpled Ford, and they headed down the back road to the seminary while the Bishop's severed body parts remained at the bridge.

***

The fog was lifting somewhat as they made their way back toward the seminary. Would they find Swain and Sven waiting at the entrance? They thought not. Would Bullock be right behind them? Not likely.

After watching the Bishop's car speed off in the opposite direction and seeing the deputy turn and give chase, fishtailing and sliding on the patches of snow and ice, Sven and Florien realized they had to make a hasty decision. Either they could go back to the seminary, or leave and head toward Pine Nut as fast as possible; the decision was easy. They had to make tracks away from there as fast as they could.

As they turned onto the back road, coming toward them in the opposite direction were two cars with red flashing lights on the dashboards. To the left was a car coming from the direction of Cruesson's slough.

They had no choice. They raced back to the seminary, and made their way down into the wine cellar. There they could stay safe, at least for the time being. Or so they thought.

CHAPTER FIFTY-EIGHT

An electrical circuit blew. The lights in the kitchen flickered and went out. Suddenly it was pitch black. Anne had found some candles in a cupboard above the sink and had three of them burning at the side of the stainless steel sink up against the outer wall.

As the ladies removed their robes, Kat said, "Oh, what a night!"

"It ain't over yet," Anne remarked as she walked to the backside of the kitchen. "Where's the Sheriff in all of this? I thought he orchestrated this whole event."

"Maybe Santa Claus took over, and the Sheriff is off in search of his deputy," Pam chimed in straight-faced.

At that moment the door flew open as Swain and Sven came rushing in, huffing and puffing. Anne backed into a corner and slouched away. Kat and Pam were left standing in front of the sink at the back wall.

"Ms. Darling!" Pastor Swain said as he gulped.

At that, Pam backed against the sink, causing two of the candles to fall. The flames went out. The kitchen was lit now by just one remaining candle. Kat stumbled as she stepped forward and fell to the floor. In doing so, she inadvertently kicked the snub nose .38 special lying on the floor. The gun slid, coming to rest at Svendly Pervasion's feet. He grabbed it, pointed it around the room, and steadied it in the direction of the two ladies.

"Okey-dokey. Hold it right where you are. Dah jig's up." What that meant, he didn't know.

251

The ladies froze and raised their hands. Sven leaned toward the Pastor and asked, "Now what?"

No one spoke a word. In the shadows, they could see the disheveled Ashton Plenn tied and gagged with a potato in his mouth. Swain asked, "Where's Doc Bullock? What did you do with him?"

Trying to come up with something to say, Pam replied, "Didn't he leave with you guys?"

"I smell a rat," Sven said. "You should never be here."

Anne edged toward a corner of the large room by the back door that led to the ball fields outside. Something caught her eye next to the door. It was an old thick wooden cross about four feet long.

With the little light flickering from the lone candle, she could see that there was an inscription on it. She couldn't make it out, and right now she didn't care. She grabbed it and began making her way to the two men of the cloth.

Sven glanced at Florien as if to say, help me out of this mess.

"Ms. Darling, Florien said, "You've caused me too much grief and money over the years. I don't know how you got in here or why you're here, but we simply can't have this situation, do you understand? I'm sorry to say, we'll have to do away with you and your friend. Go ahead, Sven, pull the trigger. We must rid ourselves of the curse of women," Florien shot a look to Sven, who held the gun.

Florien's eyes darted from Sven to the ladies and back to Sven. He was getting more and more agitated as the seconds went by. He finally whispered, "Well, do it! Do it now. We must leave here at *once!*"

"Yeah, Sven," Pam said as her eyes shot to Pastor Swain, "Go ahead, Sven, Shoot me, the mother of Pastor Swain's son. Shoot me if that's what your heart tells you to do. You are a man of the cloth? But you're an ugly bastard. All I see is ugliness when I see the two of you! You have no souls! Shoot me, the mother of a baby boy the Pastor has never known. You have the gun, *do it!*"

Sven felt as if he were frozen in time. He was in a bind as a thousand thoughts flooded his being. The only time he'd ever held a gun on anyone before was when he was a young soldier fighting in France in the cold late autumn of nineteen forty-two. When he pulled the trigger for the first time, he was a young lad of nineteen.

He remembered the Führer's doctrine of supremacy and how he came to despise the Jews. After all, they were the cause of the economic problems in Germany that led to war, or so he was told.

During a minor skirmish in a small French village, a Jewish family wearing their traditional clothing, were walking briskly through the town. The man with the traditional long beard and black hat was carrying a tiny baby in his arms. His wife walked between their two girls, an arm to the back of each as they hurried across the cobblestone street.

Private Sven pointed his rifle out of the second-story window down toward the sporadic gunfire coming from the other side. There was a small pocket of French resisters taking potshots at the German soldiers from the second floor of a burned out apartment building. Aiming toward the area the gunfire, he closed his eyes and pulled the trigger. He fired once and opened his eyes only to see that he had shot the father carrying the baby. It was an accident.

Sven had shot him in the back of the head, and now he lay in the middle of the street in a heap. A growing pool of blood and scattered gray matter covered him and the cobblestone street. His wife and two girls knelt over his body, sobbing and wailing. The girls were pleading for their father to rise. They pulled and tugged at him, at his clothing, trying to get him up. They were desperately grabbing at his thick black coat when a tall blond German soldier with SS emblazoned on the side of his helmet coolly walked up behind them with his army revolver and shot the little girls point blank in the back of their heads as their mother knelt by her husband's side.

The laughing soldier then tore at the woman's clothing, baring her breasts as she knelt in shock over her two dead daughters and husband. She was desperate to get her baby laying under the fallen father into her arms. Screaming, she flailed her arms at the smiling soldier. She hunched half-naked, reaching for her baby, as her family lay in ever growing pools of blood and brains, while the German soldier who had shot and killed her two girls just backed away from the scene and watched. It was crazy.

Sven, seeing the carnage take place as he held his rifle out the second story window, felt void of all emotions. He wasn't sad or angry, but felt as if he was in a vacuum. He could hear the baby crying as he watched the half-naked woman kneeling now, lying atop her husband and her two dead girls, reaching for her baby.

As the German soldier stood and eyed the woman cradling her baby, Sven yelled out to the soldier to back away. The soldier looked about and obeyed, not knowing where the order had come from.

Sven aimed his rifle, keeping his eyes open this time as he fired one more time and put a bullet through the back of the baby's head, smashing it like a pumpkin as the bullet pierced the mother's heart. Gurgling sounds came from her throat as crimson red blood bubbled at the corners of her mouth. She struggled hard before laying her head down on the bloody pile of her dead family. She said goodbye to them before darkness took her sight, and then her life.

Sven won a medal for his actions that day. There was no honor in any of it, least of all in his actions. He had intended to return fire in the direction from which he was receiving fire, but it was the first time he had to shoot his rifle during a skirmish. He chose to close his eyes.

"Do it!" Pastor Swain shouted, ringing his hands, "Shoot them!"

Anne crept across the dimly lit room. She was getting herself into position behind the men, running out of time. Anne toted the heavy wooden cross over her shoulder as she crouched along the floor, hugging the wall.

She got within a few feet of them. The cross was heavy. She clutched it tight as she stood up, erect. Anne put herself behind and to the right side of Sven, the side holding the gun. Raising the cross high, she stood poised and ready. She glanced up at it and the inscription faced her. *Break the Silence.* It felt as if it weighed a ton. She held it high as Sven raised the gun and moved it away from Pam toward Kat, who was standing just a few feet in front of him.

He aimed at her head and squeezed the trigger as Anne brought the heavy cross down.

The instant flash from the gun barrel and the deafening loud crack from the gunshot startled everyone, including Sven.

The loud bang echoed off the cement floor and brick walls. The force of the old wooden cross hit Sven's arm so hard it was almost severed. From the elbow down, the lower part of the arm just dangled. The arm was now held together only by the outer flesh. The rest of his arm was pointing toward the ceiling as he dropped to his knees. Sven let out a bloodcurdling scream.

Anne screamed, too. They harmonized.

His knees hit the floor while he withered in acute pain and tried to keep his broken arm up off the floor. His body shook violently as Kat leaned toward Pam saying, "Oh no." She collapsed to the floor, dragging Pam with her.

CHAPTER FIFTY-NINE

Maxwell and Zaugbaum heard the shot as they approached the back door to the kitchen. Gordon peered through the little window and saw the three shadowy figures near the wooden table and Pastor Swain standing near by. They bolted through the door with guns drawn, Mickey's police revolver and Gordon's handgun.

"Help!" Pam pleaded. "Kat's been shot."

Gordon ran to her aid as Mickey held his revolver on Swain and the kneeling, pain-wracked Sven. Sven's body shuddered as he rolled onto his side holding his broken-shattered arm. He saw the snub nose on the floor and looked to Swain.

"Pervasion pulled the trigger," Swain said, shaking.

"Upon *your* command!" Anne yelled with a scowl. "You *cowering pussy!*" She let go and dropped the heavy wooden cross to the floor as she pushed aside the Sheriff to get to Kat.

"Where?" she asked.

Kat reached for her right leg before laying back. Blood was flowing and spurting. Anne pressed hard on Kat's inner thigh to slow the blood flow from the bullet wound.

"To the hospital, stat!" she shouted.

As they moved her, a green-colored orb appeared at the kitchen window. Will and Raphael were watching the desperate scene play out.

"Is she going to die?" Will asked, looking straight ahead to his teacher, Mrs. Knee.

"She wasn't supposed to."

"Then I'd like to intervene here and get her the help she needs now."

"You can't intervene unless she asks for help," Raphael said. "That's the rules."

"She said, 'Oh God,' Ralphy, ain't that enough?" Will demanded. Raphael looked to his friend, saw the fear in his eyes, and put a hand on his friend's shoulder. "She said, 'Oh no.'"

"Hey, Kat?" Anne asked. "Does it hurt?"

She rolled her eyes. Kat had lost consciousness. Anne supported her head with one arm and shook her with the other. "Listen to me, hun. You've got to stay awake. Help me, so I can help you." Kat raised her eyelids, nodded, and passed out again.

The Sheriff ripped off a piece of Plenn's robe, exposing the birthmark on his side just below his rib cage. He saw it. He tossed the torn garment piece to Pam as she used it to tie a tourniquet around Kat's upper leg to help slow the bleeding. Anne was busy talking to keep her fighting, to stay with them.

While the attention was on Kat, Mickey cuffed Swain and Sven together to the table next to Plenn. Sven groaned and was in and out of consciousness.

Mickey slipped the car keys into Gordon's pocket as he carried Kat out to Doc Bullock's Oldsmobile. Pam kept pressure on her leg to slow the bleeding. She slid in first and helped her into the backseat, laying Kat's head on her lap. Anne jumped in the front seat while Gordon slipped behind the wheel and sped off to the Capital City Methodist Hospital. Will hovered above the vehicle, watching with great concern.

Mickey stood over his Pastor and Father Pervasions. "Men of God, huh? And you, Plenn, what an ignorant fool you turned out to be. I'd like to say Ashton-boy, you are a perfect fuck-up, but you'd like that. No, you're just an *average* arrogant fuck-up. The potato, though; I like it. You guys are pathetic. The three of you ignorant fools on the floor in your KKK outfits. You look like the Three Stooges on bad drugs."

"Stay with us, Kat," Anne demanded.

"I feel light. I see a light like way down in a tunnel and I don't hurt," Kat whispered.

Anne was in the front seat kneeling and leaning over the back, helping as much as she could to keep pressure on Kat's leg along with Pam. The oozing blood covering the seat began flowing to the floor. The nurses fought courageously to keep their new friend alive. Sheriff Maxwell continued, winding his way to the hospital.

"Hey, Kat, the Sheriff says he wants to date you. He's got the hots for you, kid, so stay awake, girl," Anne hollered from the front seat.

The yelling startled Gordon as he drove, but it got a smile on Kat's ashen face for a second before she slipped away again.

Kat's attention turned toward a bright, loving light. She felt her eyes open to it. She saw herself in a long, light blue, sheer gown walking toward the glittering white silver light. Kat was being led on a stairway of clouds by a large stag with a huge rack of antlers. She made her way up with her hands outstretched. As she neared the light, an extremely tall angel wearing a cobalt blue tunic appeared next to her on the stairway.

His face had a shiny copper color. His thick beautiful golden wavy hair draped to his shoulders. He looked at her with his oval-shaped, loving hazel eyes.

The angel broke the silence. "Where are you going, Kathryn?"

"To heaven, aren't I?"

"Now?" her angel asked as he faded away.

"I think so," she said unsuredly.

She thought, Why not now? She looked down at the blue and white orb of Earth as her eyes fixed on the speeding car just entering the city limits. She looked closer and saw her body in the backseat as Nurse Anne and Pam Darling hovered over her, doing what they could to keep her alive.

She wanted the light. Kathryn yearned for the loving glow. She wanted only good. Another bright orb appeared in front of her. She paused as it materialized into human form. A handsome, smiling young army air corps pilot wearing his leather bomber jacket and fly-ing cap appeared in front of her on the shimmering-lined white and gold stairs.

He held out his arms and touched her hands as she reached for his. "Oh, Lee, I love you so much. I've never stopped loving you."

He drifted up the steps with his arms outstretched to hers. "I'll wait, my darling. I'll wait for you, Kathryn."

Suddenly she felt herself floating down, faster and faster to the backseat, back into her body. Pam pulled her lips from Kat's mouth and said, "She's breathing again."

CHAPTER SIXTY

Back in the kitchen, two Capital City police officers were helping Mickey get the three men out of the building and into separate squad cars. Will had seen his teacher through her near-death experience and flew back to the kitchen to find Swain and Plenn being placed in the back of one squad car and Sven alone in the back of the other.

He saw Bullock standing at the door, listening to the activity as things quieted and the kitchen was vacated. The action was taking place out front now as the police had their men, including those captured by Gordon; the smelly ones, in the garbage dumpster. They were placed in the backseats of the squad cars and paddy wagon tracking up the driveway heading toward police headquarters.

Bullock opened the door with a burning candle in hand. Stepping up and out into the room, he saw the big puddle of Kat's blood on the floor. He contemplated stepping over it. Instead, he sidestepped it heading for the back door for another chance to escape the madness.

As he put one foot to the side, Will appeared before him in a green haze and startled the doctor. "Green. What's with goddamn green anyway?" he said out loud.

The light grew brighter as Will materialized.

"*BOO!*"

The doctor stood frozen as a warm flow of urine gushed down his pant legs to the floor.

"Yupper, Doctor Bullock, it's me, the country boy. Remember me? You called me a *zebra,* a country boy, and you said, and I quote, 'It's a shame he didn't die.' Remember? It's been quite a night, hasn't it, doctor *butt-fart?* Using God's name in vain isn't the wisest thing to do, either. You have defects, doctor, *personal* defects."

Trent's eyes were wide, and his pants were warm and wet. As he backed away from Will, the Doctor slipped in the thick puddle of blood and fell backward, ass over teakettle, all the way down the cellar stairs again.

Will stood at the top step and gazed down at Trent Bullock as he slammed against the cobblestone wall and came to rest with his legs apart, arms limp at his sides, and his head resting on his chest. He was passed out cold, again. Just as William was closing the door, he heard a rumbling down in the cellar. He paused for a few seconds, then it hit the nostrils.

"Oh, God." Will exited the kitchen with one hand covering his nose and mouth.

Using God-Thought, he flew above the highway to the squad cars on their way to the police station.

He zoomed in close to the lead car and, while flying next to it, he peered into the passenger window to the backseat. Inside sat the defrocked Highway Patrol captain, Ashton Plenn and his Pastor, Florien Swain. William recalled the times that the minister had kicked him hard on his backside and slapped him on the sides of his head and face. Often, this abuse was carried out on the front steps of the Lutheran church.

The Pastor was in shock. Looking out of the car window, he did a double take when he saw William. He was smiling at him. Swain turned away, put his head down. Thinking it was a mirage or his mind was playing tricks on him from the stressful evening he had had, he turned and looked again. This time Will not only smiled, but waved to him.

Swain's mind began to drift. *I must be losing it. Is this revenge from that backward bastard country boy?*

Will had read his thoughts. *I'll show you revenge.* He took a deep breath, closed his eyes, and moved in. When he opened his eyes, he found himself sitting in the middle of the backseat with Plenn on his left and Swain on his right. Plenn sat with his hands cuffed behind him and still had the Idaho in his mouth. Though rattled at the sight of Will, he could only stare. Will tapped the Pastor on his left shoulder.

Swain lifted his head and sat up straight, then turned in Will's direction. Will greeted him with a nice big toothy grin.

"You slapped and kicked me, remember?" He whispered. Pastor Swain opened his mouth and screamed bloody murder. Plenn chimed in with an Idaho-muffled yell of his own as Will made a hasty retreat through the roof of the car.

The squad car swerved hard to the left and right. The two officers in the front seat all but soiled their pants. The one in the passenger seat reached over with a blackjack and popped the Pastor hard on the forehead, several times. Swain lay back with knots emerging from the top of his forehead and didn't make a peep the rest of the night. Plenn was moaning and struggling hard to wrestle out of the handcuffs so the officer lay the nightstick across the top of his head, a time or two. Old Plenn went night-night as he slumped over and lay on Swain's shoulder for the duration of the ride downtown to the Capital City Police Headquarters.

Norm turned to his partner, Mike, in the passenger seat and said, "These guys are *fucked* up. What's with all the screaming, anyway?" Mike shook his head and shrugged.

It was almost two a.m. Gordon was posted outside the door to the room occupied by Mrs. Kathryn Knee. A Capital City officer came walking up the corridor toward him. Gordon looked his way and nodded.

"Hi, Sheriff. The Captain wanted me to thank you. He's going to write you up for a state merit award. Oh, and this is for you, too." He handed him an envelope, then walked back the way he had come. He turned just before reaching the door at the end of the hallway and said, "By the way, we retrieved the Bishop's body, his arm, and the guts and stuff from the bridge. He shook his head as he wiped his hands on his police uniform pants, as if the blood was on his hands, too. God, what a mess! He's downstairs in the morgue.

"Nobody's seen Doc Bullock yet, though. He's the only one missing." He turned, pushed the door open, and walked out.

Will hovered outside of the hospital. He'd heard the one-way conversation of the police officer and saw the concern on Gordon's face for Kathryn Knee.

He closed his eyes and moved into the hallway, almost. Once again, he was stuck, half in and half out. He stood, arching his back, doing his best to make it look like he was leaning against the wall as he eyed the Sheriff.

Gordon reached into his back pocket and pulled out his red-and-black-checked handkerchief. He brought the handkerchief to his face and blew his nose. He got a quick glance of something strange and jumped back. As he did, he cracked the back of his head against the hard marble wall. "*Jeezuz H. Christ.* You scared the hell out of me! Why do you do those things?"

"I'm stuck. Also, Doctor Bullock is still back in the wine cellar at the seminary's kitchen. You might want to get Zaugbaum back there to retrieve the bast, ah, the poor fellow. He knows where it is. He's been there. In the wooden cabinet down there he'll find more incriminating evidence, pictures, and one of your old roommates. One of the photos is of our friend, Ashton Plenn, again."

Gordon answered his little buddy. "It all came together yesterday morning. Plenn, the devious shithead, was in this up to his neck all along. I hope he lives a long life because the judge will likely throw the book at him."

"It won't hurt my feelings either," said Will. "One other thing Sheriff, ah, I'm going back to the Pine Nut Hospital now to be with my mom. I should be in her presence now."

Gordon nodded saying, "If you stay here much longer, you'll freeze your spirited little butt that's dangling on the other side of the wall."

"It *is* getting chilly," Will said sheepishly. "I'll see you later; and, one more thing, thank you for all of this, Sheriff. You helped save my little friends from holy hell, no pun intended."

"Yeah, yeah, you go now," Gordon said.

Will pushed back and disappeared. The Sheriff blew his nose again and wiped the tears from his eyes; tears of gratitude. He put the handkerchief back in his pocket as Mickey stepped out of Kat's room.

"Her breathing is much better. They just gave her another pint of blood from transfusions donated by Anne and Pam. Coincidentally, they both have the same blood type as Kat, A positive."

Gordon had Kat on his mind as he skimmed over the contents of the envelope handed to him earlier. "Thanks, Mick. There's one more thing I'd like you to do. Go back to the seminary, to the wine cellar in the kitchen. You have a friend waiting there. Bullock."

"I thought so," Mickey said right away. "That's where he would have had to be. I should have known."

"One more thing, Mick."

"Yeah?"

"Open that little wooden cabinet at the far wall in the cellar and get the contents out of it, all of it. There are more pictures down there, including our officer friend, Ashton Plenn."

"Ashton? How do you know all of this, anyway?"

"Yes, Ashton. Because I'm Santa Claus, that's *how* and that's why," he bellowed! "Sorry, Mick, I lost it."

Mickey shrugged, saying, "It's okay," as he hurried down the hallway and obeyed the last order of the night to retrieve the incriminating photos, and a mumbling doctor from the wine cellar.

Both the Sheriff and his deputy checked into separate rooms in a small motel on the edge of town precisely at 4:44 a.m. that morning.

CHAPTER SIXTY-ONE

Twelve hours later, they checked out of the motel at precisely 4:44 p.m. and were driven toward Pine Nut. The cold winter sun was down, and its last rays bounced off billowy clouds.

Mickey purchased the morning and afternoon newspapers before getting into the back of the Capital City squad car. The front pages were covered with pictures of the big bust. The morning paper had a picture of Sheriff Maxwell hurling two men at one time toward the dumpster. The headlines read: *Child smuggling ring sent flying to the garbage.*

Looking to Mick, he said, "I didn't know where the hell my partner was."

"Mick, he continued, "I'm going to write you up for a couple of service medals, and so is the Attorney General's office. One will be for heroism, one for valor. There'll be other citations for both of us from the Capital City Police Union, maybe others."

Mickey said, "I appreciate that, Boss. But, I was just doin' my duty."

"But, Mick, You'll get 'em for infiltrating an international child smuggling ring and sending thirty of them off to jail. There should be enough evidence to send 'em all to prison for a long, long, time. Your head will be so damned big, I won't know how to handle you anymore."

As the car traveled out of town, Gordon gave the driver directions to his squad car in the pines just beyond the seminary.

"This is where I get out. Mick, enjoy the limo service back to the office. Here are the keys to the office. There's one loose end for me to tie up. I have to do it alone. If you don't hear from me, come searchin'. Other than that, enjoy the limelight while you have it. It never lasts."

Gordon nodded as they drove off toward Pine Nut. He opened the unlocked door to the Ford squad car, thought about the weapons in the trunk for a second and shook his head. He sat there for a time, tapping his fingers on the steering wheel before starting the engine. Something was gnawing at him. There was a knot in the pit of his stomach, and he didn't like it. He fiddled with the radio until he found a local station. He got the weather report. *Cloudy and warmer tonight, turning to fog with a good chance of thunder showers after sunset.*

He backed the squad car around and drove out of the pines the same way he drove in. He turned and took the back road to the seminary, past the kitchen area, around the side to the convent, and stopped. The sun had set minutes earlier and, with the clouds and fog, it was getting dark fast.

"It's now or never," he said to himself. "I won't rest until I find the answer to a fifteen-year-old question."

He put it in gear, drove around to the front of the seminary, and stopped for a second to look at it. The windshield was icy. He didn't give the engine enough time to warm up enough to use the heater. He rolled down the window to set his eyes on a particular window on the third floor. It was his room all those years ago.

There were no lights in the cold building and no vehicles on site. He drove around to the side by the dumpster and touched the brake pedal. He looked over at the square metal container and chuckled before driving out to the back. Again, there were no lights, no cars. Gordon continued to the convent side and turned the lights off. He thought about driving across the yard to the back, but didn't want to risk getting stuck.

The cool, heavy air chilled him to the bone as he walked around to the back door. There was no wind at all, just a dead calm. Not a leaf moved on the lone oak tree in the backyard. Off in the distance, a dog barked incessantly. In the fields beyond, a lone coyote bayed.

Out of his coat pocket he pulled his heavy-duty flashlight. He stood at the back entrance. The screen door opened, but the main door was locked. He thought it would be. He turned around and faced the backyard and the tall pines that lined it, protecting the yard from the fields beyond. It was pitch dark now.

He shivered as he stood with his bare hands in his pockets. His eyes searched the grounds. The clouds were getting thicker and closer to the ground. Gordon felt a light mist as he shined the flashlight. He combed the yard slowly, looking for anything and nothing. He stepped down from the concrete step and walked about the grounds. Off to one side and to the back, he saw something odd. He crouched low as he looked to the ground. The crosses that were there when he was a seminarian were gone.

He found a small hole in the grass where a pole or some other object had been recently. He shined his light around and saw a series of small holes. He found twigs under an oak tree. He walked the lines, sticking the twigs in the holes and checking the depth. They were but a few inches in the ground. He counted seventeen in all.

"Let's see," he said to himself. "The place opened in nineteen-thirty and here it was, nineteen-forty nine." Gordon walked to the back row and continued forward.

From the hole he'd found nearest the pine trees to the side of the yard where he found the last hole, he placed the final twig and silently stood over it for a moment. *That many in fourteen years?* He shook his head.

At the back door, he tried turning the knob harder and harder. It didn't budge. He looked down at his Wellingtons as he stood on a hand-sewn rug used as a doormat. *No. They wouldn't put the key under the doormat.* He reached and pushed his fingers along the frame of the door. No key. He tried around the kitchen window, nothing. He went back and stood on the back step, warming his cold hands in his coat pockets.

Miffed, he kicked at the rug with his heel. He kicked it half over. Nothing. It lay in a heap. Gordon bent down to straighten it up, and under the doorframe between the rug and frame lay the key. "I'll be damned," he said.

Inside, he gave the place the once over. There was a door to his right. He opened it and shined the light. It was the steps to the basement. He knew it was heated with coal the same as the seminary. He searched with his light. Everything was neat and orderly down there as the kitchen above. "Aha!" He said as he spotted two shovels near the coal bin. One was a short, flat-edged coal shovel. The other was a spade.

He grabbed them both. As he turned for the steps, he glanced back at the coal bin. It was full. With the spade in hand, he used it to push the coal around. Nothing. Then he poked the spade in, dug out a scoopful, and turned it, then another and another. He flashed the light around the basement again from the rafters to the floor.

Not finding what he was looking for, he headed once again to the steps. Pausing, he could see his breath. The air was cool. He shined the light on the big, round, cold furnace that heated the two-story house.

Something told him to look inside it. He didn't want to. *Oh, what the hell,* he thought, maybe they're in there. He reached out to the small heavy iron door. He turned the handle, and the heavy, creaking door opened. He pointed the flashlight. Inside, he saw a scoopful of coal piled on top of pieces of wooden slats. He reached in and pulled a few out. *Two-by-twos with nails.* "Sonofabitch," he said.

CHAPTER SIXTY-TWO

The light mist turned to a drizzle. He dug as fast as he could. It wasn't easy. There was at least two inches of frost on the ground. It would have been thicker, but the surrounding trees protected the soil from the winds. He was thankful for that.

He slammed the spade into the grass to the frozen soil below. It stuck there. Then he jumped on each side of the top edge of the spade, and it went through the frost to the cold, thick, wet soil. He dug just in front of a twigged hole, lifting the frozen turf in chunks. When he finished removing the sod, he had a trench approximately three feet wide by six feet long. With the frost out of the way, he could concentrate on digging downward.

The dog had stopped barking. The coyote had found a mate. Each howled from an opposing direction. An owl flew low, just over his head, as Gordon paused to catch his breath. It landed on a lower branch in the oak and hooted. He didn't like the eerie sounds from nature. Not that night, anyway. "All I need now," he said to himself, "is a werewolf, Dracula, or Frankenstein to stop by and lend a hand. With my luck, I'd get Abbot and Costello."

The wind picked up. Gordon was working up a sweat as his coat got heavier with the drizzle. He forced the spade into the wet hard soil and turned his thoughts to the work at hand. Shovelful after shovelful, he dug deeper into the ground, cutting through thick tree roots. He stepped up and out of the three-by-six trench and caught his breath, again. He'd gone down about three feet. The drizzle got heavier, and the southeasterly wind was howling now along with the coyotes. Rain dripped off his cold wet hair.

Now I know why undertakers have the nickname, Digger.

He heard a car. It was coming his way. It rolled into the front entrance to the seminary. Gordon's heart pounded as he whispered, "I don't need this shit. I left the Walther P-38 and the shotgun in the trunk."

The car crept along the lane before stopping by the front side of the seminary. Gordon could see the bright headlights as it began moving again toward the convent. It stopped behind Gordon's squad car, and two men got out. Gordon stepped close to the house, the shovel in his hands for company. He nosed around the corner to watch.

One had a flashlight and shined it into the parked squad. "It's a county Sheriff's car. I bet it belongs to that Sheriff Maxwell guy. Why would he be here, now?"

His partner replied, "Beats me. Let's take a look." They donned their police hats and exited the squad. "This place is technically in the city limits as of last year, so if it *is* Maxwell, he's out of his jurisdiction."

"Maybe it's here from last night. It's all iced up. The tires are muddy. What do you think, Officer Mike?"

Looking around, he saw no lights at the seminary or the convent. "Well, Norm, I look at it this way. We drive Chevys. This damn thing is a Ford. Remember what the Captain said about Fords and why we didn't get 'em?"

"The batteries?"

"Yup. I bet it's here from last night, and the battery died." The rain picked up and started to pour. The wind was blowing so hard the rain came down in sheets, almost sideways. Their hats blew off. Norm's rolled along the ground on the side of the convent toward the back.

Gordon watched the hat roll by him and raced back to the trench, stepped in and laid down just as Officer Norm appeared at the back of the house. He picked up his wet hat and pointed his flashlight into the pine trees lining the backyard. The cold wind was bending them half over as they swayed fast and hard. He turned and pointed the light at the back of the house as the rain pelted the siding and windows.

He shined the light to the backyard as his partner yelled, "I'm getting soaked. I'm going to the car."

Norm stood for a second, pointing his light around on the ground in front of him. An owl hooted. He jumped, spun around and sloshed to the squad car.

"Mike, just for shits and giggles, make note of the Sheriff's car and the license plate number. I'm going to find a donut shop around here so we can dry off."

CHAPTER SIXTY-THREE

Cold, wet, and muddy, Gordon climbed out of the shallow trench and made his way inside. He found a bathroom just off the kitchen. It was small, just a shower stall, sink, and toilet. There, he saw a towel hanging on the chrome rack between the shower and sink. He used it to wipe himself off as best he could. He ripped the plastic shower curtain from the hooks. He pulled out a jackknife from his pocket and sliced a small opening in the middle of the plastic curtain.

Inside the shower stall was a rubber shower cap. He grabbed that, along with the shower curtain, and stepped back into the kitchen. The rain had become a drizzle again. He slipped the curtain over his head. Though crude, it made a good poncho. He dropped his chin as he donned the rubber shower cap. He thought to himself, *if anybody finds me in this get-up, I'll be in the hospital on the fourth floor in a padded room.*

Back in the yard, he skimmed off the watery mud from the bottom of the trench before stepping back in. His boots were getting stuck in the mud, and more than once he stepped out of one as he moved about. He dug down another foot or so all around. He jabbed the spade down as far as it would go, hoping to hit something hard, something solid. Twice he hit a hard object. Both times it was large rocks.

Lightning made a quick unexpected flash, and an instantaneous loud clap of thunder accompanied it. He cringed. He slammed the spade into the ground again. This time he heard and felt a thud.

Moving the shovel over a couple of feet, he drove it in hard. Another thud. He shoveled out the muddy earth faster and faster.

He used the coal shovel with the flat end and scooped off the soil on the long narrow object. After setting the shovel aside, he pulled out the flashlight and shined it on the object. He made a fist with his right hand, wrapped on it and ran his hand over it, removing the wet soil. As he suspected, it was a pine box decomposing in the cold wet ground.

He reached again for the spade. He dug along one side of it to make room for standing. Questions from the past ran through his mind. *It was just a rumor, Bobby said. Is it a normal practice to plant priests in the backyard of a convent? If they kicked the nuns out, it would no longer be a convent. It would become a home for the priests, in which case it would appear to be normal, whatever the hell normal is around here. After all, it is the Church that owns the land.*

The seminarians, would they be buried here? Cheney said some ran rather than face their parents. If it's true and they are here, he couldn't have been the only murderer, could he? That would be true of the others as well. Would Captain Ashton Plenn have been in on this, too?

There was another flash of light and a quick crack of thunder. It lit up the broken pine coffin and his mud hole. Gordon was spent.

He rested the shovel on the ground next to his shoulder as he caught his breath. He lifted one leg, almost stepping out of his boot again. He got himself to a corner, leaned against the muddy wall, and pondered his next move when lightning struck the oak tree behind him. It shot through the tree, splitting a heavy branch from the trunk. The huge branch peeled away and came down toward Gordon. He ducked down beside the coffin as it crashed to the ground. Another flash produced a loud clap of thunder. It shook the ground so hard, the coffin lid rattled and shifted.

Gordon put a shoulder to the fallen trunk and pushed it along the trench to one end and out of the way.

He pulled out the flashlight. *Should I lift the lid and see what's inside or get out now and get the police here to witness?* His thoughts of Kip and Allen came back to him. They obeyed the priests, their parents, and they were gullible. They were perfect candidates for grooming in the eyes of pedophile priests. They were gutsy enough to tell the rector, though, and they were going to their parents with their story of the unholy weekend. They never made it home.

Then, there was his roommate, Charlie Schlimgin, whom he hardly had time to know. He was quiet, unassuming, a real loner. He wound up missing, too.

Gordon leaned over the coffin as the drizzle came down, and lightning flashed shards of light into the muddy trench. He put his cold bare hands on the lid. It creaked as he raised it up a couple of inches.

There was an immediate odd aroma that hung in the air around him. He turned away, putting an arm across his nose and mouth to keep himself from gagging. Again, another sudden lightning strike and a loud clap of thunder shook the ground.

He set the flashlight next to the shovel and, with both hands on the lid, he pushed it up and off as it crumbled into pieces. He was breathing hard as his heart pounded fast against his chest.

Rubbing his hands together didn't help warm them. He stuffed them inside his shirt and pants below his beltline, touching his pubic hair. Gordon was cold and wet to the bone. He had a job to do, and questions needed to be answered.

He couldn't quit now. After a brief moment, he pulled them out and reached for the flashlight. "I ain't waiting for the police. Stay calm, Gordy," he said, "Don't get spooked."

He flashed the light inside the coffin. He was surprised at first. Burlap. Whoever or whatever, it was wrapped in brown burlap. He had to unwrap it. Slowly, he reached and grabbed it. Nothing happened. He tugged at it, ripping it. He ran his hand around it, feeling it. Bones. He felt an edge of the burlap. Gordon tugged and removed the burlap from the stiff bony contents.

He fumbled the ground behind him until he touched the flashlight as lightning and thunder did its thing again, this time farther away, but it unnerved him, nevertheless. He shined the light on the body. The bones were covered with brown, dried, leathery skin. Long fingernails, too.

The corpse was wearing a white dress. *A woman?* He was confused. He had to shine the light on the skeleton's face. He didn't want to.

But he did. The skin was hardened leather stretching across the facial bones and skull. His hands shook as he studied the skeletal remains. Two coins. Someone had placed coins where the eyes once were. He bent close to see them clearly. He touched one and picked it up and held it close. It had a skull and crossbones on it. He put it back and shined the light on the garment again. He tugged on it around the chest. "Ah. There it is," he said out loud, "The red cross of valor."

CHAPTER SIXTY-FOUR

He saw another light. This time it wasn't lightning. The rain picked up again. He was soaked to the bone. He heard the sound of a car engine. "Not again. Not now!" he said gritting his teeth. Gordon watched as the car came up from the back entrance and stopped behind his squad car. He found himself in a lurch. "Shit."

The harder he tried to get up and out of the grave, the more noise he made. Slipping and sliding back into the muddy grave was getting him nowhere fast. Gordon placed a foot on the side of the coffin and tried jumping up from there to the edge. No go. He slid the crumbling coffin lid, sideways, over the grave and again stepped onto the top edge of the coffin. He had to get out fast and prepare himself for his new visitor. There was no time to lose.

Gordon Maxwell had a bad feeling. His stomach was in knots. He raised a leg and knelt one knee on the coffin lid. It crumbled below him.

All of a sudden, something seemed to latch onto his ankle. It sent shivers down his spine. His neck hairs stood on end. In a shot, he looked down and flashed his light. He wanted to scream and scream loud, but he couldn't. He pulled his leg up with all his might. It was no use. He was being pulled back into the muddy, watery grave. He flashed his light at it again. From inside the coffin a skeletal arm seemed to reach out, the hand clutched his ankle again.

Gordon couldn't move. A light went on in the convent house. He took a deep breath and jerked his leg up as hard as he could. It was no use. He tried again. The skeletal arm clung to his ankle, pulling Gordon down to the bottom. He kicked at it with his other leg over and over again. The bony hand finally released its grip.

He pulled hard out of the clutches of the skeletal hand, leaving his Wellingtons in the grave. Sloshing over the wet slippery grounds to the side of the house, he stepped on his homemade poncho. It pulled on the back of his neck, and he fell face-first into the frozen watery turf. With his strong arms, he heaved himself up in a crouched position, stepped carefully to the house, and listened.

The kitchen light went on. Gordon ducked around the corner of the house. The door opened. The screen door opened. There was silence. Gordon could feel the veins around his temples pulsate.

A tall shadow of a man stepped out onto the first step and stopped. Though the rain had quit, Gordon didn't notice.

"Anybody out here?" the voice asked.

Gordon stood stiff. He held his breath. "Wherever you are, I know you're here. You left an awful mess in the bathroom. I followed your muddy footprints from the kitchen. Come out," the voice said again. "Listen. I'm a priest. It's okay. I won't harm you. I've got nothing to hide. If you're the police, show yourself. We can talk. I'll start the furnace. You can warm up and dry off inside. Say something!"

The last thing Gordon needed was for him to light the furnace. The evidence would go up in smoke. The crosses would be ashes. The tall dark figure stepped back into the kitchen as the screen door swung back and slammed against its frame. Gordon froze in place as he felt something cold and hard on the back of his neck.

"Turn around slow," the voice commanded.

He stood still, holding his breath. Gordon craned his neck. There was the sound of a click as Gordon cringed and faced the stranger. A quick flash blinded him. "Mick-Gordy." They spoke at once.

Gordon whispered fast. "You take the front entrance. Follow it through to the kitchen. There's a door off to your left as you enter. It'll take you downstairs to the furnace room. I think he's going to light it. Don't let him. I'll stay by the back door in case he comes out this way again. Hurry!"

Mickey handed him his Walther P-38 and slipped off to the front of the house. Gordon eased himself to the back door, revolver in hand. He peered through the window.

Inside, the tall shadowy man reached over the wood cooking stove for a box of wooden matches and slipped them in his pocket. He picked up the long, heavy iron poker on the side of the woodbin and stepped to the back door. He saw Gordon crouching near the window. He stepped fast. He pulled on the back door. As he did, he felt a sudden shot of excruciating pain with a crushing blow to the back of his head. He staggered out the door and missed the step as Gordon Maxwell smacked his face with the cold metal revolver. He fell to the ground in a heap. With one hand, Gordon rolled him over and shined a light on him. Mickey put his gun back in his holster and stepped out to join Gordon.

"Ever see him before?" Mickey asked.

"Nope. See if he's got a wallet."

Mickey patted him down and pulled a leather wallet from inside his coat pocket. "Yup." He slipped out a driver's license. "Ever hear of a Lawrence Burke?"

"I'll call the captain and get his ass outta bed. By the way, since you're trigger happy with the camera, shoot some more pictures around here, will you?"

"Be glad to." Mickey said.

"Thanks for showin' up, partner. Thanks for everything."

"I knew you were up to no good. I had to help."

WILLIAM IS BACK

His intriguing and mysterious flight soars to breathtaking heights as he transports from December,1949 to August,2001 from the Mainland, to the island of Hawaii, to hideous depths of evil–the dark side of the insane mind of man. . . .

FINDING MAGGIE'S BLISS

A Novel by

Augustus G Van Slyke

BOOK II

On sale via kindle, ebook, and paperback

Spring/Summer of 2014

FINDING MAGGIE'S BLISS

A Novel by

Augustus G Van Slyke

BOOK II

Scottsdale, Arizona - August 2001

A loud commotion woke the ten-year-old. His heart pounded. A shot rang out. A bullet crashed through the small bedroom inner wall just above his head, smashing the mirror on the far wall.

"Stop!" he heard his father shout. Richard slipped out from under the sheets and grabbed his gun. Two more blasts sounded from the room next door. He heard a moan. Then an ominous silence filled the air.

Seconds later he peered through a crack in the door. A stranger leaned over his father with a gun to his head.

Richard's instincts kicked in. He held his new handgun with both hands, just as his father had taught him. Then he aimed, squeezed the trigger, and pumped all nine shots in his 22 High Standard pistol into the back of the intruder...

✱✱✱

Eighty-one-year-old Richard Fleming wiped the sweat from his forehead with his sopping wet white handkerchief.

His thoughts had shifted aimlessly these past few days. He wasn't feeling well, and the nightmare from his youth never escaped him, its memory forever etched in his mind.

The rusted air conditioner vibrated in the window, blowing in warm air as the glass rattled. The old psychiatrist got up from his desk and trudged to the windowpane. Squinting, he focused on the outdoor thermometer. One-eleven in the shade. "I'll be damned," he moaned as he turned and labored back to the swivel chair at his desk.

He hated the monsoon season; even if it lasted only a few weeks, it was too damned long. The humidity took its toll on the aging doctor.

But now he had another problem to contemplate. He wasn't looking forward to his first and only client of the day. *Damn you, Margaret Lynne Hornsby!* He wanted to help, but liking the woman was impossible. She made it that way. Frustrated, he pushed the leather-bound appointment book aside, picked up his unlit Cuban cigar from the clunky glass ashtray, and stuck it in his mouth.

The old swivel chair creaked as he leaned back and peered at the framed photos, medals, and citations that lined the walls. *"For God and country,"* read one of them, though there were days, like this one, when the former FBI agent felt that God and country had nothing to do with it and he had been in it for the prestige. *Whatever. I'd do it all over again.* Why not? He was proud of his work. He knew how to keep a secret. And how to lie. The government paid him well.

He had been a professional in all the right ways. He'd saved and mended lives. It was his job. And, too, there were times when he had to take lives. If one is to play the game, one plays it to win. There is no other way.

At the beginning, when Richard Fleming was young, he wasn't full of American pride. If he was full of anything, it was questions: Why do people hate? Why do people love? Why do they kill? He was simply interested—obsessed, even—in what made people tick. So he studied and became a psychiatrist. In his youth he was a bookworm. His father, Henry, wanted him to expand his horizons and enjoy the outdoors, too.

So Henry took his son to their cabin in the woods to learn about nature. That he did; he learned about the dark side of man.

Henry had given him a pistol for his tenth birthday. They practiced with it the day before the incident, when a man broke into their summer cottage in upstate New York. That night Richard's father died in his arms from gunshot wounds. A kid grows up pretty fast after something like that, he often mused.

Two years after the tragedy, Richard was twelve and confirmed in a traditional Catholic confirmation ceremony blessed by the bishop of the diocese. He chose the name Francis after Francis of Assisi, a saint he had always admired, and not just because his life was dedicated to helping the poor and downtrodden, as honorable as that may be; it was his courage to walk a different path than most. St. Francis left his rich father and joined the army, an act of bravery. And, toward the end of his life he willingly received the stigmata. *That* was a true act of loyalty.

After the ceremony everyone filed into the church basement for refreshments. The Bishop had too much wine. That night, his mother, Patricia, was driving them home when a car sideswiped them. Forced off the road, she hit a tree.

Richard never got so much as a scratch. Patricia's neck was broken. She died at the scene. An investigation of the hit-and-run accident followed and the driver of the other car was found. It was the Bishop who had confirmed Richard. He was never charged—with anything.

Richard believed in himself and that was enough. He could bullshit an Eskimo into buying an ice cube then, and now. Fuck the rest.

The plaques, trophies, and medals were for the old guys, the survivors. *The best of the best, as they say.* Ironically, he had become one of them.

He loved to look at himself—back then, when he was young and thin. Well, thinner. It didn't matter, the extra weight made him look regal, astute, dignified, even if it was only in his own mind.

He thought of one of his oldest friends, the skinny one, who for all the world reminded him of Barney Fife.

Mickey Zaugbaum could never keep his shirt tucked in-always a half a step ahead of the others, and in a different direction. *I'll be damned if the sonofabitch wasn't right. Always! Damn him to hell.* He worked outside of the organization, contracted himself out, and never made a mistake.

And then there was Mickey's sidekick. Richard loved him, though he drove him crazy! Gordon Maxwell was a thick guy, red-haired and sly, a Sheriff Andy Taylor-country-boy kind of guy. If one thought at first meeting that he was mentally slow, he'd be wrong. He made a lot of people wrong. They paid for it, sometimes with their life. And that was the oddest thing, because he didn't believe in carrying weapons.

Gordon was a sheriff at one time, back when he was young and single (well, single since his wife had left him) and he drank too much.

He was a strange case. Mickey had set up an appointment for Gordon and Richard became his therapist. Gordon was overworked and stressed from a tough assignment. He knew Maggie and a boy named William when they were kids in distress. They had to be saved. He did his job.

Gordon was convinced that William, a fourteen-year-old boy he had protected from family abuse, could fly. He listened, took notes, and asked questions. Gordon poured his heart out from the couch. Richard didn't know whether to laugh or cry at first. He listened to the wild and wacky story. He didn't laugh. And they became fast friends.

Gordon insisted that he take one last patient, and that was when Maggie (as she preferred to be called) walked into Richard's life.

She was trouble from the get-go. She'd tried suicide and her life was a mess. It didn't start out that way. She had good parents—a good life by all standards. Lived in the country and was happy until ... until what?

PSS: An FYI about my new friends. Back when I was growing up there was only one person who cared about folks like me, Sheriff Gordon Maxwell. Today, it's a whole new ballgame.

We have friends now, lots of them, and they care about us. They are powerful people and righteous organizations looking out for kids like my friends and me. You can even be a member.

Check out the websites below.

WWW.PROTECT.org.
I have solid friends here like: Grier Week, Camille Cooper, JonAnn Glenhill, Jennifer Allen, and Lou Bank. These people are strong!

WWW SNAPNETWORK.org.
Good people such as Barbara Blaine, David Clohessy, and Barbara Dorris are working hard for folks like us.

Join us. You will feel good about it!

www.ingramcontent.com/pod-product-compliance
Lightning Source LLC
Chambersburg PA
CBHW071254170626
46809CB00001B/210